Praise for
Children of God Go Bowling

"Olson completely avoids maudlin sentimentality, allowing her protagonist to be honest . . . without losing her sense of humor."   —*The Baltimore Sun*

"Taking her cue from the principles of feng shui, she clears out the clutter in her life to make room for new friends, and, of course, a hot guy. Hilarity ensues."
                    —*Boston Herald*

"Shannon Olson is impossible to dislike . . . very funny and endearing."   —*Detroit Free Press*

"Wry, sometimes cynical and likeably written, *Bowling* really strikes out. In the bowling sense of the word, that is."
                    —*The Rake*

"A breezy, often hilarious read."—*Rocky Mountain News*

"Shannon is an engaging narrator."
                    —*Booklist*

"Remarkable talent for deft comic writing."
                    —*Kirkus Reviews*

"Olson regales readers with her good-natured and self-deprecating wit, reminiscent of Ellen DeGeneres at her best. . . . a wicked sense of humor."   —*Library Journal*

"Strong, ironic and characteristically cranky . . . Shannon's commentary on being a round peg in a square world . . . rings true."   —*Publishers Weekly*

ABOUT THE AUTHOR

Shannon Olson, whose debut novel was *Welcome to My Planet*, has taught creative writing at the University of Minnesota and the Iowa Summer Writing Festival. She lives in St. Paul, Minnesota.

Children of God Go Bowling

A Novel

Shannon Olson

PENGUIN BOOKS

PENGUIN BOOKS
Published by the Penguin Group
Penguin Group (USA) Inc., 375 Hudson Street,
New York, New York 10014, U.S.A.
Penguin Group (Canada), 10 Alcorn Avenue, Toronto,
Ontario, Canada M4V 3B2 (a division of Pearson Penguin Canada Inc.)
Penguin Books Ltd, 80 Strand, London WC2R 0RL, England
Penguin Ireland, 25 St Stephen's Green, Dublin 2, Ireland (a division of Penguin Books Ltd)
Penguin Group (Australia), 250 Camberwell Road, Camberwell,
Victoria 3124, Australia (a division of Pearson Australia Group Pty Ltd)
Penguin Books India Pvt Ltd, 11 Community Centre, Panchsheel Park,
New Delhi - 110 017, India
Penguin Group (NZ) Cnr Airborne and Rosedale Roads, Albany,
Auckland 1310, New Zealand (a division of Pearson New Zealand Ltd)
Penguin Books (South Africa) (Pty) Ltd, 24 Sturdee Avenue, Rosebank,
Johannesburg 2196, South Africa

Penguin Books Ltd, Registered Offices: 80 Strand, London WC2R 0RL, England

First published in the United States of America by Viking Penguin,
a member of Penguin Group (USA) Inc. 2004
Published in Penguin Books 2005

1 3 5 7 9 10 8 6 4 2

"Leaving" From *Maps to Anywhere* by Bernard Cooper. Copyright 1990 by Bernard Cooper.
Used by permission of the University of Georgia Press.

PUBLISHER'S NOTE
This is a work of fiction. Names, characters, places, and incidents either are the
product of the author's imagination or are used fictitiously, and any resemblance to actual
persons, living or dead, business establishments, events, or locales is entirely coincidental.

THE LIBRARY OF CONGRESS HAS CATALOGED THE HARDCOVER EDITION AS FOLLOWS:
Olson, Shannon.
Children of God go bowling : a novel / Shannon Olson.
p.   cm.
Sequel to: Welcome to my planet.
ISBN 0-670-03281-6 (hc.)
ISBN 0 14 30.3456 1 (pbk.)
1. Self-actualization (Psychology)—Fiction.   2. Young women—Fiction.
3. Minnesota—Fiction.   I. Title.
PS3565.L838C47   2004
813'.6—dc21   2003052545

Printed in the United States of America
Set in Bembo   Designed by Erin Benach

This book is dedicated to everyone who is bad at bowling

Leaving

The statistical family stands in a textbook, graphic and un-
abashed. The father, tallest, squarest, has impressive shoulders for
a stick figure. The mother, slighter, rounder, wears a simple tri-
angle, a skirt she might have sewn herself.

A proud couple of generalizations, their children average
2.5 in number. One boy and one girl, inked in the indelible
stance of the parents, hold each other's iconic little hands. But
the .5 child is isolated, half a figure, balanced on one leg, one
hand extended as if to touch the known world for the last time,
leaving probable pounds of bread and gallons of water behind,
leaving the norms of income behind, leaving behind the likeli-
hood of marriage (with its orgasms estimated in the thousands),
leaving tight margins, long columns, leaving a million particu-
lars, without hesitation, without regret.

—Bernard Cooper, *Maps to Anywhere*

Acknowledgments

I can't begin to adequately thank my editors, Karen Murphy and Carole DeSanti, for helping me shape the book, and for their patience, perseverance, and faith. I am always grateful to my wonderful agent, Gloria Loomis, and to Katherine Fausset, Gretchen Koss, and Carolyn Coleburn. Thanks to Gretchen Scherer, Elizabeth Larsen, and Neal Karlen, for early readings of the book in progress; to Katherine Lanpher and Lynn Bronson, for walks around the block, retail therapy, and pep talks; to Marie Boehlke and David Bailey, for insight and buoyancy; to Mitch Goldstein, Marty and Gary Eastman-Browne, and Amanda and Tom Falloon, for fabulous accommodations; to the nice people at the Loft Literary Center for indispensable studio space; to David and Lisa Africano and the Cottagewood Book Club; to the neighbors on Illinois Street; and to Vince Klaseus and Todd Gertchen, Michele and Bill Sonnega, Erick and Stephanie Johnson, Dan Wellick, Lori Skallerud, Shaila and Joe Cunningham, Anne Knutson, Kevin and Sue Casson, Bill Tenney, Jim Moore, Bill Meissner, Caesarea Abartis, Suellen Rundquist, Jim Heynen, Genevieve Love, Jane Hilberry, Lisa B. Hughes, Barry Sarchett, and Randy White. Thanks to my relatives, family friends, and the wonderful people from my hometown, and to Mary Beckfeld, because Bill would have something to say about this, I am sure. And finally, I am grateful to my family for their support, encouragement, and really good one-liners; and to Jon, a good friend, who is somewhere bowling a perfect game.

Contents

My Whole New Little Adult Life

Part 1

Chapter 1

It started when I began packing to go back home. Actually, it started before that.

For the last two years in therapy, the counselor and I had been working on It's Not Always About Me.

"You can have the feelings you're feeling," the counselor kept reminding me. "You can have them and notice them and wonder, 'Huh? What's that all about?' And then you need to tuck them away and keep doing what you're doing. You don't have to *live* in your feelings." She made them sound like a small mud hut. "You need to remain active, keep moving forward."

So when my younger sister became pregnant, I repeated to myself, *It's Not Always About Me.*

It's Not Always About Me.

I was actually thrilled for her, and scared for her. Wow, she was pregnant. Wow, she'd be a mom. Wow, she'd have to go through *labor. Before* me. I'd have no idea what she was feeling. But I would get to be an aunt. Yay! An aunt! I would get all the benefits of having a little person in my life without having to save for the college fund. Only the occasional diaper change. Maybe I would be the fun, jet-setting aunt who sent her nieces and nephews presents from Hawaii. Not that I had ever been to Hawaii.

I was fine until I saw a special on *Dateline* or some such thing, the kind of thing a single woman would be home watching, about how I should have gotten pregnant when I was seventeen, when my eggs were robust and petulant, daring and adventurous. When I could have become pregnant in the time it took to watch an infomercial. Women approaching forty— women in their midthirties, for that matter—shouldn't count on getting pregnant, the experts concluded. If you thought you were doing the right thing by forging ahead with a career, paying your own bills, and trying to at least curb some of your dysfunction in therapy so that eventually you'd be partner-ready, you were wrong.

It was too late. You should have had children when you could still drop them at the high-school day-care center while you went to algebra class.

Not that I had always *planned* on having children. I just always *thought* I would have children. In the same way that you count on Christmas every year. Whether you love or hate the holidays, they show up. Whether I would be good at it or not, whether I actually wanted it or not, I just thought I would be a parent someday. Like millions of people before me. I would screw up my kids; they'd go to therapy; the cycle of life would continue.

I was thirty-three. Every day my uterus, my ovaries, and my little collection of eggs were becoming more and more *compro-*

mised. Which made them sound like crooked accountants. Frustrated workers, forced to cook the books.

And suddenly all you heard about in the news, on every talk show, in special reports, was the reproductive demise of the career woman. Poor her. She thought she could have it all, and she can't.

I never thought I could have it *all*. I just wanted a *little bit*. Something.

I'd been single for almost four years, since my graduate-school boyfriend had left me to go on a fellowship in Rome. He had said that he hoped we'd always be in touch, and then he'd disappeared until he finally e-mailed a year later to say that he was engaged.

Since then I had been living in the dating world's version of the Old Country Buffet. Date after date after date after date after date. The tepid, lamp-warmed, greasy, convenient, heartburn-inducing singles buffet.

I had dated three graduate students, a sportswriter, a product designer, two lawyers, two journalists, a photographer, a deli owner, a concert violinist, a triathlon coach (much too peppy), a high-school science teacher, and a kindergarten teacher. The kindergarten teacher was perhaps my favorite; he was sweet, and because he was used to dealing with small children, he smiled and nodded encouragingly throughout our conversation. He taught students for whom English was a second language, those who had just moved to America, and when I asked him what they did each day, he said, "Mostly songs. And movement."

I wished my days were about song and movement.

I forgot the architect.

I had also dated an architect who, with every e-mail he sent me, included a photo file. Some photo he'd taken, part of his amateur photography hobby. An afternoon e-mail to ask me out for drinks might include a photo of kids on a playground. The "how's your day going?" e-mail might include a photo of an empty parking lot. He asked me out to dinner over e-mail and included a photo of his cat standing on the dining-room table. We had only been out a few times, and I didn't really like cats and I wasn't sure things were going to work out. When I sent a message back saying that I was really busy at work for the next couple of weeks, which was actually sort of true, he sent me a message saying that I'd know where to find him if I ever came up for air, and he included a photo of a drowned body.

I was tired of dating.

So when my sister had her baby, my niece, Georgia Margaret Greene, this tiny warm loaf of bread who calmed down when I sang her made-up lullabies—"Do you like Doritos? I enjoy Doritos . . ."—and who slept peacefully in my arms for hours, I still couldn't help, alone at night, sleeping on their couch, look-ing out the bay window at the streetlights, feeling like I might shrink into myself and cease to exist entirely.

My dad had come out for a couple of days while my sister was still in the hospital, and then he'd gone back home to work. My mom was staying for a week, like me, and slept in the den with the television on all night. My sister and her husband and little Georgia and the dog all slept in the master bedroom. They were up half the night the first night they were home; I could hear little Georgia crying, my sister comforting her by walking in circles on the upstairs landing. I woke up every time Georgia woke up, but I knew it wasn't my job to go up there, that my sis-ter needed to be with her.

The next morning they slept in. I was sitting downstairs reading the newspaper and around 10 A.M. I heard the master bedroom door opening, the sound of footsteps coming down the carpeted stairs, the dog tumbling after them. "Is everyone up?" my sister said. "Here comes the family."

I had never felt so lonely.

I knew she was probably getting over her own shock, at suddenly being a mother, at suddenly really being a family, a partnership cemented by baby and dog.

Still, *I* was her family, too. Wasn't I? *Not everything is about me. Not everything is about me.* This was an important moment for my sister. But my chest felt so big and empty that a dump truck could fall into it.

"How was your night?" I said. I forced a smile even though I wanted to start crying. *Why me? Why me? Why have I been sent to America's Siberia? Why am I still out here on the cold flatlands of singledom? What is the secret handshake? Let me in, let me in!*

The family I had been a part of had dissolved, become Balkanized, and formed new unions. My sister had a new family and lived in Portland. My brother was married, lived in Seattle, and spent almost every weekend backcountry skiing or hiking in the mountains with his wife. I still lived in the Twin Cities, where almost every Sunday I still saw my parents, who had known each other since they were fourteen.

Everyone else had a designated person, it seemed. Everyone else came as a Value Pack, two products of equal size, held tightly together in plastic. The more the merrier. The more the cheaper.

I was like a big bottle of lotion that came with a tiny trial size. Each date I went on was like another trial-size product. Fun to try, easy to toss away.

I spent the week cleaning my sister's house, looking after the dog, doing laundry. My sister was still in a lot of pain; she could barely lift anything.

My mom spent the week washing the windows, making dinner, correcting my posture, and telling me what she liked better about the haircut I had *now,* which was more feminine, *much better* than the way it was *before,* which was too *severe.* "What I don't like is that Hitler look," she concluded.

"What's that supposed to mean?"

"I don't like it when girls have that piece off to the side that's so severe. That one little piece that comes down. That's how Hitler wore it. It looks better now."

"I never wore it that way."

"And I don't like it when you tuck it behind your ear. Here," she said, fluffing up my hair. "That's better."

"I never wore it like Hitler."

"Well, your bangs were going across your forehead. I don't like that."

My mother is separate from me. She is entitled to her own opinion. I am my own person. I am entitled to my own opinion. My mother does not define me.

I washed dishes and held Georgia as often as I could wrangle her away from my mother. Tiny Georgia smiled when I sang to her, which I appreciated, even though I knew smiles at that age were involuntary. I believed that in my case perhaps they were genuine. Maybe I was one of those people who dogs and babies loved! I'd just never been *around* dogs and babies!

I was up to my elbows in soapy water one afternoon when my mom called me into the living room. "Oh, this dog! This dog is so, oh, *get down!* Shannon, could you get in here and calm this dog down? I want to take a picture of the new family."

"Come here, Shasta," I said, and I went to get her a biscuit. "Maybe you'll be in the next photo." She panted at me and stuck her nose in my crotch, which my sister had told me was a sign of disrespect. The dog thought she was superior to me and was establishing dominance.

What did it mean that the dog thought she was better than me? That the dog asserted herself, when I couldn't even tell my mother not to criticize my hair?

★   ★   ★

"I think Georgia feels calm around you," my sister said, sitting down next to us on the couch one evening.

"Really?" I said.

"I really do," she said, adjusting Georgia's little newborn hat. Georgia began to fuss. "I think she likes her auntie."

I sang Georgia a song about a little girl who wished cheeseburgers grew on trees and she stopped crying. I sang her a song about rain, "Rainy night. Rainy night. Here we are. It's a rainy night," and she fell asleep.

How do you get from being single to being *here,* in this condition of American grace? With my own home, my own family?

Maybe I was one of those people who was always supposed to be single, like my great-uncle Bob, a gentle, delicate, affable man. He was the one designated to take care of his parents in their old age, while the rest of his siblings married and cultivated their own lives. But they had lived out on the windy Minnesota prairie, in the early 1900s, and assigning one sibling as caretaker was a convention of the times.

Oh, please, God. Let it have been a convention of the times. Now I could put them in a home, right? With Scrabble and movie night.

Surely they would enjoy that.

This morning, my last in Portland, Shasta woke me up by licking my ear and then trying to lift my hand with her snout. I made coffee and had some toast and was watching *Today* when I started to feel shaky. I had a little flutter in my chest. I drank a big glass of orange juice and went back into the den to start packing. My mom had left a day earlier, and my sister's husband, Clifford, would have to take me to the airport that afternoon.

I packed my suitcase, but by the time I was done, I needed to lie down. My sister had been up at 5 A.M. and was taking a nap on the couch with Georgia, and Clifford was upstairs ripping through a Tom Clancy novel. I was dizzy, light-headed, and I lay back down on the futon in the den.

I woke up about an hour later and didn't feel any better. What was this? My chest felt like it was filling with air, and yet, at the same time, was strangely constricted. It didn't feel like an asthma attack, more like the worst case of low blood sugar I'd ever had.

I went into the kitchen and grabbed some sliced turkey and started eating it out of the package. I poured myself another glass of orange juice.

"What are you doing?" My sister came into the kitchen holding Georgia, who was asleep.

"Do you want a sandwich if I make one?" I said.

"Sure. How about some soup, too? There's soup in the cupboard."

I made turkey sandwiches and soup while my sister took Georgia upstairs. I got out the baby carrots and pickle spears. I shoved a couple of pickle spears into my mouth. No matter what I ate, I still felt like I was standing behind myself.

"How are you feeling?" I asked my sister while we were eating. "Do you want to share half of another sandwich?"

"Sure," she said. "Crappy. I've never been this tired. Now I know what it's like to be you and Mom."

The family joke is that my mom and I can sleep through anything. The abandoned farmhouse at the end of our block burned down when I was in fourth grade, and five fire trucks came roaring up the street, right past our house. My parents were at couples counseling, and our baby-sitter tried to wake me up so that I could watch the flames devour the old house, but I slept through the entire thing.

"Well, that sucks," I said. I felt like crying. Maybe it was hormones.

"Thanks for everything you did this week," Greta said. "I don't know what I would have done without you guys. Now it's just going to be us. Although I don't think I needed any more advice from Flo."

"Thanks for letting me stay," I said. I thought about going back to my apartment and the big messes of paperwork that were piled up near the door because I had run out of other places to store them. The dishes I had left in the sink. The pile of dirty clothes on the bedroom floor.

"Are you okay? You're kind of quiet," my sister said.

"I think I'm having one of those low-blood-sugar moments," I said. "I'm just not feeling very well."

"It's probably because you don't want to go home and deal with Flo," she said. "I don't know how you do it, girl. Viva la distance, I say. Do you want some cookies?"

"That sounds good."

"What was that business about your hair yesterday?" my sister said through a mouthful of cookie.

"I don't even know. Something about Hitler. I don't comment on *her* hair. That drives me crazy."

"She needs other things to think about. She needs a job. Or a new hobby."

"Besides me," I said.

"Amen," said my sister.

By the time my brother-in-law dropped me off at the airport, I was convinced I was getting some kind of bug. It was that vague feeling of removal you get when you're sick, when you can't move as fast as everyone else. When normal activity seems miraculous. I hoped I hadn't given it to my family, especially not to Georgia. Maybe what I really needed was just to be able to sleep it off. If I could sleep it off, I'd feel better.

I produced my e-ticket and driver's license for the woman behind the ticket counter. "Ms. Olson, have you been in control of your baggage the entire time?" she asked.

For the first time, it struck me as a metaphorical question. Have I been in control of my *baggage*? Is *anyone* in control of their baggage?

"Yes," I said, as a matter of course, though I wanted to say, *What an interesting, life-changing question! I'm going to get a beer now!*

I sat down at the airport bar, where a handful of men were fixated on a baseball game, except for one guy, who was sitting alone and flipping through an issue of *Maxim*. A woman was reading *Vogue*. The three of us not watching baseball looked like an Edward Hopper painting.

"Listen to this," the *Maxim* guy said to the bartender. "Is this really true? To be a good lover you're supposed to take care of the women's orgasm and not even get one of your own?"

I looked up at the baseball game. I couldn't even tell who was playing. Everything was kind of fuzzy. They all looked to me like they were on the same team. I took another gulp of beer. I had ordered a raspberry-flavored one so it would seem less like drinking alone and more like juice, but the beer wasn't helping. I ordered a hot dog.

By the time I got on the plane and loaded my overhead baggage, my chest felt like it was expanding, and there was a darkness spreading through it, moving up the back of my skull. I sat down in my seat by the window, buckled my seat belt, and closed my eyes.

I was starting to really worry. It suddenly occurred to me that I could die on this flight. I had always been a comfortable flyer. Why hadn't I noticed before how fragile we were in this collection of sheet metal? Why wouldn't it all just come apart? Or drop out of the sky for no reason? *What if I died on this flight?* I wouldn't get to see my niece grow up. I would miss my sister. And what would everyone think when they saw my apartment? Would the news do an exposé on it? It was so messy that they'd never even find the information on my retirement account. And someone should get that money.

My chest kept expanding, would keep expanding, I felt, into eternity, in darkness, the stars of constellations pushing away from one another, refusing to be associated and named, moving toward anonymity, free bodies, moving further into the nothingness, into the cold.

The pressure behind my eyes was less if I kept them closed. I crossed my arms around myself. We hadn't even moved away from the gate yet. I willed myself to sleep. And woke up in midair.

It was dark. The pressure behind my eyes was almost gone. My chest seemed to have recontained itself. Maybe that raspberry beer had helped. The captain announced that we were over North Dakota.

I felt like a rabbit who had darted under a bush or into a small hole during a chase. My furious heartbeat had begun to slow.

I looked out into the darkness and saw the crescent moon hanging in the sky. For some reason, it was a comfort, that bright half moon.

Until I realized it was a wing light.

"Hi, Flo," I say when my mom picks me up at the airport. I give her a kiss on the cheek and hoist my luggage into the back of her Honda wagon.

"My God," she says. "Their house must have lifted off its foundation when you left there. What's in that suitcase?"

"Cripes, it's cold," I say, jumping into the car. "Why is it this cold in May? Is it going to stay this cold?"

"It's a front," Flo says. "I find it invigorating. Did you enjoy your last day in Portland?" she says, almost nailing a Subaru as she merges back into traffic.

"Mom!"

"I know what I'm doing," she says. "Relax."

My sister believes there is some kind of magical protective force field around our mother's car; she hums her way off freeway ramps, listening to Hawaiian slack-key guitar on her cassette player and gliding into traffic like a blind speed skater on crack. "I have never had an accident!" my mother says proudly every time I bug her about her driving. She says this because she knows I can't say the same. I've been either sideswiped or rear-ended five different times. By people who drive like my mother.

"Did you go to that retirement party last night?" I ask her.

"Oh, yah," she says. "You know it's kind of strange for me to go to those events now because I keep thinking that I don't know who's in charge of what anymore in Chaska. Ever since I retired from City Council. You know, the old guard is kind of moving on. They've kind of been through the community-service portion of their lives, you know, like I have. You do that for a while, and then you feel like you've contributed what you can and it's time for someone else to learn from doing that and to make their contribution."

"So, you didn't know anyone at the party?"

"Oh, I knew everyone," she says. "But that's unusual now. You know. And Jim Swanson was there, and he's been managing the grocery store for thirty years now and I think, 'What will happen on the day when I go to the grocery store and he's not there anymore to tell me a bad joke?' And that's sad. And Lolly and Ed were there. Do you remember them? Ed's been sharpening our knives at the hardware store for years. And now he's got Parkinson's, which is a tragedy. And I don't think you know Lolly, come to think of it. She drives bus."

"What do you mean, 'She drives bus'?" I say. "Any bus? Is that some kind of Chaska slang? 'Whoa! Lolly! She's the shit! She drives bus!'"

"Don't make fun of me," says Flo.

"I'm sorry," I say. "But you dropped your article."

"She's been a bus driver for twenty-five years," says Flo. "She drives *the* bus."

"For the schools?"

"Yes."

"You always have enjoyed clipping articles," I say.

Flo starts humming and fiddles around for a Hawaiian tape.

"Thanks for picking me up," I say.

"That's me. You can count on Mom. Always there whenever anyone needs anything."

Mother takes bow and accepts Emmy for starring role in a dramatic series.

"I thought it would be better if I left my car at your house," I say. "I don't like leaving it on the street for a week."

"Mhmmmm," she says.

"I'm sorry," I say. "I'm not in a very good mood."

"Well, don't take it out on me. I'm not your whipping post."

"I just thought it was funny. When did you start talking that way?"

"What way?"

"Old-fashioned Chaska," I say. "The old farmer's accent." The old farmers in Chaska were first-generation Americans whose parents had come from Germany. They had a grammar all their own, English with a German structure.

My mother is quiet.

We drive in silence for a while, except for the campy twang of the Hawaiian guitar coming from the tape deck.

I don't think my mother and I have ever had a normal fight. The kind you're supposed to have in therapy, where each person says how they *feel* and you move toward some mutual resolution.

The summer that I turned nineteen, for instance, I was home and she was going through menopause, which I did not understand at all. All I knew was that every time she mentioned her "hot flashes," it sounded dirty to me and I wanted to throw up.

My mother had placed oscillating fans around the house so that no matter where she was when a hot flash struck, she would be visited by a cooling breeze. The fans moved around the hallway, the laundry room, the kitchen, the upstairs living room, the television room. They were like exchange students rotating through different host families. They would appear as if from nowhere, *ta da!*, stay in one place for a while, and then move on to a new location, just when you'd become used to them.

And because my mother kept moving the fans around, I assumed for variety, I kept tripping over them.

I was racing down the hall for the phone one afternoon when I tripped over a fan that had just been placed just around the corner where the hallway turned. "Fuck!" I screamed, and grabbed my toe, which felt like it was broken. I tried to bend it, but it wouldn't move. "Fuckity fuck fuck!"

My mom came screeching down the hall like old brakes. "*Shaaaaannon!* Why are you swearing? There's no call for language like that. What's wrong with you?"

"Why do you have to keep these damn fans all over the house?"

"These *damn* fans are moving the air around in our house. These *damn* fans are circulating the air, young lady. These damn fans keep us all fresh, and it would help if you would stop tripping over them."

The fan was on its side on the carpeting, and because it

was still set in oscillating mode but was essentially stuck in one place, it was vibrating violently and looked like it was having a seizure.

"I don't trip on them on purpose!"

"Well, be more careful."

"Well, if you wouldn't move them around so much, I might stop tripping over them." I was standing now on my good foot, holding on to the door frame of my bedroom for balance.

"You know, you might try just being considerate and thinking about someone else's feelings for once," my mother said sharply, with her hands on her hips.

"Fuck you!" I blurted.

She stared at me with wide eyes. I was waiting for a hand to fly up and slap me in the face. It did not. She left her hands on her hips and raised her chin defiantly.

"Young lady," she said, "I will not."

And we both burst out laughing.

What else could she say?

It was as if we'd been mud wrestling. Dignity had been eliminated. At this point we were both just trying to get our balance, a little traction.

And it seemed that in that moment the division between mother and daughter, authority figure and fledgling, had melted away.

"Are you going to stay overnight?" she says now, as we're pulling up our street.

"It's pretty late," I say. "I guess that's probably a good idea."

"You could do your laundry tomorrow," she says. "Have you got anyplace you need to be?"

Tomorrow is Saturday. My plants probably need watering, but they've gone longer. I should have somewhere to be, I suppose, someone to be responsible to, but I don't. "No," I say.

I had left my apartment a total disaster area. Why not prolong the inevitable? The sinking into psychological despair upon returning to The Piles, which is how I'd started to refer to my seemingly unmanageable one-bedroom space, as if it were some kind of estate or gated community. *The Piles.*

"Can you still go out for your dad's birthday dinner tomorrow night?"

"Of course." That was the benefit of living near home. Free meals.

And laundry.

I am napping on the couch in the living room, waiting for my last load of laundry to dry, when my mother says, "Come here. You've got to see this."

I open my eyes to see her standing at the kitchen sink, binoculars in hand.

"The squirrels are *really* going at it," says my mom.

"Ish," I say. "Why don't you just get cable?"

"Get your mind out of the gutter," she says. "And we have cable. Come here and look."

I get up and stretch. I can feel that my hair is sticking out and doing something weird, and my mother confirms this by saying, "You're quite a vision."

"Give me those," I say, grabbing the binoculars.

"Third tree over by Millie's yard," says my mom. "See? Look for a bright yellow spot."

"What is that?"

"The squirrels have stolen our windshield scraper," she says. "We have a broken one that I was using to stir the birdseed in the big crock there, but I always put it back in the crock. I think your father must have left it out. That's so like him."

"So what are they doing?"

"They've taken a liking to it," says my mom. "I think they're trying to drag it up into their nest. I saw one trying to drag it up the tree earlier, and he got about halfway up before dropping it. See? That yellow spot is the brush on the end."

"It's pretty exciting around here," I say, handing her the binoculars. "Where is the windmill?" I say, looking back out the window. For as long as I could remember, a windmill had been spinning in the fields behind our house.

"Twiggy sold it at auction," my mom says. "He needed the money. Go get ready for dinner."

In truth, I kind of envy my parents the little woodland dramas that take place in their yard, the life that shows up there. The seeming domestic grace and tranquillity of it. One morning, my mother woke up to find a plump wild turkey sitting in the middle of the backyard. She called me at work to tell me about his colors, the iridescent blues and rusts. Another morning, five deer were nibbling in the fields. "It's nice to have new life," she had said, "now that the cows are gone." Twiggy Johnson had had to sell off the dairy cows that used to graze in the open fields behind our house. He was getting old and they were too expensive to maintain.

"I thought you were going to say, 'Now that you kids are gone,' " I had said.

"No," she had said, "I don't miss you." And she started laughing. "I just miss the cows." And she laughed some more. "I'm funny!" she said.

For dinner we go to the Mall of America, a retail structure so big that it is probably visible from space. My dad and I mill around Nordstrom's, waiting for my mom to finish looking at handbags.

"So, what are these shoes?" says my dad, picking up a pair of heavy-lugged loafers. "Dr. Martians? Why would you want to wear Martian shoes?" He's not trying to be funny. When the sales attendant asks us if we need help, I tell him we are *beyond* help.

"Okay," says my mother, approaching us from the handbags. "I'm ready."

We maneuver our way around the enormity of the mall, up escalators and around kiosks, past huge herds of tourists standing in front of the Green Bay Packers store, a couple of smoothie places, Macy's, Bloomingdale's, Banana Republic, Stuck on You (a store devoted entirely to magnets), the Body Shop, and Camp Snoopy, with its indoor roller coaster, a gigantic swinging ride shaped like an ax, and an enormous fountain shaped like a dog dish.

"You know," says my mom, stepping carefully onto yet another escalator, "people come here to spend the day, but you'd think it would just make them depressed, and overwhelmed."

"Why is that, do you think?" says my father.

"I mean, look at all this stuff. You think people would come here and just start to feel bad about what they don't have. You work and work and work and come *here* and think, 'My God, if I just made more money, I could have *all this stuff.*'"

"That's true," I say, watching a store called Cut Up, devoted entirely to knives, get smaller as our escalator goes higher.

At the California Café we get a good table, away from the noise of Camp Snoopy's roller coaster, and my mother is delighted with the design of the chairs and with the tile that's been placed on the middle of the table to hold the olive oil. "What a beautiful purple!" she exclaims. The hostess smiles.

My dad orders a Jack Daniel's and my mom and I each order a glass of white wine.

"Hey," my dad says, looking over at the bar, "that's Roy." Roy is my mom and dad's divorced friend, who's now dating eligible sixty-somethings. Roy and his date have their arms around each other.

"Go sneak up on them," I tell my dad.

"I'm not going to sneak up on them," he says.

"I think that's the woman Roy keeps talking about," says my mom.

"I think Roy's getting a little action," I say, nudging my dad on the elbow and winking.

"More than you're getting," says my dad, "hanging out with your parents. What's wrong with you?" He bursts out laughing.

"Hey!" I take a swig of chardonnay.

My mom and dad want to know about my friends who are pregnant and buying homes, which is almost all of them. I tell them instead about this guy at work who has just been diagnosed with manic depression and who just got someone pregnant. *His mania,* I tell them, *manifests itself in uncontrolled sexual impulses.* I hope, by telling the story, to make my life seem enormously adequate in comparison.

"I *thought* he was manic-depressive," says my mom. "I mean, I thought that right away." She is devouring the crab-cake appetizer that she said we should go ahead and order, even though she didn't want any.

"You've never met him, Mom," I say.

"From what you said about him before," says my mom, "I thought that right away."

"So, he's getting married?" asks my dad.

"No," I say, "he's going to be a father, but he's not marrying the mother."

"Edward," says my mother, "wouldn't Bill like these?"

"Who's Bill?" I say.

"Bill likes all food," says my dad.

"Who's Bill?" I say.

"But he loves crab cakes," says my mom.

"That's true," says my dad.

There are theories and measures of relativity that haven't been adequately explored.

For instance, Bill (whoever he is) liking crab cakes holds the same interest as someone else being a sex addict and fathering a child with a woman he doesn't love, depending on your vantage point. When you are sixty-five, the crab cakes are more interesting.

"The, um, whatever this is on the side," says my mother, forking some purple shredded something or another, "is real good, too."

"I think it's some kind of fancy coleslaw," I say.

"So, he doesn't want to be a father?" says my father.

"Who, Bill?" says my mother.

"He would love to be a father," I say, "just not with this woman."

"Hmmm," says my dad.

"It's quite a responsibility," says my mother. "Parenthood." She is holding up her empty chardonnay glass and looking around for the waiter.

In the fifties and early sixties, it was a given that you'd get married. You were single, and then you got married. Once you were married, you kept the same job for thirty years.

If you were like my parents, you were the first generation to go to college. You learned; you drank martinis; you smoked Lucky Strikes; you got married. You had kids and had to stop smoking. You bought orange and green furniture. Green and gold phones and refrigerators. You bought your kids orthodontia, better teeth, a more American smile. You took some trips to Florida, *before* it got overdeveloped. Collected shells on the beach and brought them back to set on your kitchen windowsill, where you watched the drifting fields of snow and waited for spring. Kept an eye on the squirrels. Soon you were redesigning your interior with *beige,* and experimenting, tentatively, with those new microwaves. Reminding yourself not to put aluminum foil in them. And before you knew it, you were giving your now college-age kids the green and gold and orange leftovers, the butterfly and beanbag chairs, now available in upscale catalogs at super-inflated prices. Angular ashtrays and horn-rimmed glasses. Audrey Hepburn's capri pants, the kind of thing you wore in your twenties and thirties, in between pregnancies. You haven't lived that long and already it's all coming around again.

"I'm going to say hello to Roy before he leaves," says my dad, plopping his napkin down on the table just as the waiter comes with our dinner.

"Damn," I say to my mom. "I should have married a doctor. I can't afford to eat this way."

"Well, you're not married yet," says my mom.

"There's no hope for me, Mom. It's too late." I'm a little drunk, I realize. "Take the lifeboat, you!" I say to my mother, with one hand over my chest. "You have such promise! You," I say, "have a future!"

"Oh, cripes," she says, waving her fork around, separating the air from the air, "you've got time."

There are cute babies everywhere at the mall tonight, and I begin to feel palpably empty.

"There's a cute one," I say.

"I was watching that one earlier," she says.

"I don't think we can have kids in my building. Pets or kids. Fish, maybe."

"Read those articles I clipped for you," she says. "Then you won't feel bad. They're really comforting, those articles. You know, I bet some of your married friends envy your freedom."

"That father is cute, too," I say.

"Yes," she says, "I noticed that. Here, try some of this." She plops some kind of potato concoction on my plate. Potato slices baked with layers of mushroom.

I take a bite. "Oh, my God. That's really good."

"Isn't it?" says Flo.

My dad brings Roy and his date back to our table for introductions, and when they leave, we order dessert.

"So," says my dad, "what's new? How was the rest of your time in Portland?"

"Pretty good."

"Did you whoop it up?"

"Yeah, we whooped it up," I say, rolling my eyes. "We sent Georgia out to get us more beers."

"She's pretty cute, that little one," he says. "I bet you miss her."

It's true. I did. Her little baby smell. The commotion of a new life.

"Anything exciting going on this week?"

"Just work," I say. "Oh, I ordered a new bed and they're delivering it on Thursday. It's my first piece of real furniture. My first adult-type purchase." I had been in graduate school for five years, and I'd run my credit cards up to their limit. Finally, I had paid them off and was making some money.

"Really?" says my dad. "Hooray! Good for you."

"Are they delivering it to *your* apartment?" says my mother. "Where is there room for more furniture in *your little* apartment? What size is it?"

"Queen," I say.

"What's wrong with your old bed?" my mother asks, looking like she's just swallowed a filling. "What are you going to do with the old one?"

The old one was a twin-size bed that I'd been lugging around for years. It had been my brother's bed when he lived at home. It was the bed my brother had made out on with his high-school girlfriends.

"I hate that thing," I say. "It's too small. I can bring it back to the house if you want it."

"You know," says my mother, "just because you get a new bed doesn't mean a boyfriend comes with it. You need to be careful."

"Mother," I say, "I'm thirty-three."

"What does that mean, 'I'm thirty-three'?" she says. "Edward, what does that mean?"

I am waiting now for her to launch into a speech that she's been giving me since I was in junior high school. "You know, sex requires a lot of emotional maturity. You have to be ready to *handle* it . . ."

"It means she's thirty-three," my dad says, taking a sip of his coffee.

"Never mind," I say. Note to self: *In future, do not mention bedroom, bedroom furniture, anything in bedroom to mother.* Note to self: *This is why brother and sister live so far from home.* "How about those squirrels?" I ask.

"What about the squirrels?" says my mom.

"Do you suppose they'll ever get that windshield scraper up into their nest?"

"Maybe," she says. "You know, they're always eating my birdseed, and I suppose, since the scraper was in the birdseed crock, to them it must smell like dinner."

"Sure," says my father. "Why does anyone do anything?"

Chapter 2

Maybe that *was* the reason anybody did anything. Simple comfort.

What did it really mean to choose someone to be with for the rest of your life? Maybe I'd been holding out too long, for something that didn't exist. Maybe chemistry had nothing to do with it. Maybe that person just smelled like dinner.

My friend Ellie, for instance, got married a couple of years ago, and with that had come an enormous house on the golf course in Wanita—the kind of place where in Victorian times you might have been invited to spend a fortnight—complete with a security system, a big-screen TV, a bar, a sauna, a golf room where you could drive or putt, a Jacuzzi, and an enormous built-in fish tank. Ellie keeps having to buy new fish because she still hasn't figured out how to clean the tank, and because the fish swim so quietly, she keeps forgetting they are there.

Like me, Ellie never had a huge income of her own. She was an English and art history double major, and when we finished college, she got a job in marketing at a small local publishing house. She did all right, but without David, who is a partner in his advertising agency, she would not have fish or the premium cable channels.

The furniture Ellie had in her apartment when she was single had been donated by family friends: old corduroy chairs with worn arms, her grandmother's old loveseat with a print of geese wearing bonnets. That furniture was in the rec room now, where David and his buddies could spill beer and it wouldn't matter.

I wondered if married people sometimes simply woke up and thought, *I'm so glad we have a house! I'm so glad we have premium cable!*

Being married, as far as I could tell, was like having a roommate after college. Two people could always get a better space than one. You *qualified* for things you would never qualify for as a single person. It was like a race. In the qualifying heat of life, being single meant that you always came in last. Not only were you *single,* you still had to live in an apartment. You saw your married friends when they could squeeze you in between feedings and baths and diaper changes. You went to their homes because it was easier.

Most of my married friends had never even seen my apartment because it was never convenient to come all the way to St. Paul, which was fine, I guess, because my space was small and it was always a mess. But the fact that no one ever came over made things worse. The more it was only me there, the more I began to live like a yeti in my little drifts of paperwork.

I remember that Ellie, when she first started dating David,

had had a crush on one of her coworkers. Her coworker drove a Geo Metro, had a ponytail, came in to work at 11 A.M., and spent the summers fishing in Alaska. I knew, even though Ellie never said it, that that was why she had chosen David instead. David had short hair and came home every night for dinner. He left for work early every morning. He drove a car that performed well in crash tests. And there was comfort in that.

The weekend after I got back from Portland, Ellie invited me out to their house for a getaway. She and David had just remodeled the guest room, and she wanted me to be the first guest. Plus, David was going fishing with his buddies.

We spent Saturday morning sitting on lawn chairs, reading *People* magazine, and drinking iced tea. We planned to go shopping later that afternoon. I was reading about who was on the Zone diet when my vision began to blur around the edges. I began to feel tired; my muscles were limp. Maybe I did have diabetes.

"Ellie? Do you think I could make myself a sandwich?"

"Seriously?" It hadn't been that long since breakfast.

"I'm just feeling kind of shaky. I think I'm having one of those low-blood-sugar kind of moments."

"Help yourself," Ellie said. "If you don't mind, I'll stay out here." She tilted her face up to the sun and readjusted herself in her lawn chair.

I went into the kitchen and drank a big glass of milk. I made myself a peanut butter–and–jelly sandwich. I ate a banana. Then I went back to my lawn chair to lie down again.

I still felt like my heart was pounding too fast. I couldn't say that I was thinking much of anything. My mind was like white bread, insubstantial. I looked out at the people playing golf on the course behind Ellie's yard. The pond was up this year because it had rained all spring. Men in shorts were chipping onto the green. I was dizzy and all I could think about was going to sleep, but we had only been up for a few hours.

I went back into the kitchen and heated up a bratwurst in the microwave. I ate a piece of cheese and a pickle. I drank two glasses of water and another glass of milk.

"Are you having a growth spurt?" Ellie said when I sat back down again. "You have your period, yah?" she said, imitating the nurse in our college infirmary. The nurse had had a German accent and, no matter what your reason for coming in—you could have a nail through your palm—if you were a woman, she would say, "You have your pewiod, yah? Cwamps?"

"Cwamps," I said, settling back into my chair.

The sun was high in the sky and two dragonflies were mating in midair, floating over Ellie's dribbling fountain. The world, I thought, was pulsing and procreating and my chest was going to seize up. For ten minutes, while Ellie flipped through the *People* I had abandoned, I watched a swarm of gnats congregate around the hydrangeas.

"I think I need to go in and lie down for a while," I said. "I'm sorry. I'm just not feeling very well."

"Well, we don't want you not feeling well," said Ellie. "Especially when you're our inaugural visitor in the new guest room. Maybe it's the heat?"

"Maybe."

"It's starting to get to me, too," she said.

I went into the dark, air-conditioned guest room, where Ellie had left a mint on my pillow. She had also presented me with a first-guest welcome kit, including sample-size shampoo and conditioner, a tiny fragrant soap, and some body splash.

I moved the mint and set the stuffed bunny that was nesting in between the pillows on the floor.

I lay down sideways on the bed. When we were small, my

mother always had us lie sideways at the end of the bed during nap time. Or, we could lie with our heads where our feet normally were, and put our feet on the pillow.

This was to differentiate it in our minds as a *nap*.

It meant that we weren't giving up on the day.

"Feeling any better?" Ellie asked when I came back downstairs a couple of hours later. She was curled up on the couch watching *Terms of Endearment* on the Lifetime channel.

I had fallen into a deep sleep, in which I had drooled and woken myself up snoring. I think, in my dream, Prince had kissed me. Everything else I had felt that morning was still buzzing inside of me, but now it was mediated by my groggy half-sleep.

"Not really," I said. "Do you think I could make myself a drink?"

"It is the weekend, isn't it?" Ellie said. She got all the ingredients for gin and tonics out, and stuck a jar of olives on the counter and handed me a plastic sword. "Go for it," she said. I was grateful for this small recognition. Ellie knew I loved olives.

I wished that I could entertain Ellie and David in my own lovely home. That at the end of a lovely dinner, I could put the dishes in my lovely dishwasher, give everyone a lovely glass of dessert wine, and ask everyone to retire to my lovely living room.

Approximately three people could fit into my living room, but that was stretching it. I had an old futon couch and a rolling office chair with a torn seat and old foam spurting out of it. The bathroom and kitchen were tiny. The bedroom was big enough for my queen-size bed and that was about it.

Cleaning the apartment was a task of Sisyphean proportions. If you wanted to move the bed to get the dust out from underneath it, you had to move piles of magazines into the living room, put the nightstand and the alarm clock and the lamp out in the hallway, and shove one of the dressers partway into the closet, and so on. It made cleaning so depressing that I couldn't remember when I'd last done it.

The apartment had the occasional and inexplicable smell of an old man who has never dry-cleaned his leisure suit. I wondered if it was dust, or the old books I had, or maybe all the piles of paperwork I had been accumulating and couldn't bear to sort through. The smell waxed and waned. I got used to it.

Ellie and David had come over for drinks once. "I haven't been in an apartment for ages!" David had enthused. "Radiators! Awesome! Sometimes I wish I still lived in an apartment."

He was nice. That's why Ellie had married him.

"Hey!" Marty, one of the Web designers, sticks his head into my office while I'm looking up my daily horoscope. Every morning I check Joyce Jillson, Sydney Omar, and AstroLadies on my computer, and create a composite prediction. The most promising advice from each site. "Check it out," Marty says, handing me a sheet of paper with shades of gray on it. "I found a really cool Web site."

"What is it?"

"Federal satellite photos," Marty says.

"Satellite photos?"

"Yeah, old government photos. But you can get them now on the Web. I found my house in Albert Lea. The house I grew up in. The whole farm. You can see the barn."

"Really? Albert Lea? Why on earth would anyone be keeping track of what's going on in Albert Lea?"

"They have everything."

"You could see the barn?"

"It's, you know, a gray block. It's an eagle-eye view. But it's the barn. And I could see our house and the oak grove by the pond." Marty holds up a sheet. "See? Look." He points to the printout, shades of gray where there must be grass. Something lighter where the cornfields are. A dark block for the barn. A dark block for the house. A circle for the top of the silo. A lima bean–shaped blob for the pond. Dark splotches for the trees.

"Hey, that's cool," I say. I don't know why the idea is appealing, when actually the surveillance should be mortifying. Maybe it's just nice to imagine that somewhere out there, there's a record of everything. A picture of all of us.

Marty pulls the Web site up on my computer and then goes back to his desk.

It takes me a few minutes to find my hometown. I zoom in and out, looking for familiar landmarks. The photos take up a lot of memory. I fiddle with the coordinates and try to find downtown Chaska, the few blocks of it, the Minnesota River, and the two tiny lakes where they used to dig up clay for the brickyard.

We used to swim in the smallest one; after the brickyard went out of business, it became a public beach called the Clay Hole. My sister and I spent hours with our snorkeling equipment in the shallow end, diving for Freezie Pop containers that we'd filled with sand so they'd sink. Later, when we were big enough to swim out to the dock, we'd spend the day with our friends, eating Chips Ahoy cookies on the beach and marveling at the girls who smoked and wore crocheted bikinis.

Finally I find the Clay Hole, and the Dairy Queen that used to be down the hill from us. The Dairy Queen was torn down last year so that the city could expand Highway 41, but on the satellite photos, the Dairy Queen is still there. So are the houses that used to line the brickyard. And where there are now subdivisions, the old photos still show cornfields.

Then I find the Lutheran church at the end of our street. And here's Twiggy Johnson's farm, with fields of corn and soybeans, the barns and silos. Hey! Our house, the second-to-the-last gray square at the end of the street. And in our backyard, blobby conglomerations of crabapple trees and a small grove of Russian olives. A big dot for the maple tree that I used to run into with my sled.

I zoom in as close as I can and print it out. A sheet of ink-jet hieroglyphics. Strange symbols that mean nothing if you don't already possess the Rosetta Stone of familiarity.

Here we are.

If you're up there, looking down on us, this is what we look like. Trees and homes and grass. We're pretty simple.

"Hey, Flo," I say when I call my mom. "You're never going to guess what I found today."

"A husband," she says. And then laughs at her own joke for a while.

"Satellite photos," I tell her when she stops. "Of our house. I've seen our house from space."

"You're kidding," says Flo. "Now, is that on your computer?"

"Yeah. There's this Web site. You go to the site and you enter the town, and then you can scroll around and zoom in until you find what you're looking for."

"You *zoom* in? You *zoom* in. Huh. And they have Chaska? See?" she says. "Other people think Chaska is special." My mother is the poster child for our hometown, always talking it up to strangers as if it were some earthly paradise. She believes that people who live in a small town support one another, while everyone in California is crazy and people on the East Coast are bitchy and/or will mug you. Growing up, I believed her. "Did that Marty show you this one?" Flo says. "What does he do all day? Last week he had those dancing gerbils."

"Hamsters. Marty found it."

"Doesn't anybody work anymore?" says Flo.

"Well, he *is* one of our Web designers. He has to see what's out there. Anyway," I say, "I found our neighborhood and I printed it out. I'll send you a copy."

"Okay," says Flo. "So, did you see me?"

"Where?"

"On the satellite photo."

"No, Mother. I did not see you on the satellite photo."

"Nuts. Well, then, what good is it?"

It's true. The satellite view doesn't begin to explain much of anything. The real picture would show Flo adjusting her bifocals, sitting down with the *StarTribune,* clearing her throat, and taking a sip of the coffee she claims she doesn't drink anymore. It would show her reading the obituaries, which she does first thing every day "to see if I'm dead yet." It would show her leaving the neighborhood for water aerobics and coming home to sort through the mail. Making something interesting for lunch with cottage cheese. Walking next door to check on Millie, her ninety-year-old neighbor, to see if she needs more cream, white bread, or craft supplies.

But I guess I also found it kind of comforting, this picture of home, my little corner of the world. Where on Sunday nights we got to have steak and watch Disney at the dinner table. Where someone always warmed the car up in the winter before we got in. The place where I lived with a family. It wasn't a thing I felt very often anymore, like I actually belonged somewhere.

"Don't you think it's neat that someone is keeping track of all of us?" I say. "I think it's kind of cool that you can go back and see where you've come from."

"Well, excuse me," says my mother, "but I'm still here."

On Wednesday nights I go to group therapy, which was my counselor's idea. She had been nagging me for two years to join Toastmasters, a public-speaking group for businessmen who want to learn how to tell jokes, and I'd finally agreed to go to group therapy instead.

"You do isolate yourself, honey," she had said.

"I know," I had said. We were working on that. The counselor is sort of a cognitive behaviorist. We were working on a lot of things. Getting up early. Being comfortable with my own anger. Not letting shame paralyze me. (*Guilt and shame are two different things and only guilt is useful.*) Being comfortable with conflict. Putting work first, before leisure. Recognizing my priorities and establishing long-term goals.

"How am I supposed to *not* isolate myself if I'm putting work before leisure?" I asked the counselor.

"Just do your work," she had said, rolling her eyes.

It was a lot to keep track of.

Not telling my mother everything. That was another one.

Which seemed to be making my mother angry, though she wouldn't admit it.

"I am not someone who gets angry," my mother would say.

"Well, you seem angry," I would say. "Everyone gets angry."

"I don't get angry," she would say. "And if do, I will tell you."

"The counselor says that anger is a gift," I would say. "It means that you care enough to engage with someone."

"Well, that's interesting," she said. "Your father never gets angry with me. He just brushes everything off."

"We're not talking about Dad. I've already told you that I don't like it when you talk about Dad with me. Dad doesn't criticize you."

"Fine," she said. "I know. I know. We don't talk anymore. You've got your new rules and your whole new little adult life."

My whole new little adult life.

It was just one more reason not to tell her anything.

"I think you're ready and I just really think you'd get a lot out of group," the counselor said. "Everyone there has already done a good deal of individual therapy. It's a good group."

I see the counselor every Tuesday night. Lucy, my only girlfriend who is single, and only because she's divorced from what she calls her "starter marriage to Troy the asshole lawyer," asked me if I ever thought I would be done with therapy. Did I ever wonder if I depended on it too much? But I told her I was learning a lot and that it seemed worthwhile.

"It just seems," Lucy said, "like you're always referencing what your counselor said about something. And like you don't make any big decisions without checking with your counselor first."

I checked with the counselor to see if that was true.

"I don't know," the counselor said. "What do you think? Do you think your therapy is helping?"

"I think it's helping," I said.

"Good," she said.

Still, I wondered when I would feel comfortable making decisions on my own.

Trusting my own voice. That was another thing I was supposed to be working on.

"But my mom always had an opinion about everything," I told the counselor in our last session. "On what looked good together. The way the table should be set. How to fold the towels and T-shirts. How green, blue, or mauve plates were disgusting. You should serve food on white or black plates, so that the food can stand out and be its own decorative element. Which makes no sense when you're serving casserole."

When I was little, I told the counselor, I had a nightstand at the head of my bed. One day, I moved some of the books from my little bookcase onto the nightstand. I put a little plant there, too, along with my alarm clock.

My mother made me put it all back where it had been. Except for the alarm clock. She had given us each an alarm clock when we turned five, and we were responsible for getting ourselves up and ready for school.

"Why would you want all that clutter by your head?" my mother had said.

"I don't know why I remember that," I told the counselor, "but to this day, I feel guilty if I have anything besides the alarm clock on my nightstand."

And until I left for college, I told the counselor, I could barely leave the house without asking my mother what she thought of my outfit. Sometimes after I go shopping, I'll bring the new clothes out to my parents' house to see what my mother thinks of them.

"Well, that's got to stop," said the counselor. "You can wear whatever the hell you feel like wearing. We've got to get you trusting your own opinion."

"Do you think so?"

So we were working on that, too.

On this particular night, I'm ten minutes late for group, which is a big no-no, but I needed to stop at McDonald's. I think it's really hard to listen to other people's problems when you're hungry.

Group starts right at 6:00 P.M. with Old Business—anything you need to say to another group member that you didn't have a chance to the week before or in response to something that happened in group that week. Sometimes Old Business winds up taking almost the whole time if people are really pissed off at one another, which means we don't get time for New Business and have to rush into Closing Statements and Optional After-Group Hugs.

I've been coming here for six months and I still dread Closing Statements—even more than Optional After-Group Hugs, because that's informal and you can quietly disappear or send out negative body language.

With Closing Statements, we all hold hands in a circle like a bunch of fucking campfire girls, and then you're supposed to say something sincere about what you learned that night and what you're taking with you as you leave. Once I said, "This throw pillow. I'm going to take this throw pillow, thank you very much. And maybe this pen here that someone left on the coffee table." A couple of people in the group giggled, but the counselor and her partner, Dr. Douglas, just looked at me until I said something seemingly heartfelt.

Maybe that was all that was in my heart anyway, I wanted to say to them. Why do we always have to go scrounging around in our feelings like we're at some damn rummage sale?

It's the formality of Closing Statements that is hard for me. Formality and sincerity are two things I've always disliked. Along with harmony. Groups that sing in harmony, like Manhattan Transfer, make me want to shoot myself in the head.

When I'm really at a loss for Closing Statements, I say that I learned tonight that I'm not really lonely. That other people have similar feelings, even if our experiences are different. Which is true, but not specific to the evening's discussion.

The other members are generally better at saying what they really learned. After a few months, I started to notice that they were referencing one another in their Closing Statements, saying things like, "Dana, I was really moved by what you said about your mother tonight. And it helped me think about my girlfriend's shoplifting problem in a different way." Things like that. Which hadn't occurred to me to say. I am usually busy trying to solve their problems in my head, moving the pieces around like one of those puzzles that has only one missing square.

Tonight, Old Business takes about an hour because Harvey is pissed at Eileen.

Harvey says that Eileen thinks he's boring, that she rolled her eyes last week when he was talking about his ex-wife.

And Eileen says, "It's not that you're boring. It's just that you go on and on and on about your wife, and you're missing the point. Entirely."

"How would *you* know?" says Harvey.

"What's that supposed to mean?" Eileen crosses her legs.

"You go on and on and on about your husband."

"And?"

"Well, clearly he's an asshole. Why don't *you* move on?"

"I didn't say you needed to move on," Eileen says, crossing her arms over her chest. "That's not what I meant. And *don't* tell me what to do."

"Good!" says Dr. Douglas. "Eileen, I like how you're standing up for yourself."

"Well, he's pissing me off," she says.

"Can you tell Harvey why you're feeling angry?"

"I guess I'm not even angry," she says. "I mean, that's his problem. I just don't like him."

"Right now," Dr. Douglas adds.

"Maybe I don't like him at all," she says.

"Can you separate what you know about Harvey from his behavior right now?" Dr. Douglas asks.

"Not really," says Eileen. "He reminds me of my husband."

Dana looks like she's going to cry, and the counselor asks her to talk about it.

"This just reminds me of how my parents used to fight," she squeaks.

The Kleenex box is right underneath my chair, so I grab a handful and give them to Dana.

"Why don't you hold on to that," the counselor says gently. She means the feelings and not the wad of Kleenex. "And we'll come back to you when we're done with Harvey and Eileen." Dana nods.

Eileen says that Harvey pissed her off because he seemed to have no sympathy for her predicament. She's thirty-nine and wants to have children, at least one child, and just found out that her husband, soon to be ex-husband, has been having an affair with his secretary—how unoriginal—for three years. When Eileen found out, he didn't make any excuses; he just moved in with the secretary right away and told Eileen that if she hadn't spent so many nights working on her certification as a yoga instructor, they'd still be together. That downward dogs were ruining their marriage.

"Well, how do you think it feels to put your wife through medical school and then watch her run off with a male nurse?" Harvey says.

"Well, maybe there's a reason she ran off," Eileen says.

Old Business kind of merges into New Business. Harvey and Eileen keep fighting and then we move on to Dana, whose parents were alcoholics. "I know they did the best they could," she honks into a Kleenex.

I hardly ever bother to bring anything up. I always feel like I'm interrupting, like my issues aren't worthy of group attention. I could talk about my visit to Portland, how I felt kind of lonely but at the same time didn't want to go home. How nice it was to be around a baby. I had no idea I would like one so much. Or how I'm wondering if I should get checked for diabetes or something because of what happened on the plane and at Ellie's.

But when the counselor asks if there's anything else, I stay quiet. Just like when I was in college: I would want to talk in class, but I'd start shaking and turn red, my mouth would go dry. I'd practice what I wanted to say and just when I'd finally get up the courage to say it, the professor would move on. While we might have been discussing aspects of epistemological theory a minute ago, now, in the middle of a discussion of something else entirely, I might blurt, "If we create our own existence, why would we make it so depressing? Isn't that proof that it's real?"

"Let's go to Closing Statements, then," says the counselor.

"Shannon," she says, startling me, "what is your Closing Statement? What are you taking with you, from the group?"

Crap. I look over at Harvey, whose curly dark hair is flaring from his head. Harvey teaches math at a community college and always comes here straight from class; tonight he has half a sandwich and three pencils in his shirt pocket. I appreciate his eccentricities because he is completely unaware of them.

"I like the way Harvey says what's on his mind," I say. "I'm going away thinking about that. And I like the way Eileen stands up for herself."

"Good," says the counselor. "Maybe next week you'll say more about you."

Chapter 3

Ellie said I should at least *try* going out with Ian once. Like a parent insisting that her toddler take at least one bite of something before leaving the table.

"I know, I know," she said. "I don't envy you and I'm glad I'm not out there anymore. But I always thought Ian was nice."

Ian had worked at the press when Ellie was there. She'd recently run into him at a dinner party and found out that he was single, and thought that since I'd done my graduate work in English, Ian and I would have something in common.

"If he watched television all the time," I'd said to Ellie, "we would have something in common. If he's too lazy to cook, we will have something in common."

I had found over the years that people usually set you up

with people *they* would like to date if they were still single. I had been set up with a flight instructor, a chiropractor, and a lab technician. Somewhere in the middle of each date, I had realized what it was about each man that would appeal to my married friend. The flight instructor was more passionate than her husband. The chiropractor was a good listener. The lab technician looked like my friend's ex-boyfriend. Each date had ended with the guy saying, "Well, it was nice to meet you."

The more I thought about it, dating had become like going to the grocery store on sample day. You walked by, you tasted, you kept walking.

"I honestly think you might like him," Ellie said. "He has very good manners."

"Good manners?" I said. "Well, Jesus! Why didn't you say so?"

"Really," said Ellie. "Come on. Don't be that way. He's just nice."

Ian and I met at a little wine bar in the warehouse district. We made it through the night coasting on the fumes of introductory conversation: number of siblings, college, work. He had lived in Seattle for a few years and finally moved back to Minnesota. He hated camping.

"You really hate camping? Have you ever gone camping?"

"No," he said.

"Then how can you hate camping?"

"It seems like an awful lot of work," he said. "For a vacation."

"That's what I thought," I said, "the first time I went. But the great thing about camping is that you kind of get into a groove after a while. All you worry about is finding your way to a campsite, what you're going to eat next, and where you can go to the bathroom. It's very relaxing."

"I don't like the idea of not washing my hair."

"But that's the best part," I said. "No pun intended."

"Ha," Ian said. "I don't know. Being in the middle of nowhere freaks me out." There was just the right amount of product in his hair to make it look both coifed and neglected. And I suppose because we were talking about hair, he ran his hands through his, shaking his head a little as if to free the few dark strands that then fell over his forehead. He tucked them back behind his ear.

"How did you manage to live in the Northwest and not camp?" I said, thinking of my brother and his wife and friends, who went camping almost every weekend.

"I don't know. There are other things to do. I'd rather see a good movie and smoke a cigarette. Mind?" he said, pulling out a pack of Marlboros and offering me one.

"I better not," I said, although it looked appealing. "I have asthma. My dad smokes those every once in a while."

"Marlboros? Oh, great. I smoke a dad cigarette. I remind you of your dad. That's great."

"No, you don't," I said. Despite his slick hair, Ian had a softness in his cheeks, something dewy around the eyes. My dad looked like a Republican.

Ian knew a lot about Stanley Kubrick and I was embarrassed by the fact that the only Kubrick film I'd seen was *Dr. Strangelove*.

"How? How is that possible?" he said.

"I don't know," I said.

"That's tragic," he said, blowing smoke at the wall. He went on for a while about *A Clockwork Orange*—it was his favorite movie; why was it every guy's favorite movie?—and I was beginning to get pissed off. I didn't tell *him* that *his* life was tragic because he never watched *Frasier*. Or because he'd never gone camping. Maybe I was just in a bad mood. Maybe this date hadn't been such a great idea. I had hoped for instant chemistry.

The end of my long, bad streak. So far, it wasn't happening. So far, it seemed we had nothing in common.

"Doesn't that movie open with a rape scene?"

"Yeah," he said.

"That's the only thing I know about it, I guess," I said.

I hadn't read Ian's favorite author, either, though I'd heard of him.

"What *do* you read?" he said with a disarming smile, broad and warm, but which felt somehow hostile. Or maybe I was projecting.

"Isn't his big book about a stockbroker who's a serial killer?" I asked. "And it opens with a woman splayed out on the trading floor? Didn't that book make a lot of people really mad?" *What do you read? What was that about, Mr. Culture Police?*

"They don't know what they're talking about," he said. "He writes with this incredible satirical sense. He's really describing the downfall and decay of American culture. The commodification of everything," he said, blowing smoke. "Our craven selfishness." The strands of hair he'd tried to control earlier sprang back out.

"Our craven selfishness?"

"Okay, that was on the back of the book," Ian admitted.

"Can't he do that without butchering women?"

"That's the point," he said. "That women represent what's beautiful, the attainment of an unrealizable dream. A Holy Grail. It's a representational murder."

"That's just a nice way of saying *misogyny*," I said. "There's no such thing as a representational murder."

"Sure, there is," he said, blowing smoke up at the rag-painted walls, which were supposed to make the restaurant have an Italian-villa feel.

"Only if you're a guy," I said, "would it be that. Why does she have to be nude?"

"You've got a little feminist streak," he said, which made it sound like I'd put highlights in my hair—Saffron Suffragette, or Gloria Stun 'Em #45. "It's kind of sassy." He smiled again.

"Thank you. I guess," I said. I couldn't decide whether Ian was one of those guys who would actually treat a woman well despite his misogynistic taste in film and literature, or if underneath his pleasant voice and decent manners, there really was a snorting, drooling pig.

"It's appealing," Ian said, cupping his chin in his hand and gazing at me.

Maybe he actually liked women who said what they were thinking. In graduate school I had been on dates with men who had perfect feminist politics and who had read all the right theory but, when it came down to it, were too insecure and at the same time too egocentric to really notice anything about you.

When the bill came, I offered to split it, but Ian said, "Hey, you're the brave soul who agreed to go on a date with me. My treat."

Maybe it was me. One of my moods. Maybe I was too quick to judge. But I kept hoping to meet someone who I'd have a *feeling* about, and I didn't feel much, for whatever reason, for Ian.

"Can I walk you to your car?" Ian said.

It's just that here I was again. In the gray area. Nothing *really* wrong. Nothing fantastically right, either.

"Do you want to do something during the week?" Ian said. We were standing by my car and I was wondering if he would try to kiss me. This particular moment on a first date always made me incredibly nervous. It was like Optional After-Group Hugs. It was too free-form. There were no hard-and-fast rules; there was no structure in place. The triathlon coach, for instance, at the end of our first date, had simply grabbed me by the back of the head, pulled me into him, and planted his lips against mine. Which was more caveman than I'd been ready for.

"We have a big presentation this week," I said. It was true, although if I'd felt more strongly about Ian, I probably would have wanted to see him during the week, at least for dinner. And I might have wanted more for him to kiss me. I kind of did; he had nice lips, a nice smile. But on the other hand, it was easier just to go home.

"Okay," he said. "Talk during the week?"

"Sure," I said.

"If you're not too busy," he said. He turned and began walking down the street.

"Where's your car?" I said.

"Right there."

"Oh."

"Well, good night," he said. "I'll wait until you go."

Ellie was right. He did have good manners. Why didn't I like him more? Maybe it was first-date jitters. Maybe my heart just wasn't open to it in the first place. Maybe the whole problem was me, making everything more difficult than it needed to be.

Chapter 4

I guess I've always thought of Adam as my standby. Another passenger on a flight that might never get off the ground.

We met during our first month of college. He lived in the women's dorm at St. Olaf, one of twelve men in our freshman year who had the dubious distinction of being Harriet Larsen Men, housed in the basement of the only women's dorm left on campus. Why there was still, in 1985, a women's dorm and why they were in it that year was not clear, but it produced the Lutheran college's most racy dorm T-shirt to date: *Larsen: Where the Women Sleep on Top*. How approval for the shirt had slipped past the dean at a school where you couldn't buy condoms, cigarettes, or *The New York Times* on campus, no one knew.

And how Adam and I ever became friends is as unlikely as the fact that I wound up staying at St. Olaf for four years.

One night I had walked by the open door of his dorm room, where he and his roommate and some girls I didn't know were sitting on the floor playing Trivial Pursuit.

I had my laundry with me, and I remember that I was wearing a powder-blue sweatshirt that said *St. Olaf College* on the front. My entire wardrobe consisted of three sweaters and a few shirts, all from The Limited Outback Collection. I had always thought I was kind of fashionable, but I now realized that I had only been fashionable in a Chaska way, in my small town, where we'd developed our own particular, parochial ideas of what looked good. And where, ultimately, people didn't actually care all that much about what you wore. The girls in the dorm room next door to mine were best friends from snooty Wayzata High School. One of them had come into my room one night, ostensibly to see what my roommate and I were up to. She had peered into my closet and pronounced its contents "interesting." Her closet (I had already noticed, because none of the closets had doors) was filled with matching shoes, sweaters, and hair accessories, all organized in those plastic hanging units. Like hundreds of other women on campus, she dressed every morning for class in a color-coordinated outfit and went to the campus chapel service every morning at 10:05—which everyone simply called "Going to Chapel."

At another school, "Going to Chapel" might have been a funny euphemism for illicit sex or smoking pot in some hidden stairwell, but at St. Olaf, it really meant going to chapel. I took advantage of that time, a time in which no classes could be scheduled, to sleep.

Two women down the hall from me were in the St. Olaf Choir, and would burst spontaneously into sacred song on their way to the showers, on the paths walking to class, or as they filed into the dining hall.

Was this what the world outside of Chaska was like? I had always lived in one place. The people at my brother's school were a bunch of granola-genius types. And here was the rest of the world, I thought. I should try to adapt.

I had bought the St. Olaf sweatshirt hoping that it would transform me into someone who felt like she actually belonged where she was, and I was on my way to the laundry room, when Adam's roommate shouted out that I should join their Trivial Pursuit game.

Adam's roommate, Greg, was cute. He had dark curly hair and was on the swim team. His shoulders were broad and he had an infectious giggle that sounded like Elmer Fudd's. He was a pastor's kid, but he wasn't like any of the other PKs I'd met. At St. Olaf, being a PK was like being one of the heirs to the Hilton fortune. You came from a certain social elite, and with that came certain pressures that you needed to blow off by partying your brains out as soon as you were out of your parents' view. The pastors' kids had the most sex, smoked the most pot, and were most likely to throw up, dance on the bar, or flash their breasts at strangers. They went wild as soon as they got to school; the entire academic calendar became a kind of Mardi Gras, because at home they had been forced to behave as good examples of Christian Youth. At St. Olaf none of this wildness damaged their status as sacred social cows. On the contrary, they were revered for their previous suffering and afforded complete grace. They were like Homecoming Queens.

But Greg was quiet and shy and smart and kind of nerdy, and I liked that. We were in Music Appreciation class together and he had tripped and knocked over all of the professor's presentation slides. Then he had put them all back in the carousel upside down.

I stopped at Greg's door, dropped my laundry basket, and sat down in a small open space. I wasn't sure whose trivia team I was supposed to be on, or if there even were teams, and when I finally knew one of the answers, I just kind of blurted it out. Greg started laughing.

"Be quiet! Don't shout the answers," some tall guy with curly red hair and an argyle sweater vest said to me. "It's not your turn."

That was Adam, and I immediately hated him.

Adam was dating one of the women in the St. Olaf Choir. They seemed to have been hooked at the mouth from the moment they'd arrived on campus. Like Adam, she was tall and bony and wore sweater vests. Like Adam, she planned on being a prelaw-and–political science double major.

I resented their patrician builds and practicality. I resented the fact that they not only seemed to belong here but that they had each other. And so when I went down to the basement to visit Greg, I generally ignored them. Which they didn't seem to notice because they were always making out.

Greg was as shy as I was, and we mostly just turned red when we saw each other and had trouble speaking our native language. Greg and I would get drunk at parties and make out, and when we'd see each other again, we'd be too embarrassed to talk. In the back of my mind, I was terrified. I had never really had a boyfriend, and Greg was Lutheran. What if he wanted me to have sex? I didn't know how. And if you dated someone long enough, you were bound to have sex. Plus, my mother had always said that she didn't think I could *Handle It*. What did that mean? *Sex takes a lot of emotional maturity,* she would say. Why? Was everyone else emotionally mature? What did she mean by that?

I was afraid that inevitably Greg and I would have sex, and then inevitably, if he was my boyfriend long enough, he would want to get married and I'd have to become Lutheran. I didn't think I wanted to be Lutheran. They were so *positive,* so *proactive.*

They were always going on *missions*. Sharing their positivity with the *less fortunate*. Catholics were depressives, and I trusted that.

Years later, I would meet a preacher's kid who said to me, "I grew up thinking that I always had to be happy. That I had to act happy even if I wasn't." This explained a lot to me. But at the time, I drew from what I knew. Catholics, I thought, were more relaxed and had more fun. The Catholics I knew felt incredibly guilty about everything, which made them really fun when they started drinking. Plus, I didn't ever want to move to Washington State, where Greg was from. Didn't they have active volcanoes there?

So when Greg, sometime in the late fall of our freshman year, asked me if I wanted to go to the St. Olaf Christmas Concert with him, I panicked and told him I couldn't see him anymore. There was an enormous social pressure about going to the Christmas Concert. It was like attending the prom, only God was involved. The concert was held in a big gymnasium, which was decorated with enormous paper doves and stars and other optimistic symbols. It was *televised*. If I went to the Christmas Concert with Greg, we would have to have sex and then I would have to become Lutheran.

A few weeks later, Greg had a new girlfriend. She was Lutheran and she liked to sing. And I was jealous.

I went down to his room and knocked on the door. To say what, I wasn't sure, but Adam answered.

"Is Greg here?" I asked, crossing my arms over my chest.

"No," he said. His eyes were pink and his face was splotchy. His nose was twitching. He looked like an albino rabbit.

"Do you know where he is?"

"He went to a movie with Kristen." Adam sniffled a little.

"Oh." He looked vulnerable in a way that he never had before. He was wearing a worn blue T-shirt instead of his usual ironed oxford shirt and argyle sweater-vest. "Are you okay?"

"Margot broke up with me," he said.

"Oh," I said. *Tee hee,* I thought. And then I felt bad. He looked miserable. "Um, I'm sorry."

"She's dating a senior now."

"Oh," I said. "That's too bad."

"I know," he said. "I can't compete with that. He's in the Olaf Men's Choir."

Being in the Men's Choir was the equivalent of being in the Brahman caste.

"Wow."

"I know!" Adam's shoulders slumped and he began to cry.

"Listen, I'm sure there's someone better out there for you," I said, and I reached up to pat his bony shoulder.

"Do you think so?" he said.

"I'm sure of it," I said. What else could I say? "Can I get you a soda or something?"

"I was going to make some tea," Adam said. "Do you want to come in and hang out for a while? Do you want some tea? *Cheers* is on."

"I guess so," I said.

"She *was* kind of clingy, anyway, I guess," Adam said. He wiped his nose on his T-shirt sleeve and flipped on the television. "I'm sorry about you and Greg."

"Why?"

"Well, it must have sucked when he broke up with you."

"*He* broke up with *me? I* broke up with *him.*"

"That's not what he said."

"He kisses kind of weird anyway," I said. "His tongue is really big."

"Really?" Adam started laughing. Or really it was more of a guffaw. "I won't tell him you said that."

"Thank you," I said.

★   ★   ★

After that, Adam and I hung out all the time. We met for lunch almost every day, and he'd invite me to sit with the Harriet Larsen Men in the cafeteria at dinner. Greg was so happy with Kristen that he didn't care. And most of the time, because of swim practice, he ate with the team instead.

Next to Chapel Service, the largest daily social pressure at St. Olaf was the attendance of, and proper seating at, meals. The cafeteria was shaped like a great horseshoe. One of its arms was the cool side. The middle was also cool, but in a more experimental way; it was for outlaws and those so cool that they didn't care about being seen, since the sightlines in the middle were not as good and your cool might not be witnessed. You might not also be able to scope on the people you wanted to scope on.

The other arm of the cafeteria was the nerd side or, alternatively, the loser side. This was for people who didn't have anyone to sit with, or who were math and computer-science majors.

It was verboten to sit by yourself at a meal and to sit on the cool side; you could *maybe* get away with it at lunch, but it wasn't recommended. And at dinner, you may as well have worn a scarlet *A* around your neck.

I still wasn't getting along very well with the girls on my floor. If it weren't for Adam, I would have had to sit on the loser side every night.

"Doesn't sound like the date went all that well," Ellie says, rolling a full house on her first try.

We were playing Yahtzee and drinking gin and tonics at her place. David had gone camping with some friends, and Ellie hated camping. Maybe that's why she had liked Ian.

"It wasn't a total disaster," I reply. "On the other hand, it wasn't a total—what's the opposite of 'disaster'?"

"Aster?" ventures Ellie.

"It wasn't a total aster, either." I swish the ice around in my glass; I'm on my first drink, but already I have a nice buzz going. "I know I shouldn't be, but I'm still waiting for Mr. Fabulous to ride up on a white horse. You know? I don't even like horses. I'm allergic to them."

"David is my white knight," Ellie says, shaking her cup of ice. "It can happen. Want another one?" she says, getting up and going over to the bar.

"Not done yet."

"You and Adam are totally going to wind up together," she says.

The sip of gin and tonic I've just taken catches in my throat and burns on the way down. Where did *that* come from? I feel my face go hot.

People have been saying that about Adam and me for years, but never Ellie. It is always people who only sort of know us.

All through college, people had mistaken Adam and me for boyfriend and girlfriend. A girl on my floor senior year had said to me in the bathroom one day, "So what's the deal with your boyfriend? You guys been going out a long time?"

"My boyfriend?" I had said.

"Yeah, that guy you always eat with. That guy with red hair?"

"Oh, that's not my boyfriend," I said. "That's Adam."

Right after college, Adam and Ellie and I were the only three who stayed in the Twin Cities. The rest of our college friends went to Seattle to wear flannel, or to invade Prague by chain-smoking, or to graduate school in other cities, or into the Peace Corps. Adam and Ellie and I made dinner together at least twice a week and usually went to brunch together on Sundays. Until Ellie started dating a chef. And I started dating a good-looking loser who worked at Kinko's. And then Adam started his M.B.A.

But whenever Adam needed a date for a graduate-school function, he called me. And later, whenever either one of us needed a date for the office Christmas party, we called each other.

Now Adam and I were the last two single people in our group of college friends. It didn't mean that we were the last two single people in the *world,* but sometimes, in Minnesota—where people seem to settle down in their midtwenties, buy a house and a lawn mower, and start going to church again so their kids will have something to reject—it felt like we were.

I cough up an ice cube and spit it into my glass. "We are not!" I blurt like a teenager whose parents are accusing her of going drinking.

It's not like I hadn't thought about why we never dated. I had. But wouldn't that be like dating a cousin? I had never looked at him as anything but a pal, until a couple of years ago, after Michael and I had broken up, when suddenly it seemed Adam's chest had broadened and he'd stopped slouching; he had taken up running and his legs were thick with new muscles.

I didn't know *what* to think about it, but whenever I did, my mind was a tire stuck in mud. It just kept spinning in place. I had never said anything about it to Ellie. The only people I'd told were the counselor and my sister.

So where did Ellie come up with this?

"I'm just saying." Ellie starts giggling. "He wouldn't have called to check in if you weren't here."

I got up to make myself another drink.

Adam had called earlier to see what we were doing. Ellie had invited him to come and stay for the weekend, too, but he had said that his parents would be visiting. Ellie volunteered that there was room for all three of them, but Adam told her that they had tickets for some choral festival and were otherwise having dinner with his parents' friends, the Rolvaags.

This is the part where my brain starts to spin, a stuck tire splattering mud all over the place. Does Ellie really think that?

You two are totally going to wind up together. Does she know something I don't?

I dump in extra gin and spear some olives with my stir stick.

Every once in a while I wondered why I got along so much better with Adam than with any of the guys I'd been out with. But I kept holding out hope. Adam was like a brother. There had to be someone out there for me who was more like a lover. Ellie saying that Adam and I would wind up together was a confirmation of my worst fear. That my fantasy about what *might* be out there for me, some hot guy I just hadn't met yet, was only a fantasy.

Suddenly I feel like a little lab rat who's been observed for years under the technician's eye without knowing it. They've finally decided I won't get out of the maze by myself. *So here,* they say. *The cheese is over here. The thing you've been looking for, it's over here. Duh,* they say. Since I can't smell it myself. If they could, they would pick me up and place me in front of it. Is that what Ellie's up to? *In case you didn't realize it,* she's saying, *you two totally belong together. You're putting off the inevitable.* Which has occurred to me, but then always seems wrong. Or something.

"Shut up," I say, sitting down with my new drink, my mouth full of olives. "We are not." *Shut up. We are not.* The refuge of the truly inarticulate, embarrassed, or defenseless. I sounded like an eighth-grader.

"Sure. Whatever," Ellie says, and starts laughing.

Now I kind of want to slug her. Why is it that married people always get the equivalent of the lifeguard's chair? The better view. *Hello, silly little single people splashing around down there, flailing around in the choppy surf.* It's not good to feel like there's something about your life that everyone else sees and you don't.

"Adam's all wrong for me," I say.

"Okay. Whatever you say." Ellie rolls another full house.

"You don't even need that," I say. "Can I have it?"

"But he wouldn't have called if you weren't here."

"That's not true," I say.

"Never mind," Ellie says.

I can feel a flutter in my chest. My throat begins to itch.

Why *haven't* Adam and I ever gone out?

"You're getting to be one of those uptight feminists," Adam had said to me when I was in graduate school. "Don't get too high and mighty and literary on us."

Which had made me really mad, though I'd never said anything.

The counselor had said that Adam simply felt threatened. He saw an old friend moving into a new life, new interests. "He doesn't want you to change, to leave him behind," she'd said. "That's natural."

It had occurred to me since then that part of the reason I wasn't meeting any other guys was because I was always hanging out with Adam. Everyone thought I was spoken for. Though I supposed there were plenty of other reasons, too.

After I started graduate school, Adam and I saw less and less of each other. I had ditched the Kinko's guy and was living with Michael in a tiny apartment, working and studying all the time. And Adam had a different life. A corporate job. A house in the suburbs. All by himself.

"Do you really think Adam and I will get together?" I say, rolling the dice. Why was I asking when I didn't really want to know? When I was pissed already? "Do you honestly think that?" What if she saw something I didn't see? Knew something I didn't? Had Adam said something to her?

"I'm keeping my mouth shut," says Ellie, taking a sip of her drink.

"No. Come on," I say, tossing out a bad third roll. "Why did you say it?"

It is her turn. Ellie rolls the dice and considers her options. It isn't fair that she is married. It isn't fair that, in the musical-chairs game that is dating, she's been able to sit down. And keep her seat.

"You still need a small straight," I say.

"Oh, thank you," she says, gathering up two of the dice and shaking them in the cup. "I just think," she says, releasing the dice and watching them tumble across the table, "I just love the both of you. And of course it would be nice if things worked out that way, but I'm not holding my breath."

"You got your straight."

"So I did!"

"What do you mean, you're not holding your breath?" I take a big gulp of my gin and tonic and finish it off. My eyes feel fuzzy. Her nonchalance—no, it isn't really nonchalance—her cryptocrappitycrap refusal to say anything is driving me crazy, and my throat feels like it is tightening up. Am I developing an allergy to gin? I bring the empty glass up to my mouth and tilt it, tap the bottom for any last remnant of booze. All of the ice comes flying out at my face.

"It's your turn," Ellie says.

I roll the dice three times and get nothing. I cross out my large straight.

"I quit," I say. "Can I quit?" I am feeling kind of drunk.

"But I'm winning," Ellie says. "I never win. Do you want another drink? I want another drink."

"If you're having one, I want one." I go over and plop onto the recliner. "You never answered my question."

"About what?"

"About Adam. What do you mean, you're not holding your breath?"

"I just think, I don't know. I mean, I think it would be great to have two people I love be happy together. But I don't know. Maybe you want something different."

What does she mean, *different*? Adam is nice. The people

I've dated have not always been nice to me. Michael, for example, used to tell me my arms were getting fat and that my clothes were weird. Does she mean that I pick the wrong guys? Does she mean to say, *Maybe you want bad relationships?*

That isn't fair. David was the first nice person *she* dated.

"What's that supposed to mean?" I say.

"Oh, I don't know," Ellie says. "I'm just speaking off the cuff." And she waves her hand around in the air. "Maybe you both want different things, or it just won't happen, for whatever reason. I hope you both find whatever will make you happy."

This is the problem. I am not entirely sure what *would* make me happy.

I sometimes wondered if having some idea about what you wanted was dangerous, if it fell into the "be careful what you wish for" category. You might be attracted to someone who was charismatic and later find you'd mistaken charisma for narcissism. You might be attracted to someone who is hardworking and later you'd hate him for putting in so many extra hours at the office. You could fall in love with someone who was a free spirit, and later resent his unpredictability.

You could get exactly what you wanted, and then not want it. And then imagine how lonely you'd be.

Few people around the world expect to be happy. Being *happy* seems like a distinctly American notion. But if happiness were available, then shouldn't you try to get it? Like going through the drive-thru: Why go in if you can remain seated? If you can get the food easily, why not? If you could measure and locate happiness, why not try to find it? Which brought to mind, for some reason, the orienteering unit we'd had to take in elementary school, in which most of the class had become lost in the school ravine.

"What makes *you* happy?" I ask Ellie, who has stretched out on the couch and is now sitting in the glow of the television, her slippered feet hanging over one end, a gin and tonic in one hand. "How did you pick David?"

"I don't know," she says. "You just know when you know. He just felt right."

I hate that answer.

"Falling in love and living together every day are two different things," she says, sipping her drink. "Not that I'm not still in love with David," she adds, crunching on her ice. "It's just different."

"Do you think Adam and I would make a good couple?"

"I don't know," says Ellie, staring into her glass and shaking the ice around. She looks over at the aquarium, with its fish swimming next to the television. A stream of air bubbles constantly pushes to the surface behind the plastic seaweed. "I'm not the one to say."

Even though living on Lake Wanita would probably drive me crazy, I envy Ellie's life. She and David have wool carpeting. Espresso and bread makers that have been used only once. CD players in their cars. Ellie has full health coverage, including dental. The heat doesn't go off and on at random intervals in their home, and Ellie doesn't have to turn the shower on and go make coffee and microwave oatmeal while she waits for the water to heat up. She doesn't have to jump out of the shower when it produces a sudden scalding blast. Maybe more than a husband, I want a lifestyle upgrade. But the two seem to come together.

"Don't you think he's gotten better-looking since college? He's filled out," I say.

"Uh-huh," she says. "Yeah. I do."

Ellie flips through the cable channels for a while and stops to watch *Saturday Night Live*. I try to pay attention, but I am thinking about the day, a few years out of college, that Adam and I had gone cross-country skiing in the bitter January wind, across Lake Minnetonka, from Cottagewood to Wayzata.

We hadn't known how long it would take us to get across, and when we got to the other side, we were hungry. We clomped down Main Street in our ski boots, carrying our equipment, and found a little bistro that neither of us knew existed. We knifed our skis into a snow bank outside the restaurant and went inside to warm up. We had meatloaf sandwiches made with rosemary and sundried tomatoes, and shared a bottle of wine. Then we bundled back up and made our way back across the lake, our skis scudding over ribbed snowmobile paths, the sun beginning to set on the ice-fishing houses that dotted the lake. There were only a few of the tiny temporary shelters at the time; the lake had just frozen and occasionally, where the wind had blown the ice clear of snow, you could see air bubbles just under the surface—the lake still breathing—and the occasional crack where it might, if it were warmer, give way.

When we got back to Adam's place, we opened another bottle of wine and decided to make pasta. We dug around in the refrigerator and cupboards and found garlic, olive oil, and dried mushrooms.

"We can make something out of this," I had said.

Adam said, "See? You can cook, Shan. I think you sell yourself short. You're a good cook."

It came to mind now, I think, because it was one of the most easy times I'd ever spent with a man.

But maybe that's because, at the time, I didn't think of him as one.

What if the right person has been in front of me all along?

My chest was kind of pounding. My throat tickled and felt like it was closing.

I told Ellie I was tired, excused myself, and went upstairs.

Up in the guest bathroom, I looked at myself in the mirror.

I was pale. I felt like I was looking at a foreigner. *Who are you? How did you get here?*

Maybe it was the gin and tonics, but suddenly my existence felt so *tentative.* Like I was here on earth on a tourist visa. I felt like I could evaporate at any moment. Combust. Leave a little pile of dust here on the bathroom floor. *Why wouldn't I? Why on earth wouldn't I?* And who would miss me? Would people be sad if I were gone? I would miss my family. I would miss Ellie. Even though, at the moment, I was resenting her domestic comfort.

My vision was getting blurry. My throat was still tight. I went to bed, hoping that in the morning I would feel normal.

"Why didn't you tell your friend you weren't feeling well?" asks the counselor. "That concerns me."

"I didn't think of it. It was late. We were tired. I went to bed."

"It concerns me that you keep things like that to yourself."

"No one wants to hear about it if you're not feeling well. I mean, what's she going to say? 'That's too bad'?"

"You and I are alike," says the counselor. "We could lose an arm and we'd tell people we'd lost a thumb."

"I think they would notice anyway."

"You know what I mean."

"I thought I complained *too much,*" I say.

"About the wrong things," says the counselor. "You pick at the little things. And then when something's really wrong, you keep it to yourself."

"This one time I had lasagna and red wine and the same thing happened with my throat. I just thought it was like that again, like an allergy. And it went away eventually. There wasn't anything Ellie could have done."

"But that's how you get lonely, honey," says the counselor. I love it when she calls me *honey*. The cost of each session is worth that occasional endearment.

"I know," I say. "But that stuff she was saying about Adam, that was kind of freaking me out. She was so calm, and it was like she knew something that I didn't know, but she wasn't going to say it. Which pissed me off. You know how much I freak out about this Adam thing. I mean, what if? *What if* he is the right one for me?"

"I know," says the counselor. "I know. But I really think that's that place *in you* where you want someone else to figure out your life."

"Maybe," I say. "But I mean, *Why don't we go out?* I mean, really. Adam is nicer to me than some of my ex-boyfriends have been. Why didn't I date *him* instead of them?"

"I don't know," says the counselor. "But it keeps coming up and I guess we'll keep talking about it until you get it figured out. In the meantime, I think you need to keep getting out. See what's out there."

"Maybe the right one for me has been in front of me all along, and I just didn't notice," I say. "Maybe that's why none of the other dates are working. That happens in the movies. It happens on television," I say, thinking of *Friends* and *Moonlighting*. It seems to be the eventual plot of most sitcoms.

The counselor rolls her eyes. "Do you think that's true? That he's the right one?"

"I don't know."

That night I went home and made myself a frozen pizza. I flopped onto the futon couch and ate the whole thing. I talked to my sister for a while. Georgia still wasn't sleeping through the night, but my sister couldn't bring herself to do that thing where you're supposed to let them cry it out for three nights.

"Then don't," I said.

"Everyone else is doing it," Greta said. "All the women in my mom's group."

My sister had joined a new moms group at the hospital where she'd also taken birthing classes. It had turned out to be the best way to meet people that she'd found since she moved to Portland. In the five years that she'd lived there, getting pregnant had come in the most handy socially.

"I think it's more important that you do what feels right to you," I said.

"Letting them cry it out is supposed to teach them to be self-sufficient. That you're not always going to come running."

"Why should you be self-sufficient when you're three months old?" I said. "If anything, they should learn that you *will* always come running. Why be lonely and disappointed now? There's plenty of time for that later."

I was still sitting on the couch, getting sleepy, watching reruns of *Frasier,* thinking about Greta and Georgia, thinking about the client meeting I had in the morning, about the second date I had coming up next Saturday with Ian, when I became inexplicably weepy.

And the feeling I'd had at Ellie's came back. I went into the bathroom and looked at myself in the mirror. I was still there. I still looked the same. But I felt like I was looking at a stranger; my peripheral vision was closing in and my chest began to feel light and heavy at the same time. I felt my own death approaching. It would happen soon. My God! It would! It wasn't a thought. It was a *feeling,* a deep premonition. In my heart. In every vein. In my fingertips. I would die in the next couple of weeks. Would it be a car accident? Yes, it would probably be that. I could picture the mangle of metal. But I didn't want to die. I sat down on the edge of the bathtub and began to sob. *Please, God. Please don't let me die.* I'm not ready. I'm just getting going. Georgia needs an aunt. And who would make sure my sister would be okay? She needs a sister. And I would miss my family. And I think they would miss me. Although what if they got used to me being gone and began to forget me? *Please, God, don't let me die,* I bargained silently on the edge of the bathtub. I'll get my life straightened up. I'll get my apartment straightened up. I'll do some volunteer work. I'll work harder at work. I won't Web surf.

I slumped down onto the floor, sobbing, doubled over in grief.

Oh, God. I don't want this vision.

I'm not ready to go yet.

Please, not now.

A feeling of dread hovered over me for the rest of the week, and when Marty came into my office on Friday to show me a Web site with a strange man dressed as a pixie, I just smiled politely and told him I was on deadline. I was trying to keep my promise.

On Sunday, while my dad and I were driving to the golf course, I told him what had happened. I couldn't stand it anymore; I had to tell someone. If I was going to die soon, I wanted to be open about it, to warn someone, to have a chance to say good-bye. And I figured that my father, the unflappable physician, was the best person to tell.

"So, you really felt like you were going to die?" my dad said.

"It was more like I *knew* I was going to die soon. Like I'd been given a premonition. Maybe it's my time."

"So then what did you do?" my dad asked. He was calm and kept his eyes on the road.

"I sat on the edge of the bathtub and I bargained with God." It sounded so stupid when I said it out loud.

"May I ask what you bargained?" My dad was sort of giggling, and it actually made me feel better that he thought it was funny.

"It's embarrassing," I said.

"Okay," said my dad.

"I promised to get my life straightened out and to do something for someone else."

"It sounds like you had a panic attack. You've described, to a tee, how some of my patients have described their panic attacks."

"Really?"

"Sure. That bargaining with God, that's pretty normal. And usually, the things people wind up bargaining are things that they want to change in their lives anyway, things they've been holding back on."

"Really?"

"Has this happened before?"

"Sort of. I thought I had diabetes."

"Sounds like a panic attack, Shanny," my dad said, pulling into the golf-course parking lot. "Oh, Lucky Pierre!" he said, getting out of the car and stretching his arms. "What a day! It doesn't get any better than this."

"So, I'm not going to die in the next two weeks?"

My dad started laughing. "None of us ever *knows* that. But probably not. Come on. A little golf is just what you need." My dad's prescription for most anything was "a little golf." He was usually right.

We were paired with a couple who looked like they were in their early forties. The husband kept calling his wife "Mother."

"Come on, Mother," he would say, "smack it out of here. Come on. *Send it,* Mother!"

I couldn't figure out why she didn't club him with her driver. He chain-smoked through the front nine and made my dad and me so nervous that we both ordered beer when the cart came around.

"Why do you think she puts up with that?" I whispered to my dad.

"It's probably what she grew up with," he said. "You know, those old Germans here in Chaska, that's what they called their wives. She's probably used to it."

Well, that was at least one thing I knew I didn't want.

I wondered if, when they were in bed together, the guy shouted, "Send it, Mother!"

It was too much to think about.

At least Ian didn't call me "Mother."

Maybe I was too picky after all.

On our way home, my dad and I stopped at McDonald's to pick up dinner. "What do you want?" he said. "I can't even read this menu."

Unfortunately, I have the menu memorized.

"I'll have a Big N' Tasty," I said.

"What's that thing your mother likes? The Thick N' Spicy?"

"Yes, why don't you go ahead and order a Thick N' Spicy?" I said.

"I don't see it on the menu."

"It's the Big N' Tasty," I said.

"Oh. Is that what you're having?"

"Yes," I said. "Good Lord. And you do surgery?" My dad once drove through the McDonald's drive-thru and ordered three packs of McDermotts. "Well, hello there," he'd said. "Mc-Dermotts. I'll have three of those. And a cone, I'll have one of those."

"McNuggets," my sister and I had been in hysterics. "Mc-Nuggets!"

They had told him to pull to the first window and he had gone blasting past it to the next one.

Now he pulled forward to the intercom and a young girl's voice blared through the static, "Thank you for coming to Mc-Donald's. I'll be with you in a moment!"

"Okay, then. Hi," said my dad. "I'll have two Big Macs . . ."

"I said I'll be with you in a moment!" she snapped.

"Geez," said my dad. "Does she have to be so touchy?"

I was convulsing in the passenger seat.

"Did *you* hear her? Did she say that earlier?"

"Yes."

"Kids. I couldn't understand her. You're young. You're lucky."

When she was finally ready, he ordered two Big Macs, a large fry, a chocolate shake, and two Big N' Spicys.

"Big N' Tasty?" she said.

"Sure," he replied.

At home, we divide up the fries and turn on *60 Minutes*.

"How was your game?" my mom asks my dad.

"Mine was just okay," he says. "Shannon hit some beautiful shots."

"Really?" she says.

"She's a natural," he says.

"I used to be good at golf," says my mother. Then she looks at me. "You have your mother's natural ability."

Why couldn't it just be mine?

Tonight *60 Minutes* is doing a segment on Italian men. Many of them still live with their parents. They have their own homes, but they're waiting to occupy them. The houses sit empty, waiting for a wife. Until then, the men go to work and return to their parents' home at night, where their mamas have made their favorite meals.

Do you feel like you're being taken advantage of? Leslie Stahl asks one mother.

"Yes," says Flo to the television screen.

"What are you talking about?" I whisper. "You didn't make dinner. We're eating McDonald's."

Why? says the Italian mama. *Why should I feel taken advantage of? People shouldn't live alone. People were meant to live together. With other people. Otherwise, you go home to an empty house, you watch TV. It's no good.*

"Maybe you should move to Italy," Flo finally says at the commercial break.

"I knew you were going to say that," I say.

"I'm predictable," she says, sticking a fry in her mouth.

"I think that's true, though," I say, thinking about how nice it would be to move into a big house with a hunky Italian man. "People weren't meant to live alone."

Although I suppose he would expect me to cook.

"You want to talk about lonely," says my mother, "I'm here alone all of the time."

I do not want to talk about my mother's version of lonely, and am relieved when Andy Rooney comes on to bitch about light switches.

"Why didn't you tell me this was going on?" says the counselor.

"I sort of did," I say.

"You didn't tell me the whole thing," she says. "That's interesting."

"I don't know," I say. "It's embarrassing. I didn't know what it was."

"Honey," she says. She grabs my hand and gives it a squeeze. "I've got lots of clients who've had those attacks. You've got to come out of yourself," she says, which I thought made me sound like a crustacean or a turtle.

"I just wanted it to go away."

It's the body, for whatever reason, the counselor explains, *kicking into survival mode.*

The counselor asks if I would consider seeing Dr. Douglas, who runs group with her, for a while. Dr. Douglas is a psychiatrist. He could administer some tests and, being a medical doctor, could prescribe things for me that the counselor couldn't. I could see both of them at the same time, if I'd like. "Would you be comfortable doing that?" she says. "Meeting with each of us once a week for a while? I think we need to get this under control."

Always happy when someone else has an idea about my life, I agree.

Chapter 5

Dr. Douglas's office is what I always expected a therapist's office to look like. Cherry-wood tables and chairs. Upholstery that isn't ripped. Persian rugs. A coffeemaker in the corner. It differs from the counselor's office, which is filled with hand-me-down furniture and macramé throw pillows. She has two clocks and neither of them works; it is like being in Las Vegas.

"So, I think we should start with some tests," says Dr. Douglas. "I think that would be fun. It would be fun for you to see what shows up, and it would give us a base. Even though I know through group some of the things you've been working on, I think this would give us a nice foundation." He nods at me with his big blue eyes, takes a Jolly Rancher out of the bowl in the middle of the coffee table between us, and indicates that I should help myself. Dr. Douglas is an average-looking man with salt-and-pepper hair and small round glasses. He has broad shoulders and long arms, with large hands at the ends of them, like paddles; he looks like he'd played basketball in college or had been a swimmer. "So, what do you think?" he says, sucking on the Jolly Rancher and crinkling the wrapper.

For four weeks I came in at different intervals to take various tests with Dr. Douglas's graduate-student assistant, Julianne, who looked like a supermodel and would compile the data for Dr. Douglas to evaluate.

One week she gave me an IQ test. She asked me who Gandhi was and my mind went completely blank.

"He was peaceful," I finally said. "From India. He believed in being passive. He didn't wear much clothing, you know, just a thing wrapped around him. And he was tan, with little round glasses. Ben Kingsley. Ben Kingsley played him in the movie."

She asked me what the continents were and I couldn't remember. I included India. And then remembered it was a sub-continent. "No, wait. How many are there, again? Five? Seven?" I said. "Does Greenland count?"

"I can't tell you that," she said gently. Her hair was cut in a perfect bob and she was wearing leather pants. I wished I could look good in leather pants, but I had been through the McDonald's drive-thru far too many times to be able to pull that off.

"The continents," I said. "It's been a long time since I really needed to know them."

She asked me how many people were living on the earth at this moment and I said, "Well, how many people have been served at McDonald's?"

She smiled at me.

"I bet Gandhi never went to McDonald's," I said.

She wrote that down.

She gave me tests in which I was supposed to copy down numbers as fast as I could, and tests that had me searching for patterns in a series of seemingly unrelated shapes that looked like Calder mobiles. She showed me pictures and asked me to find what was missing.

"Everything that's not there is missing," I said. "By definition. I could say Elvis is missing. And why isn't there a banana in the picture?"

"These are specific things," she said, "that should be there."

I stared for at least ten minutes at a colored drawing of a barn in winter. I made sure there was snow on all of the branches, that there were no missing footprints from the tiny path of prints heading out of the barn, that there were no missing fence posts—even though, on a typical farm, fence posts *would* be missing. I made sure that every direction was represented in the weather vane.

"I have no idea," I finally said. "There's a girl in the barn and she'd like a nice boyfriend. That's what's missing."

The graduate student wrote that down and offered me a Dove-bar miniature.

The next week she showed me pictures—of a man lying in bed with an arm draped over his eyes, of a child staring into a violin, of two women working in a field with a shirtless man—and asked me to tell stories about them.

"I feel stupid," I said. "This seems stupid. This might be fun for kids, but it's not fun for me."

She nodded.

"Couldn't you just write down that I feel stupid?" I said, motioning at her pad of paper. "That should indicate something."

"Just try something," she said. "Say anything. What does the picture make you think about?"

"I feel silly. What does this have to do with anything? Anything I say I'm going to feel stupid about. It's not like I feel like, 'Weeeee! It's the story hour! What fun!' Like I'm on *Mr. Rogers.* The Happy Land of Make-Believe. *Ding, ding!* Here comes Miss Kitty!"

She nodded.

"Plus, I know everything will have some hidden meaning, and that's what you're *really* looking for. This is weird."

"It's hard," she said. "I know. But just look and, well, what do you think these people *want*?" She tapped the drawing with a pencil.

"I think that girl would like to lick that guy's back," I said, pointing to the shirtless man. "Look at those muscles. He has nice back muscles."

"Okay," she said. "Good." And she wrote that down.

The next week she gave me Rorschach tests. I told her that one blob in particular looked like Louis XIV.

The week after that she gave me the Minnesota Multiphasic Personality Inventory and stayed in the room in case I had any questions while I took the true-or-false test.

"Here, on number forty-two," I said to her, "it says, 'I have had very peculiar and strange experiences.' I mean, I don't know how long you were single. It looks like you're married now. But if you spent any time dating, you've probably had strange experiences. Right? I mean, that's just true. But I mean, the right answer, if you just have a normal kind of a life and, like, dogs and stop signs aren't talking to you, is to put false, right?"

"Just put down what seems true for you," she said.

I marked true, and she went back to reading a textbook.

"Here," I said. "On number seventy-three. 'Someone has

been trying to influence my mind.' I mean, I watch TV. I read the paper. All of that advertising. It's all around us. All of the time. Someone is always trying to influence you." I thought of my mother and all of her opinions about how things should be done. "Unless you live alone in the woods."

"Just answer with what seems the most true for you," she said. "To the best of your ability."

I marked false so I wouldn't get put on Lithium.

When I got to number 123, "I am being poisoned," I put false. Even though I thought that, with all of the frozen dinners I'd been eating lately, and all of my trips to McDonald's, and the big tub of diet pop I always get at the movies, the real answer was probably "true."

Number 145, "Everything is going too fast around me." Who in America wouldn't mark that one true? Especially if you drive on the freeway?

"These are hard," I said to the graduate student. "These don't really seem like true-or-false questions to me."

She smiled.

So when I got to number 189, "I know who is responsible for most of my troubles," I put true.

I figured it was probably me.

It took the graduate student a week to compile all of the data, and another week or so for Dr. Douglas to review it.

"You've tested off the charts for secretarial skills," he tells me, leafing through the folder that holds my results.

"What does that mean?"

"Well, that part of the test is the part where you wrote down all of those numbers really fast. It means you do best when you've got something specific to focus on. An immediate task. Otherwise you tend to second-guess yourself into the ground. You overthink things and sabotage yourself."

It explained why I could never get anything done at work

unless I was on deadline. "I was kind of hoping the tests would show that I was a genius."

"Well, the good news is, it seems like you've worked your way out of your depression. You tested normal for depression."

"Hey, that's good."

"And quite high here on the anxiety scale. Yes," he says, taking a sip of coffee from a Styrofoam cup, "here we go. You've got a real healthy anxiety disorder."

"Oh." Well, at least my disorder was thriving. That was something positive.

Dr. Douglas explained my anxiety disorder as a fight-or-flight impulse gone haywire. Back in the good old days, the anxiety might have protected me from the saber-toothed tiger about to pounce on me. Would have helped me run or fight. Now I was pretty much chasing my own tail.

"There are some nice meds for that." Dr. Douglas nods and smiles at me. "To help take the edge off, so that simple things don't seem overwhelming. We can talk about that later." He turns back to the folder. "Let's see. Your libido looks good."

"The test showed that?"

"Uh-huh. The storytelling part. Okay, on the section where you had to look at pictures and figure out what was missing, you remember that?"

"Yeah."

"You did really badly on that."

"I would have thought that would be my best area," I say to Dr. Douglas.

I was always trying to figure out what was missing, why I always felt a little empty and alone.

"Anxiety," says Dr. Douglas. "I think your anxiety interferes. But look, you were very honest in answering questions. You had the highest possible score there."

"They measure for that, too?"

"Sure."

"At least I'm honest," I say. "I'm the world's most gifted and honest secretary. Fabulous!"

I wanted to die. The IQ tests I'd taken when I was little had shown me to have much more promise. I'd tested nearly as well as my brother, who was a genius and who would have been able to say exactly who Gandhi was and on which continent he lived and who probably could have figured out what the fuck was missing in that barn.

My brother, who was always flying off to philosophy conferences. Who had hobbies that required equipment, knowledge, and patience: hiking, camping, backcountry skiing, bird-watching. Cooking dinner.

The only pieces of equipment required for my favorite hobbies were the remote control and a credit card.

My brother and his wife were always going on some vacation where they had to ski all of their equipment and supplies into some isolated hut.

When had I become so much less than I had hoped to be? Or maybe I had never known what I wanted in the first place. And was it too late to change?

I was waiting for someone to come along, I realized, who would make my life meaningful, more exciting.

How was he going to find me on the couch? Or hiding in a barn?

And why would he find me interesting?

"Well." Dr. Douglas lets out an enthusiastic sigh and slaps his hands on his knees. "This gives us a good place to start."

Chapter 6

By then it was the end of September, that time in Minnesota when flies get slow and bees get mean. When one day you're wearing a tank top and sandals, and the next you're digging out your polar fleece, and the next you're back to sandals. When the leaves have turned a muted yellow-green, on their way to brilliant crimsons, to oranges and yellows the color of highlighting markers. And then death, of course, a tumbling onto the sidewalks, a fall from grace, like Norma Desmond. *I am not ready for my close-up. I am on the sidewalk, dying.* Leaving a faint imprint after the street sweepers come by. Where leaves used to be, light brown imprints on the pale gray concrete, like the Shroud of Turin, the impression of delicate veins and stems, signs of former life.

It's a bipolar season, exhilarating and depressing at the same time.

Adam and I were waiting for Ellie at the Hard Times Café, and Adam was stirring honey into his herbal tea with some dissatisfaction, holding his chin in one hand.

"Does it hurt?" I asked him.

"Kind of. The novocaine's wearing off," he said. "Am I drooling?"

"Just into your tea. I thought you were doing it on purpose," I said.

Adam looked down. "No, I'm not, am I?"

"No."

Adam smiled at me and kept stirring.

When he was ten, he'd been playing hockey at a rink in his neighborhood. It was a pickup game, after dinner in the cold, under the rink lights. The boys in the neighborhood probably should have been wearing mouth guards, but of course they weren't. Adam took a puck in the mouth, and ever since then had worn a bridge with four artificial front teeth. About every ten years, the bridge had to be replaced. Adam was grateful that he had insurance coverage through work, and referred to himself as "dentally challenged."

This week, they'd pulled the bridge out and had done a root canal on a back molar. They'd given him replacements, which Adam kept calling his "Chiclets," insisting that the temporary teeth were being held in by gum and luck.

"I'm hungry," Adam said, "but I'm kind of afraid to eat here."

He stuck his nose in the air, turned, and looked longingly at the cooler, where sandwiches with sprouts and cream cheese were piled high.

"You're not supposed to eat, anyway," I said.

"But I could have soup," said Adam.

They were serving carrot-ginger soup today, which sounded

promising, except we had already noticed that the kid behind the counter had practically a garden's worth of dirt under his nails. And when I had asked him where the baked goods came from, he had said that he didn't know but that he thought "Ned might have made them yesterday." When I asked him who made the soup, he said, "Ned might have made that, too."

I was having drip coffee and trying to act normal around Adam, though I was having trouble harnessing the wayward idea that we might be right for each other. Increasingly, every interaction with Adam was a matter of compounding evidence, either for or against a partnership.

The Hard Times had been around forever; it was an enclave for aging hippies and a hothouse for young hippie wanna-bes. The place was furnished with rusting patio furniture, and the walls were covered with old Hendrix, Joplin, and union posters. There was a closet in the corner where people could leave clothes they didn't want anymore, for other people to take. FREE CLOSET, it said. On the adjacent wall a poster read FREE MUMIA.

"Someone must have picked him up already," I had said to Adam when we first sat down, and Adam had started laughing and cupped his mouth.

"Don't make me laugh," he said. "My Chiclets will fall out."

From what we could tell, Adam and I were the only people in the place who might have showered that week.

"What does it smell like in here?" Adam said. "Is that the carrot-ginger soup?"

We stuck our noses in the air and took a big whiff. Adam sneezed and quickly cupped his hands to his mouth again, checking to see that no tooth had flown out.

We thought, after a few more whiffs, that the secret recipe for the café's longevity was one part cumin, one part turmeric, two parts espresso, three parts clove cigarettes, one part American Spirits, and two parts pot.

"And a dash of b.o.," said Adam, sticking his nose in the air one last time.

"Perfect," I said. "A dash of b.o."

That was when Ellie came through the front door, looked around, spotted us, and raised an eyebrow.

"I haven't been in a place like this in a *long* time," Ellie said, pulling up a chair. What she meant was, she hadn't been in a place like this since she got married and moved to Lake Wanita.

"I wanted to see what it was like," said Adam. "I drive by it every day."

"Huh," she said, surveying the café. Ellie had been more ad-venturous in college, had smoked covertly, had been known to dance drunk on the bar (one of us usually pulled her down), had once dumped a pitcher of beer on an ex-boyfriend's head. But now her taste for adventure was limited mostly to field trips. "It's nice to come into the cities," she had said two weeks ago when we met for beers, "but I think life in Wanita suits me."

Wanita was beyond the western suburbs, where Adam lived, even farther out into the country than my parents' place. Once a sparsely populated farm town, it was now filled with SUVs; where there had once been modest lake cottages with septic tanks and sand on the floors, there were now sprawling execu-tive mansions. The kind with ceilings so high they made you feel like you were in a beige-carpeted cathedral.

"Is something wrong with your mouth?" Ellie looked at Adam.

"I had root canal yesterday," he said. "So they were digging yesterday and then today they were sanding things down, sand-ing and leveling or something like that."

Adam's mouth sounded like an urban renewal project.

"Well, I only have about a half hour," Ellie announced. "I'm going to pick David up and we're going to the Minneapo-lis Club for dinner."

Adam looked perturbed. "Well, aren't you fancy?" he said,

cupping his mouth. He was kind of mumbling, afraid of enunciating too much. "How did you get in there?"

"One of David's clients gave us a gift certificate for Christmas last year. We've got to use it up before it expires."

"Lucky duck," I said.

"Well, it's not like you two don't have your fair share of perks," Ellie said.

"And just what might those be?" I said. I hadn't been in a fancy restaurant since I'd been out with the architect.

"Adam, you had that dinner for work last week," Ellie said. "That sounded pretty swank."

"What was that?" I said.

"We had this black-tie thing to honor one of the senior partners," Adam said. "It was at the Metropolitan."

"How was your date?" Ellie asked.

"What date? Hey," I said. "How come I wasn't invited?"

"I don't know." Adam shrugged. "You've been so busy lately. I brought this woman from my graduate-school program. You remember Megan."

"You know," I said, "I *can* behave at events like that."

"I know," Adam said. "I know, I know, you're fine, you're very charming. It's just that Megan knew people there," he concluded.

Why didn't he bring me? He used to always bring me. What if Ellie had said something to him?

"You know who I ran into the other day?" Ellie changed the subject. "Beth Franklin. Do you remember Beth Franklin?"

"Beth Franklin?" Adam puzzled, taking a delicate sip of his tea, as if he were expecting a tooth to fall out in the cup and float around like a life preserver. "Oh, Beth Franklin! She was in my biology class."

"The one where you had to stuff dead things?" I said.

"No, that was Field Studies."

"She married Warren Divine. Remember him?"

"You're kidding," Adam said. "Did they even know each other at Olaf?"

When Adam and Ellie would start to reminisce about St. Olaf, I usually drifted off and stared into the middle distance. They had both liked the school, while thinking about it for too long gave me the shivers. I was sort of half-tuned in, and half gazing at the clothes in the Free Closet, wondering if there might be anything in there worth taking.

"I always liked Beth," said Adam.

"Really?" said Ellie. "I always thought she was a little different."

A Minnesotan's most damning adjective. Anything a Minnesotan does not understand by direct experience is dubbed "different," usually meaning unacceptable. Presented with theater of the absurd, for example, a Minnesotan might, still sitting in his seat as the house lights are coming back up, scratch his head and say, "Well that was *real* different." It really meant that he was longing for a traditional narrative, something he didn't have to work at understanding.

"I kind of liked that about her," said Adam. "I thought she was funny. She was a really good violinist."

"Well, Warren has his own software company now."

"I don't think I remember him," said Adam.

"You know Warren," Ellie said. "From Decorah? His dad was a math professor at Luther? He was on the soccer team? His cousins sing in the choir at Central Lutheran?"

"Oh, Warren," said Adam. "I know his cousins."

"Real quality people," said Ellie.

"Uh-huh," said Adam, nodding. "Definitely."

Quality was a descriptor I'd never before heard applied to people until I went to St. Olaf. When the Lutherans were describing someone they liked, they would all nod and agree that he was "quality" or "a quality person." This puzzled me. Growing up Catholic, we never discussed who was "quality" and who wasn't, as if we were all subject to manufacturing inspections. We all felt like pieces of shit, damned to hell, and were grateful for the company.

But the Lutherans, in conversation, would all nod and someone would offer, "Quality people." And they would all nod again and someone else would say, "Yep. Real quality people."

What I realized after a while is that "quality people" was shorthand for "he's just like us."

My worst fear was that when I wasn't around, they referred to me as "kind of different."

Sometimes I wasn't sure why Ellie and Adam even liked me, and at moments like this, during conversations that left me completely out, I wasn't sure why I liked them. I had vague memories of Beth and Warren. I knew who they were but didn't really know them. It only reminded me that Ellie and Adam had this connection, and had had all these experiences at St. Olaf that I'd never been privy to. Somehow I'd missed out on them. I hadn't attended chapel. Or perhaps I'd been in the library, which is where I'd spent most of my time.

"Did you know Beth helped build a mission in Africa?" Ellie continued. "Now she teaches elementary school. She said she incorporates African folktales in her lessons."

If I could, I would cross my eyes into the back of my head. "Missionary work makes me want to puke," I blurted.

"Are we not paying enough attention to you?" Ellie said, in a tone that I found snide.

Adam patted me on the back. "Let's talk about you, Shanny," he said. "What's new?"

"I don't want to talk about me," I said. "I just don't want to talk about them." Now I was embarrassed. Why did I act like such an emotional cripple sometimes?

"I brought it up because they're thinking of moving to Lake Wanita," said Ellie. "And they would join my church, which would be great for me," she said, with a resolved sigh. She had been working up to this and I'd ruined it. Ellie was usually so gracious with me; what was my problem?

"That would be nice," I said. "To have them there."

"I'll go to church with you someday," Adam said. "I'd like to see what it's like."

"More conservative than yours," said Ellie, "but it's nice."

Ellie got dressed up for church every week, and often went by herself, because David liked to sleep in on the weekends.

"Well, I should get going," Ellie said, looking down at her watch. She gave us each a polite hug, reapplied her lipstick, and asked us to check it.

"You look beautiful," Adam said matter-of-factly.

"David's going to think I've been smoking," Ellie said, sniffing the sleeve of her jacket.

After Ellie left, Adam went up to the counter to get some more hot water for his tea. He came back with a steaming cup and a Special-K bar.

"Why did you get a Special-K bar?" I said. "You can't even eat that."

"It looked so good," Adam said. "I'm going to save it, for later."

"But later on, it's going to be hard as a rock," I said. "Later on, you wouldn't even be able to eat it if you had regular teeth."

Adam looked down at the chocolate-covered bar sitting on a square of waxed paper on the table in front of him.

"I guess I just want to believe," he said with a heavy sigh, "that I lead the kind of life where I could eat this bar."

Which made me laugh so hard that I snorted some coffee out my nose. It sprayed the table.

Adam started convulsing in his seat, the way he did sometimes, laughing with his whole body. He was laughing so hard that his face was all red and his eyes were watering and he began to cough, and couldn't stop coughing.

Which is when one of his fake teeth flew out of his mouth and landed on his Special-K bar, lodged in the frosting.

"Look!" I said. "It comes with a complimentary Chiclet!"

We were beside ourselves.

That was the thing about Adam. He was comfortable with his flaws. With the parts of himself that might go flying off and land in his dessert.

He was a creature of habit in a way that was almost eccentric. He got up at the same time every day. He had the same amount of orange juice every morning in the same glass, three-quarters full. He had the same cereal, Grape-Nuts, and watched the *Today* show from 7:25 to 7:45 A.M., and then left for work. He did not drink coffee in the morning. Only decaf dessert coffees in the afternoon. He enjoyed the predictable and yet he was patient with what couldn't be controlled.

And I had started to wonder, I'd told the counselor, if that might not just be the perfect type of person for me to be with.

Adam knew that I hated St. Olaf, but for some reason, he put up with me anyway, in general, and with my criticisms of the school, specifically, even though he had loved it there.

I called Ellie the next day to ask how her dinner was.

"The dinner was lovely," she said.

I apologized for being such a crank at the café.

"Don't worry," she said. "We're used to it. We've come to expect it from you. We love you anyway."

What was that supposed to mean? Who was "we"? Had she been crowned queen? Was it a royal "we"? Or were regular conferences held to discuss my behavior?

Instead of asking her what it meant, which is what the

counselor would have told me to do, I mumbled that I'd just wanted to check in and say I was sorry and that I had to go, but that I'd talk to her later. And I hung up the phone and cried.

Every once in a while, Ellie said something like this, invoked a group opinion that made me feel she'd just thrown down her trump card, her membership card as One of the Lutherans. She and Adam had known each other before they met me, and now they had talked about me when I wasn't around, and here was the evidence: *We're used to it.* And I hated them in those moments. In the same way that I hated my mother when I was thirteen, how I would tell her I was running away and then I would walk down the hill to the Dairy Queen and drink Mister Misties until it got dark.

Sometimes I hated my friends and yet I needed them. And maybe I hated them because I needed them. It was a big, cold world and we were like puppies from the same litter, squirming around and nipping at each other, keeping each other warm. We'd been small together once, had grown and joined other packs. Oh, hell. What did I know about dogs?

"I think the friends you make in college are like that," says the counselor. "You become like siblings."

"I guess I behaved badly," I say. I was thinking back to how, in college, Ellie had dates every weekend. She was on the tennis team. She had long legs. I spent all my time in the library. "I think sometimes I'm just jealous."

"Maybe," she says. "But I'm encouraged. You said what was on your mind, and if they don't like it, too bad. You're entitled to your opinion. Missionary work makes me want to puke, too. Unless they're really helping with the quality of the water, or something useful like that, and leaving the God part optional."

"I think I hurt Ellie's feelings," I say. "But, 'We've come to expect that from you.' What's that all about? I hate it when she acts like there are things she knows about that I don't."

"People gossip." The counselor shrugs.

"Sometimes the whole college thing, when I see those guys, it just feels so *insular*," I say.

"Well, then you need to keep expanding your world," says the counselor. As if it were the waistline on a pair of elastic pants.

It reminded me of something one of the guest psychologists had said on *Oprah*. "You need to get over your ex-boyfriend," the psychologist had admonished one young woman. It was a subject I identified with. "You've been sticking your fingers in the pie of the past," he had said, "and jeopardizing the filling that is your future."

Then he had repeated it. "The pie of your *past*. The *filling* of your *future*."

And she had nodded and burst into tears.

Chapter 7

The new Super Target in Chaska opened in October. Flo and I went on a Sunday and I tried on every pair of pants, all of the menswear-style pants that look so good on supermodels, the capri-cut pants, the microfiber stretch pants. In all of them, I looked like I was wearing an ill-fitting fast-food uniform. My gut was sticking out, my legs were rubbing together, and if I had a little matching baseball cap to meet health-code regulations, I might as well have been refilling Horsey Sauce bottles at Arby's.

Apparently, I had not only been sticking my finger in the pie of the past, I had planted my whole face in it.

My mom was singing the praises of dressing for your figure, wearing colors that make you look alive, choosing the proper neckline and sleeve length for your proportions, and, once you've figured out what works for you, repeat that success! Capitalize on a winning formula! And then, across the top of the fitting room, she started handing me size 14 pants with elastic waists.

"Elastic is for people who wear diapers," I said. "Toddlers and seniors."

"Excuse me," said Flo, "but I wear pants with elastic waistbands all the time."

"Oh," I said.

"You know, you have to learn to accommodate your figure. You keep saying you can't find pants that fit, so you should buy for the legs—you know, wider—and then something with elastic will fit your waist. You have a small waist."

"You've basically just told me that I have fat legs."

"You keep saying you can't find pants that fit. Now, look at these." My mom held out a pair of purple knit pants with flared legs; they came with a matching tunic top that had a scarf sewn onto the neckline, to be tossed over one shoulder.

"Perfect," I said. "That'll be great when I dress up as fucking Bea Arthur for Halloween."

"I'm just trying to help," my mom said.

"I'm serious. That's a perfect Halloween costume. 'And then there's Maude.'"

"I'm going to find the bathroom," said Flo.

We wandered silently after that through Notions. And when we got to the checkout lane, I bought a pack of sugar-free gum and shoved three pieces into my mouth.

Back at home, I helped my dad spread fertilizer on the lawn. We had rented two machines and we got done fast, and because we got done quickly, my mom didn't believe that we'd actually done what we were supposed to.

"You aren't done," she said.

"Yes, we are," I insisted.

"No," she said. "You aren't either."

"Yes, we are, Mom. We did it already."

"What did you do?"

"The lawn."

"How much of the lawn?"

"The whole thing. The front and the back."

"Did you do the sides?"

"I did the north side and Dad did the south side."

"Oh, you didn't either," she said. "Where's all the fertilizer? What did you do with it?"

She was standing in the garage with her hands on her hips, looking around for signs of deception.

"I stuck it in a balloon and shoved it up my ass and now I'm going to make a break for Mexico," I said, thinking myself incredibly funny.

My mom just stared at me and went back into the house, shutting the door behind her.

"Sorry," I said, standing alone in the October chill.

Chapter 8

That week, Marty came into my office and told me that he and his wife had bought a house and that their apartment was going to be available. He'd had a bunch of us over after work once; their place was huge compared to mine, with tons of closet space. It wasn't any more expensive than the place I was living in now, plus it had the distinction, he said, of being the Dillinger apartment.

"What does that mean?" I asked.

"It's the apartment where John Dillinger lived."

I looked at him with what I imagined was a completely blank face.

"The gangster. In the 1930s? You know, *John Dillinger?*"

"Oh, of course," I said. It sort of rang a bell.

"He shot his way out of the apartment when the FBI came to try and arrest him," Marty said. "I can show you a cool Web site."

"Sure," I said. "Are there bullet holes in the wall?"

"No. But there's always tour buses stopping outside the building. You get used to it. Do you want the apartment?" he asked. "If you want it, I'll tell the caretaker that I've found a renter."

I wanted it.

Marty e-mailed me the Web address and I pulled up a page with the flashing red words, *Public Enemy Number One!*

Here, said the Web site, was a modern-day Robin Hood. In the height of the Depression, he took from the faceless, foreclosing banks and couldn't be caught. The FBI hated him; the public adored him. He was charismatic. And though there were occasional casualties during his bold daylight holdups, he did his best not to hurt anyone.

And here was a photo of the apartment he'd shot his way out of in St. Paul, escaping with his gun moll.

The Dillinger Apartment. With enough closet space for all of my piles.

I would take no prisoners!

It was time for me to be more bold. To stop hiding in the barn. To start changing my life.

The Gospel
According to B. F. Skinner

Part 2

Chapter 9

I decided that before I moved, it would be a good idea to get rid of anything I didn't want anymore. Anything I didn't want to lug over to the new place.

Anything that I didn't want to lug over into my new life. I would leave behind the pie of my past.

Months ago I had bought a book on feng shui, *Transforming Your Space, Transforming Your Self,* which had since been lost somewhere in my apartment.

I dug around in the dusty piles until I found it.

The book said that you should put your head as far from the door of your bedroom as possible, because that would make you safer in case of intruders. You would sleep more peacefully and feel more powerful. I had been sleeping with my head right next to the door.

The book said that your head should be to the north, and your feet to the south. I had been sleeping upside down. No wonder I woke up every night, even though I'd been in the apartment for three years, wondering where I was. Things were spilling out.

The book said that you should never keep dirty clothes in your clothes closet or in the bedroom. The dirty clothes would taint your sexual life, make it sour.

Wow! I had always kept my dirty clothes in a laundry basket in the closet.

The book claimed that if you got rid of the things you considered to be clutter, you were making room in your life for new experiences. You were streamlining your life and opening yourself up to the mysteries of the universe. And you would also have better bowel movements.

"According to the book," I said to Flo, "I'm having the wrong kind."

"Are they supposed to come out shaped like bonsai trees?" she asked.

Almost everything I owned had belonged to Michael, my ex-boyfriend. When he'd left graduate school in Minnesota for his fellowship in Rome, he'd left almost everything with me. I used to hope that it was a sign; he'd meant to come back. For the furniture, for me. But I now realized that it was just easier to leave everything with me than to figure out what to do with all of it.

He'd left his kitchen table and chairs, the television, the TV cart, the futon and frame, the microwave, the blender, the mixer, some dishes and silverware. He'd also left his bike and bike rack. Some old sweaters. A jacket.

"Maybe he just thought those things would come in handy for you," my mother said.

"Well, they're weighing me down," I told her. "They're messing with my feng shui."

"Well, having those things has certainly saved you from having to go out and *buy* them, Lady Astor," my mother said.

Here it comes, speech number 57: *I think it's exhilarating to rely on your own resources! When I was single, I made do with what I had. You have to be a little imaginative . . . blah, blah, blah.*

"But having them around just reminds me that I used to have someone to eat dinner with every night."

"I guess I can understand that," my mom said. "Well, get rid of them. You know what Harry Truman always said."

Here comes speech number 23, in which Harry Truman is cited as an example of someone who made decisions and never looked back. I had once said to my mom, "But, Mom, Harry Truman killed hundreds of thousands of Japanese people."

"That's not the point," she had said.

"Well, then, what is the point?" I had said.

"Don't look back is the point," my mother had said.

"But don't you think maybe he should have looked back? Don't you think it's worth looking back on that one?"

"The point is, sometimes you have difficult decisions to make and you just make them."

So now, when my mother says, "You know what Harry Truman always said," instead of arguing, I simply say, "Never look back."

"Oh, good! I didn't know you were ever listening!" she says.

Still, I thought, if I got rid of the kitchen table and chairs, what would I eat on? If I got rid of the futon, what would I sit on?

"Now, see," says the counselor, "these are just the kind of issues you can bring to group. Some of them are divorced.

They've had to deal with stuff like this. Why don't you ask them?"

"I'm supposed to take up group time with my furniture issues?"

"Why not?" says the counselor.

I remember then that Louise spent forty-five minutes last week talking about how she couldn't stop ordering takeout, an issue I had actually identified with. And it turned out it had something to do with her mother. Everything in group eventually had something to do with your mother.

"Shannon, you have something you want to talk about this week, don't you?" says the counselor when we get to New Business.

Everyone in the group is blinking at me. Dana, who used to be a nun and hardly ever says anything, crosses her legs and eats a potato chip. Every week, Dana brings a new bag of potato chips. This week she's eating BBQ-flavored.

Harvey looks at me intently and takes a bite of his sandwich.

"I feel kind of stupid," I say, "but I'm moving into a new apartment, and I don't really want to bring anything along that has a memory for me of Michael." I explain to the group how everything I have is a hand-me-down, how I don't feel like I have anything I've ever chosen. I explain to them that I understand this to be a distinctly American and banal problem to have, but that the microwave Michael left with me never turns on the first time that you hit the "on" button. I explain how you have to pop the door open a couple of times and fiddle with the timer and then this seems to release the "on" button from being stuck, but occasionally you might have to unplug it and plug it back in again and then open and shut the door before it will work.

"You have *way* too much of a relationship with that microwave," says Harvey. He takes a big bite of his sandwich and picks a sprout out of his teeth.

"You think so?"

"I do," he says with his mouth full. "It's like you have this intimate relationship with an appliance. Like only you know what makes it work."

"Like, if you're holding on to the microwave," says Wayne, "it's like you're still in that relationship, subconsciously. When it might be better just to move on to something new." Since I joined group, Wayne has had four new girlfriends.

"What do you think of that, Shannon?" asks the counselor.

"It seems kind of true," I say. "I mean, Michael moved on and established a new life, and I'm still living with all of the re-minders of my last failed relationship. I just don't know if I can afford to replace all of the stuff."

"When I got out of the convent," says Dana, clutching her potato-chip bag, "I didn't have anything, and it was kind of freeing. To start from scratch."

Because she hardly ever says anything, I always pay attention when Dana talks.

"You don't really need a microwave," says Harvey. "You can heat stuff up on the stove."

"Plus, just because it is reminding you of an old relation-ship, I think you should get rid of it," says Eileen. "I mean, I un-derstand that. I had to get out of the house my husband and I lived in. I needed to have a new place. He can move back in with his new tootsie if he wants," she says, and waves her hand around as if there are flies in the room.

I am surprised by how much people have to say about this, and I don't feel nearly as stupid as I thought I would. "I guess that it's just, like, *everything*," I say. "The kitchen table and chairs, the couch, the TV, my bike."

"If it's bugging you, get rid of it," says Eileen.

"It's like the stickleback fish," Dr. Douglas jumps in. "The male stays outside the nest and fans it with his fins. If he doesn't provide water with fresh air to the eggs inside the nest, those eggs will die."

"Wow," I say. "I have no idea what you're talking about."

"You need to let some air in. In order to incubate your life. Give it a chance to breathe."

When did Dr. Douglas start watching Animal Planet? Still, it seemed like sound advice.

"It's about just taking a chance and *doing* something. Getting rid of things that have a heavy association and making room to figure out what *you* want."

Dr. Douglas has been married five times. He is an optimist.

It took three trips, but I brought everything Michael had left with me to Goodwill. I also got rid of my desk—an old door balanced on crooked file cabinets whose drawers would no longer open—and took the old rolling chair that seemed, from its torn seat, to produce foamlike baby rabbits.

I got rid of a bunch of clothes that I suddenly realized were ugly. When had that happened? When had I become my high-school French teacher, who throughout the eighties wore bell-bottom pants with a rainbow running up one leg, around her crotch, and down the other leg? Who spent the decade wearing green eye shadow and dangling Eiffel Tower earrings?

I threw out all kinds of old magazines, took a few books to the used-book store. *The Girl's Guide to Changing Your Own Oil*, for instance. It had seemed like a good idea at the time, but maybe feminism was also about recognizing your limitations.

I had spent so much money, I realized as I dug through cheap clothes and earrings and magazines and bath beads that made my skin itch, on things that I didn't really value. On things I didn't even remember I had. What a waste.

Then I went to Sears and bought myself a new television.

★　　★　　★

My mother is dusting every book I have, and developing categories for them. "Over here. Shannon, excuse me, listen for a second," she says, holding a moist rag. I am trying to assemble my new desk and rolling chair, which I've put on credit. "Over here I've put most of your paperbacks. The small ones. And this is an area where I've put all your books that seem to be instructional. You know, your old books from school. And this is kind of a self-help area." She points to a small row of books, mostly books she has given me, with titles like *Being You Is All There Is to It!* and *Beating the Blues.*

"Why are all my travel guides in that section?"

"That counts as self-help," my mother says, beaming.

"Thank you, Mom," I say.

Adam and Ellie are putting things away in my new kitchen. They're giggling and chatting and I can't hear what they're talking about. Lucy brought over beer and is standing outside, taking a cigarette-and-beer break.

"That Lucy is kind of sharp," my mom says. "She's got an edge on her."

"She's fine, Mom," I say.

"Is she a lesbian?"

"No, Mom, she's not a lesbian."

"She's sharp," my mom says. "She speaks in such directed tones."

"That just means she's confident, maybe," I say.

"Well, isn't that a blessing," my mom says. "Lucky for her."

"Why don't you like Lucy?"

"I mean it," says my mother. "The more you know about what you want, the better."

I am waiting for speech number 432: "Sometimes You Just Have to Pretend That You Know What You're Doing Until You Really Believe It," which always starts with "That's how Sue

Johnson's daughter got where she is today. She just keeps getting promoted because she fakes her way through everything and eventually figures it out."

I hear a burst of laughter from the kitchen, followed by El-lie shouting, "Duh!"

"What are you guys talking about in there?" I ask.

"Nothing," says Ellie, laughing again.

Did Ellie tell Adam what we had talked about at her house?

Adam comes into the living room with a dish towel slung over his shoulder. He puts his arm around me and gives me a big squeeze. "It's coming together, Shan," he says. "I like your new place." Then he bends down to where my mother is sitting on the floor, establishing the reference-book section.

"How's it going, Flo?" he asks.

My mother's face lights up like Times Square. "Well, hello! Come and sit by me!" she says. "It's been too long. Tell me about your life!"

Right after my freshman year of college, Adam had invited me to go to Europe with his family for the summer. My mother had said no. "Just who is this 'Adam Hanson' person, anyway? We don't know anything about his family."

Now she was embarrassed. Adam was nothing if not polite and honest. Every mother loved him.

While Adam tells my mother what he doesn't like about his job—too much paperwork, nothing that seemed truly mean-ingful—I go into the bedroom and put fresh sheets on the bed. Here in my new apartment, my head would still be toward the south, but at least it would be far from the door.

Chapter 10

I had asked Dr. Douglas a few weeks ago what it should feel like when you meet the right person. How do you know?

"You have to be met and matched," he said. He then went on to explain exactly what that meant, most of which I have since forgotten. It had something to do with timing and symbiosis, complementary attributes. He drew from theories of social psychology, explaining how likes attract likes. How we subconsciously seek someone of the same general level of attractiveness, the same level of intelligence, the same socioeconomic background. Though a model who had grown up poor in a small town in Iowa might marry a short and unattractive man from Paris if he was rich. There were various measures of power that could neutralize inequities. Beauty neutralizing poverty. Money or intellect neutralizing hair loss. It was like Diane Keaton in *Manhattan,* describing Wallace Shawn as her most devastating lover.

And all of this happened because you were in the right place at the right time to meet the right person.

You could otherwise meet someone and not feel well matched. In graduate school, I went on a few dates with a beautiful guy who had grown up in Colombia. He had short, dark, curly hair, deep brown eyes, and perfect white teeth, but I couldn't understand half of what he said. I would stare at his purple lips and at the end of the night not have retained anything he had said about Edward Said, or Benjamin, or Wittgenstein, or being and knowing, or the signified and signifier. The only thing I could remember was that the fries at the bar we had gone to, he said, were made of real potatoes.

You could feel well matched and yet not ready to be with someone. Or maybe that person wasn't ready to be with you. Matched but not met, was how Dr. Douglas had explained it. Perhaps you were in another relationship at the time. Perhaps you were too frightened to be with someone. Maybe you used your career as an excuse to remain lonely.

You had to be ready when that person came along. And then the person had to actually come along, Dr. Douglas said.

It sounded to me like winning the fucking lottery.

And according to all of the guest psychologists on *Oprah,* which I had started to tape religiously because I was sick of *Frasier* reruns, you could not force this. *When you had become complete on your own, when you were doing the good work you were meant to do on this earth, the right relationship would come into your life. When you are ready, you will bring the things into your life that you need.* It seemed to involve both practical measures and a certain amount of mysticism.

And it all reminded me of something I had read in an Intro Psychology text during college. Maslow's hierarchy had impressed me years ago, because it divided the elements of our existence into something like the food pyramid, and incredibly special people got to be at the top, like fat and protein.

The premise behind Maslow's pyramid, as I remembered it, was that once your basic biological needs—food and shelter, the base of the pyramid—were met, you were free to work your way up as you were able, to engage in intellectual pursuits and spiritual concerns, to give back to the community. Those who had been able to cultivate their intellect and their gifts and to contribute to society were at the top of the pyramid, and were considered to be self-actualized. *Surely the right person would have come into their lives!*

But in our textbook, at the top of the pyramid were Mother Teresa, Gandhi, and Eleanor Roosevelt.

I took this to mean that once you were doing important work, you hardly ever got to have sex anymore. That the work itself was satisfying enough.

Was it wrong to want more?

Or maybe that was the simple question of a person near the bottom of the pyramid.

"But what does it *feel* like to actually meet that person?" I asked Dr. Douglas. "The right person? When you feel both met and matched?"

"It feels," said Dr. Douglas, "well, you wake up every morning and you think, 'I'm so glad this person is in my life!' There's a joy about it."

"A joy? Really? A *joy?*" When I woke up in the morning, the first thing I could even feel remotely joyful about was coffee. And I assumed that most married people felt the same. Maybe it was just my parents.

But maybe that also meant that Adam could not be the right person for me. Being with Adam was more like a cup of hot cocoa on a cold day; it had a predictable warmth. But was it joy? And would it ever be enough?

★　　★　　★

"I have a theory for you," Dr. Douglas says in our session today. "You're scared and I don't think you take chances. You're waiting for someone to come along and find you, but you're not going out to look for what you want."

"I don't think I know what I want," I say.

"Well, then you have to go and see what's out there. You can't know until you go," he says. "Every animal, in every species, at some point, separates from the nest to mate."

"Thank you," I say. Maybe I should order cable so that I could watch Animal Planet, too. He seemed to be learning a lot.

He then goes on to tell me about a particular experiment, in which rats were raised in three different kinds of environments. In the first environment, they could only move around horizontally. In the second, they were restricted to mostly vertical movement. In the third, they were raised with complete freedom to explore in any direction.

Then they were all released into an enormous, three-dimensional maze.

The rats in the third group did spectacularly well. The rats in the second group did well, too, after a short time.

The rats who were raised on flat terrain were horribly confused and disoriented and took a long time to get used to their more complicated, more layered environment. The question the scientists posed, Dr. Douglas says, was this: Could a rat raised in a one-dimensional, restricted environment grow up to be a functioning adult?

"You've been letting people choose you, but you haven't actually *pursued* anyone. You're used to having someone taking care of you, but you haven't learned how to step out in the world and demand something of it."

"Do I get a little piece of cheese if I do?"

"That's probably where your panic is coming from. The

anxiety. You're getting older. You're moving into new territory. You've been so close to your mother," says Dr. Douglas. "That's easy. It's familiar. And clearly she's fairly entertaining. But it keeps you limited. It's time for you to get out and explore life's complexities."

Chapter 11

Lucy and I had been standing around by ourselves at Lee's Liquor Lounge for over an hour, drinking Bud Light, hoping someone would give up a barstool or a booth so that we could sit down. Earlier, a woman Lucy used to work with had come over and said hello to us. She had squealed about Lucy's new glasses. "Your hair's different, too!" she'd said. "You've grown it out." Then she asked Lucy where she got her handbag. "Is it Prada?" she said.

Lucy sheepishly admitted that it was.

"Love the shirt, love the bag!" said the woman, who, like Lucy, was wearing low-slung jeans. "Okay, don't get freaked out by this, because I have a boyfriend," said the woman, "but you'd definitely be my kind of lesbian!"

Squeals, big laughs, a hug, kiss, kiss.

I stood there, in an outdated pair of relaxed-fit jeans, feeling like a dairy-fed girl who just fell off the hay baler.

This is why I would rather stay home. This is why I would rather be married. Watching movies on the couch in my fleecy pants.

"There are no good guys here," Lucy says now. "Normally there are cute guys here."

"There was that one," I say, "but he left. Why do the cute ones always leave early?"

"I still say we should go to the Fantasy House and get you a vibrator," she says.

"That's not a bad idea," I say.

"A vibrator never makes you feel bad about your body," notes Lucy, whose husband used to tell her from time to time that she was "getting a little pudgy," which was, of course, never true. If anything, Lucy was always in danger of being a little too thin. "A vibrator doesn't hog the bed and channel surf. I love mine," Lucy says.

Just then a guy wearing leather pants and his shirt opened halfway down his chest comes up and says that he's been watching us for the last half hour. "Although you girls don't look all that approachable necessarily, I'm feeling brave," he says.

"Why is that?" asks Lucy.

"Why am I feeling brave?"

"Why don't we look approachable?" asks Lucy.

"I don't know," he says. "It's the way you're carrying yourselves. The way you're looking around. You don't look like you're here to pick up guys."

"Hmmm," says Lucy.

"Do you girls want to take a quiz?" he asks.

"What kind of quiz?" I say.

"Sure," says Lucy.

"Okay," he says to Lucy. "First question. Do you love your parents?"

"Yes," she says with confidence.

I have never been able to answer any kind of question that way, even when I had to fill out tax forms for my job. They asked if I was an American citizen, and I circled yes, because I am, but for some reason I still felt like I'd done something wrong and might get caught. Was I really an American *citizen*? I couldn't even tell you who my district representative is. *What did it mean to belong to a country?* I paralyzed myself with abstractions, which Dr. Douglas and the counselor attributed to The Anxiety.

"Do you have a big circle of friends?" the guy asks Lucy.

"Yes," Lucy says again without hesitating, and she smiles. It's true. Lucy knows tons of people; she always manages to find a job where the people are fun and like to go out after work. She worked at my office for a while, that's how we met, but Lucy found it too sedate and moved on.

"All right," says the guy. "Last question. Do you wear sexy underwear?"

"I'm not answering that," Lucy says.

I think to myself, that's the one question I *am* comfortable answering. *Yes,* I would answer, even though all of my underwear came in Hanes multi-packs from Target.

The guy decides that Lucy is stable, because it's clear she loves her parents. It is clear that she's an extrovert from the way she answered the friends question, although he might add, he says, that she is probably pretty sensitive and wears her heart on her sleeve.

"I don't think I wear my heart on my sleeve," she says.

"All right," he says. "It's just my impression."

"I really don't think I do that," Lucy says.

"Do me," I say. "I want to take the quiz."

"Okay." He asks me, "Do you love your parents?"

"Sure," I say. "Sometimes. Most of the time." I start laughing. "Who loves everyone all of the time?"

"Okay. Do you have a big circle of friends?" he asks.

"Yes," I say. It's true that I know a lot of people, from work and high school and college, but some of them have moved away, and most of them are married with kids and too busy to go out most of the time. But I see them when we can manage to coordinate our schedules. "Mhmm," I add. "Yes."

"Do you wear sexy underwear?" he asks.

I smile as wolfishly as I can and say that I won't answer, because that's what Lucy had done.

"Well, then I can't tell you what it all means," he says.

"You told *her*," I say. "Speculate. What would it mean if I said yes, and what would it all mean if I said no?"

"It depends on *how* you say it," he says.

"Well," Lucy says, "what qualifies as sexy underwear, anyway?"

"It's whatever is sexy to you," he says. "That's all that matters." Then he looks at me. "Now, with you, the way you answered the parents question probably means, and no offense"—he grabs me by the shoulders—"that you're kind of unstable, like an emotional roller coaster of a person. That you'd get really upset, say, in an argument and walk out and drive around for six hours. Don't take me wrong, I'm sure you're a great person." He shakes my shoulders in what I suppose he thinks is a reassuring gesture. "And as for the extrovert question, the way you answered it, I know you said you have a big circle of friends, but I think you're someone who keeps pretty much to herself and has a few really close friends that you share things with."

Then he tells us that he thinks Lucy looks Polish and is probably from Chicago originally. And that I look Scandinavian and am probably from Duluth.

"Duluth?" I say. "What's that supposed to mean?" Did I

have bad hair? Did I look like I got wasted at Grandma's Saloon every weekend and went driving around on my snowmobile with boys from the Iron Range?

"Polish?" says Lucy. "I grew up in Florida. I'm Scandinavian and Italian."

Did he mean that I was fat? Lucy was about five inches shorter than me and had a flat stomach. She had the build of a gymnast. "What, exactly, are your impressions of Duluth?" I say.

Lucy spots a couple getting up from their bar stools. "Hey," she says, nudging me and ignoring the guy, "there are some seats opening up over there. Do you want to sit down? Or are you ready to go? Just tell me when you're ready to go."

"I think I'm ready to go," I say.

"Yeah," she says. "Me, too."

The guy holds out his hand to Lucy and shakes it good night. Then he invites her to his annual holiday party; he actually says that he's having a party and that "you two ladies are invited," but he is gazing at Lucy and shaking her hand, passing off his business card.

"Good night," he says to Lucy as we're putting our coats on.

"Good night," I say, extending my hand, which seems to surprise him. I give him a crushing handshake, the kind men use to establish dominance. The kind I've been on the receiving end of so many times at work.

"Wow," he says, as Lucy and I are walking away, "strong handshake."

I shouldn't bother going out to clubs. Why do I do this to myself?

"I don't think I look Polish," Lucy murmurs, looking at herself in the passenger seat's vanity mirror.

But Lucy had nothing to worry about. Clearly, in the Darwinian survival game of dating and barhopping, she had opposable thumbs and was swinging vine to vine. I was some kind of sedentary land animal who nibbled on marshy plants and moved too slowly to avoid predators. Soon I would be extinct.

"He was wearing his shirt buttoned halfway open," I say. "He was a Guido. Why are you letting him bother you?" I say to her, though I am saying it more for myself.

"You're right," she says.

"And anyway," I say. "He liked *you*."

"Ugh. Whatever."

Maybe I am too weird for anyone to want to date. Maybe there really is something wrong with me.

Chapter 12

"Dating," I say to Adam while we're walking around Lake Harriet that Sunday. He had called me for a walk and as usual I was trying to act normal, though my mind was shifting in and out of gears, forward, reverse, forward, reverse, trying to rock itself out of its rut. Maybe if we just talked about our dating lives like we used to, everything would return to normal. It would feel like old times. A nun and a monk, out for a stroll.

"Yeah?" he says, holding his mitten in front of his mouth, blowing air on it.

"What do you think about it?"

"What do you mean, what do I think about it?" Adam liked walking with me, he had once said, because I was the only short person who could keep his stride.

"In general, I'm getting sick of it," I say.

"I always think I should do more of it," he says, "but I don't feel like it."

Around the lake: the usual couples with babies and dogs, designer strollers, microfiber running pants, the circle of life, the pageant of ordinary humanity and coordinated outerwear, happy domestic living.

"I'm starting to get bitter," I say.

"You'll find your person, Shan," says Adam. He puts a hand on my shoulder and I feel better. It feels like it used to.

"I'm starting to wonder if I'm too weird to be coupled."

"I don't know," Adam says. "My sister found someone."

It wasn't really a comforting example. Adam's older sister had suffered two nervous breakdowns in her early thirties, although my counselor had told me that there really is no such thing as a nervous breakdown. Several times when I thought I'd been on the verge of one, she'd pointed out that they didn't exist; the nervous breakdown was theoretical, without true definition. As a psychological condition, it exists as a specter. "If you decide that that's what you want to do," the counselor had said, "you can go ahead and have a breakdown. And we'll hospitalize you."

"No, thank you," I had said.

"What I think it means for you," she said, "is that you'd like someone to take care of you for a while. And you're not very good at that, so you may as well give up on the idea. You would criticize them for taking care of you the wrong way."

"I kind of wonder sometimes if there's something wrong with *me*," Adam says now.

Just then, a heavy man with short spiky bangs and a mullet braided down his back shuffles by with two golden retrievers.

"I just don't want to be him," Adam says.

"For all we know," I say, "he might be a *Jeopardy!* champion. Maybe he's a millionaire software genius. Maybe women go nuts for him."

"True," says Adam. "Thanks a lot. That just makes me feel worse."

"You're not going to wind up like him," I say.

We are on the south side of Lake Harriet, where there is a knot at the base of a tree known as the Elf's House. Where there had been an open hole in the knot, someone had long ago put a tiny hinged door with a lock on it, and had planted tiny bushes next to the door and created a path to the small entrance. People left notes for the Elf, asking him for advice, or to grant wishes. They shoved their requests through a slot in the door, and when the Elf's house got too full, they left them on the tiny doorstep, jammed halfway under the door, protected from wind by the tiny plantings. Urban legend had it that the Elf replied to each letter. Although legend also advised correspondence in warm seasons, because the Elf wintered in Florida.

"Let's go look at the Elf's House," I say, veering off the walking path. "I don't think there's anything wrong with you," I add.

"Thanks," Adam says. "You don't?"

"No," I say.

"It's just that I feel like everyone's having more sex than me," he says. "Like I think I should be having more sex."

"Really?" I could say the same for myself, but I didn't feel like it.

"Yeah. I mean, it's been a while. And what if I'm no good at it when I get another opportunity? I'm starting to lose the urge. I'm starting to prefer watching TV."

"I think sex is like priming an old, rusty pump," I say. "At first it's difficult and noisy and not much comes out, but then, once it's primed, it's pretty much lubricated when you need more water."

"Good." Adam nods. "Is that true?"

"It's my theory," I say.

"Maybe I should go talk to a shrink," he says.

"I think when you meet the right person, someone you're comfortable with, you'll be fine. Your pump will be fine," I say.

We are hunched now before the tiny, knotted Elf's home. There are letters crammed in the door's slot, shivering in the wind but holding their places.

"I hope they don't sit here all winter," I say.

"I think Calmzene is helping you, don't you think?" says Dr. Douglas.

It seems to be helping, a little, I tell him. I feel a little more settled. Yet, I add, the back of my mind still always feels like a teenage pep rally, kind of loud and bouncy.

"We could up the dose a little," he says. "But I'm not sure I want to do that. You've got a nice brain and we don't want to dull things for you."

"Oh, things are already plenty dull around here," I say.

I love Dr. Douglas. There he is with his big blue eyes and his Jolly Ranchers and his Jungian theories and I just want to jump into his lap.

"Why are you crying?" he says. "Gosh, it's nice to see you cry. I'm so glad you feel like you can do that here."

"It's nice to feel accepted," I say, reaching for a Kleenex on the side table. "I don't know. I'm just kind of worried that I'm always going to be alone." *When?* I ask him. *When had everyone else gone on to have a life? When, in the NASCAR race of life, had my gas tank emptied? Where had the pit crew gone? And why had I been given the Cheerios car?* "And you know those dark framed glasses that all of the women are wearing now? That make everyone look intellectual and hip? They make me look like Jerry Lewis."

I'm not sure if Dr. Douglas knows what I mean, but he nods reassuringly. His wife is lucky, I think. He is kind, with just the right amount of weird mixed in.

"You're fine the way you are," he says.

Which reminds me of something Adam would say.

Chapter 13

There is a bus idling outside the building. The third one this weekend. This one says on the side, in glittering cursive, *Lake Lillian Tours*. Outside the bus, a tour guide is pointing up at my window, and the eyes of twenty or so senior citizens follow his finger. I walk my cup of coffee over to the couch, pick up the calendar that's lying there, and sit where I am out of view.

I know the guide is telling them the story of John Dillinger, the story of the unlikely getaway. *If only that cop hadn't gone off to the bathroom. If only they'd broken down the door instead of believing that Dillinger's girlfriend needed a chance to get dressed.* But I imagine that the guide is saying, *In that apartment, up there on the third floor, is One of the Last Single Women in Minnesota. In her thirties! Gasp!*

Click, click, click, flashbulbs going off. Sometimes I think I'll go over to the window, open my robe, and flash them back.

This week, in the middle of our session, the counselor had gotten up, walked across the room to her desk, and pulled the calendar that's now in my lap off the wall. "Here," she had said, coming back to sit. "Take this calendar. This should be just fine."

An Easter Seals calendar. The current month featured a close-up photo of poinsettias and mistletoe, and down in the corner, where the month has ended and there were extra spaces, a small girl with leg braces.

"Here's what I want you to do," she continued. "I want you to track, every day, some of your anxiety about Adam. If there's none, write none. Or, say, if Adam calls and you begin to feel anxious, write that down. And write a little note about what you're thinking."

"There's not much room," I said.

"I don't want you to make a big production out of it," she said. "I just think it would be useful if you kept track of The Anxiety. If you had some notion of cause and effect. There's just enough room for you to make a note."

My grandparents had lived through the Depression. Would there be a time in history when we would claim to have lived through The Anxiety?

So I am sitting on my couch, calendar in my lap, tour bus idling outside.

What would it be like to be married to Adam? Would we live in his house? How would I feel about living in a suburb? Or would we buy a loft in the city that we could fix up together? Adam would probably like that—he liked to have projects—and we have compatible decorating tastes. Would we socialize with his friends from work? How often would we get takeout? And what if I had to work late at night to make a deadline? Would he say, "I'd really like you to come home so we can spend time together"? Adam hardly ever worked late, whereas I had to go in on the weekends all of the time. Would I have to make sacrifices in my career in order to make the relationship work? What if I wanted to spend money on new clothes and Adam thought we should stick to our budget? He was conservative that way. But maybe it would be good for me to order a shirt from Lands' End and wear it for thirty years. I impulse-shop too much, anyway. We could agree to the Mark Rothko print he had in the living room. We could keep that. But what would it be like to come home to Adam every night? To eat what Adam liked to call "nutritious dinners"? And what about the sex? How would we even get to that point in the first place?

Here is how it could happen:

Adam is in my kitchen; he leans over to pull something out of the oven. I am looking at his butt. When did it get so firm and round? When had his long, lanky frame filled out into this? His back is broad, his shoulders squared off. "Not done yet," he proclaims, closing the oven door, and when he turns around, I leap up on my tiptoes, place my hands on his broad shoulders, and kiss him, planting my lips against his surprised mouth.

I'm surprised, too. I'm the one doing all the kissing—no response from Adam—and when I pull away, he says, predictably, "Why did you do that? What are you doing?"

"I don't know," I say. "I guess I wanted to know what it would feel like."

I am waiting for Adam to get upset, to leave, to lean over and kiss me back. But he's just standing there, looking sort of puzzled, like someone who can't find his car keys. He wipes his mouth with his sleeve.

"Well, don't do that again," he finally says, trying to laugh it off. And then he adds, "I guess we had to get that out of the way, eventually."

"I guess," I say. "Right."

Dinner is awkward, a frozen pizza whose edges are burned and whose middle is still doughy, and we are quiet through the movie we've rented, *The Last of the Mohicans.*

"Time to go home," Adam announces when the movie is over, stretching his long legs across the carpeted floor.

"It's late," I say. And at the door there is this awkward moment where we just wave good night at each other, as if one of us were a tourist taking off on a cruise, the boat pulling out of harbor, and the other remaining on shore.

Or, it could go like this:

Adam and I are in his kitchen. He opens a bottle of wine. He hands me a glass and as he is pouring my wine, he stops, gazing into my eyes, noticing me as if for the first time. *Who is this woman, fresh as dew and yet so familiar?* He leans in and kisses me gently.

Soon, we are in the bedroom having passionately tender sex.

Although it is more likely that we would be sitting there in flannel pajamas playing Yahtzee.

For some reason, the thought of actually having sex with Adam gives me the shivers, but maybe it's just because we've never tried it. Maybe it's like Vegemite; it's gross unless you're used to it. In the same way that the French don't like peanut butter.

It could go like this:

No one does anything.

I can hear the gravelly engine of the bus below, its revving and burbling. The bus heaves into first; I can hear it pulling away.

I write in today's small square: *Help.*

★   ★   ★

"So," says Dr. Douglas. Today he is wearing an ice-blue cashmere pullover and his eyes have changed color to match. "What if you were with Adam and you found someone you *really* wanted to be with?"

"That's true," I say. "That would pretty much suck."

"Might you feel trapped?"

"I might."

It has occurred to me lately that half the reason I'm still coming to see Dr. Douglas is just to spend time with him. Here is a kind, good-looking man who seems unflaggingly interested in me. Of course, I pay him to be.

"So, that's not the best sign," he says.

"But the thing is, I'm out there now," I say. "And I'm not meeting anyone."

"But you have faith that you will?" Dr. Douglas nods encouragingly.

"Not really," I say. "I used to. I don't know where it went."

"That worries me," he says.

"It's like standing in the soup line," I say. "If you stand there every day and they never have soup, then eventually you don't stand there anymore."

"It is not like being in the soup line," says Dr. Douglas with a deep sigh. "I think you're not meeting anyone because you don't really want to. I don't think you're trying."

"Maybe I don't really want to," I say. "That could be true. It's scary. Meeting someone new is scary."

"Uh-huh," says Dr. Douglas. "Good. It is scary. That's honest. But I think you've got pretty good judgment."

"It's not me I'm worried about," I say. "It's the other guy. Drive defensively, I always say. Leave yourself an out."

"If you're worried about the other guy," says Dr. Douglas,

"you're probably actually worried about yourself. That's a projection."

"Oh."

"So, maybe we need to work on getting your confidence up. Your confidence in being able to say no. To decide what's right for you. To set limits."

"Couldn't we just sit here and chat?"

"Of course we could sit here and chat, but I don't think that's ultimately useful to you."

"I just don't see it ever happening," I say. "Meeting someone I feel comfortable with. Someone where everything clicks. I mean, maybe that's not happening with anyone because I've already met that person."

"Who, Adam?"

"Yeah, Adam. He feels comfortable. I mean, his taste in music kind of bugs me. I don't like choral music all that much. And he doesn't like it when Ellie and I talk about books. He gets mad and makes us change the subject. But we have fun. Usually."

"Or maybe he's just holding that place for you."

Chapter 14

Here we are, in Adam's kitchen. I'd read an article about holiday gift giving, which suggested that sometimes the best gift to give is a homemade one. *Why not make up an assortment of homemade cookies?* Since we'd lost a major client and weren't getting holiday bonuses this year, making cookies sounded like a good idea. I mentioned it to Adam, who always forgets to give people presents, and he suggested we make them here at his place. This would be the year that he finally remembers to give everyone something.

Once we buy all of the ingredients for cookies, we may as well have bought everyone a nice present.

So far, we have made those Russian tea balls with the powdered sugar all over them. Next, we tackle spritz cookies, though ours, which are supposed to be delicately shaped stars and trees, come out basically as formless little blobs with a Red Hot tossed on top. And my arm hurts from pushing on the spritzer.

"Well," says Adam, "they leave room for interpretation. It's more fun that way."

"They're like little Rorschach cookies," I say. "This one looks like a crooked leg," I point out. "And the Red Hot is a painted toenail."

"Maybe we won't make all five kinds in the magazine," says Adam. "Maybe we should stick to three."

"Three's a good number," I say.

We start making the macaroon pyramids. You are supposed to shape the coconut mix into pyramids, bake them, and then dip the tips in chocolate. We feel it is our most distinctive cookie. "But if we don't make the Special-K wreaths, or the candy-striped celebrations, then every cookie is going to be white," I say. "And that's kind of boring. Visually."

Adam thinks we can fix it by putting green food coloring in the pyramid batter.

"Doesn't that kind of take the dignity away from it?" I say.

"Then they would look like little Christmas trees," he suggests.

"Should coconut be green?"

"You never like my ideas. You know, we could try one of my ideas for once."

"Okay," I say. It occurs to me that I sound like my mother.

But when the pyramids come out of the oven and we dip the first few tips in chocolate, and after Adam has stopped giggling because he feels he is adding a nipple to each cookie, he says, "These look awful. Maybe we should just give the Russian tea balls."

"No one even likes those, anyway."

"Then why did we make them?"

"They're traditional," I say.

"I kind of like them," says Adam.

"I know," I say. "I like them, too."

"They're not a very *sexy* cookie," says Adam, picking one out to eat. "They're more of a staple." He has powdered sugar on his lips.

"Predictable," I say, picking one out for myself.

"Reliable," he says.

"Remember at Olaf when they used to have those date bars for dessert?"

"I loved those," Adam says.

"Me, too," I say. "This is what I'm saying. Even though they were kind of a grandma dessert."

"This is what I'm saying," says Adam. "That's from *Seinfeld.*"

I flash a mouthful of powdered sugar tea ball at him. "Like you never quote *Seinfeld*. You quote it all the time."

"I do not quote it all the time," he says.

"Occasionally," I say through a mouthful of cookie.

This was the thing about Adam. We could sit around and talk about nothing forever. Where on a date you might be thinking, *This conversation is going nowhere,* with Adam it was like being with family. Who cared if the conversation was boring? These were your people. It was like being a wolf, sleeping in a den in the winter. Breathing together, keeping each other warm. Oh, hell. What did I know about wolves?

But still, when we had nothing left to talk about, all Adam had to do was look at me and say, "I am now free to grieve with and for the lone honker," which was a line from a book he'd had to read in college, while he was taking Field Studies, a course where they had to find dead animals and stuff them. The book had something to do with migration, something about a bird being left behind. A bird who, for some reason, couldn't keep up with the rest. And while no one else thought the line was particularly funny, we found it to be hilarious.

Pretty soon we find that we have eaten half of the Russian tea balls.

Adam surveys the counter top. "Let's see," he says, putting his hands on his hips. "We have a dozen tea balls."

The spritz cookies look like abandoned prosthetic limbs, and the macaroon pyramids look just plain disgusting.

"I am now free to grieve with and for the lone honker," I say.

"I think we should just go to the mall and buy stuff," says Adam.

Maybe the counselor was right: Your college friends were like family. Maybe Dr. Douglas was right: Adam was holding a place for me, that place someone less familial should occupy.

That Christmas was quiet, and the snow we'd had earlier had melted or blown away, leaving frozen brown ground. My brother and sister were celebrating the holidays with their in-laws, and weeks ago, my mother had effectively uninvited me from the family celebration.

"Of course, you know," she had said to me when I was home on a Sunday and we were having dinner, "that your father and I will be here for Christmas, and you're more than welcome to join us if you'd like. But you're certainly not obligated to be here."

"Where else would I go?" I said. My father kept cutting his steak.

"Well, I don't know," my mother said. "I mean, you're an adult. I know you have your own things going on. I'm assuming you might have made other arrangements. I mean, you've clearly peed on your territory."

"Do you still have any of those little imaginary friends?" my dad said, and he started laughing.

"Very funny," I said. "Mom, who, exactly, would I spend Christmas with?"

"*I* don't know," she said. "That's up to you. I'm just respecting your space."

Chapter 15

I had never seen so many adults so drunk. Someone left the heel of her shoe in Lucy's ficus. Someone else fell down the stairs. Luckily, his fall was broken by someone who had already passed out on the landing. Another guy had stripped out of his clothes, put on one of Lucy's bedsheets, and was running around giving Baby New Year kisses. I admired him.

Adam had had a couple of beers and had finally gotten up the courage to ask a woman to dance, and I could overhear them on the dance floor.

"Hi, I'm Adam," he said. "What's your name?"

"Margaret," she said.

"Margaret," he said, moving his hips to the rhythm. "Hey! That's my mother's name."

She immediately danced off to another corner of the floor. I couldn't stop laughing.

"Shut up," Adam said.

"Well, now you know not to say *that,*" I said.

"I think I need another drink," Adam said. "A real drink. What about Lucy? Is she still single?"

"She's dating that Amway salesman," I told him, which was true, although she was thinking about breaking up with him.

"Why is she dating an Amway salesman?" Adam said.

"She's dating him *despite* the fact that he's an Amway salesman." Lucy's new boyfriend believed that he was going to get rich selling laundry detergent. He didn't understand his place as vassal in Amway's feudal system, and even though he was a good kisser, his naïveté was driving Lucy crazy. Lucy had given up on looking for another husband. Now she said she was just looking for good sex. "I'll go get us a couple of drinks," I said, and I left Adam on the edge of the dance floor.

Why was he interested in Lucy? I felt oddly jealous. What if the two of them actually hit it off? I'd be the only single one left.

There was a guy at the bar who asked me if I wanted a drink. He had a dimple in his chin and a nice smile, and I could see the outline of his arm muscles through his shirt.

"Really? Are you going to buy me a drink?" I said. It wasn't a cash bar. All the booze was free; Lucy threw great parties.

"Yeah," he said. "Anything you'd like."

"I actually need two," I said.

"Rough night?" he said.

"Normally I hate New Year's Eve," I said.

"Me, too." He introduced himself as Paul and asked me how I knew Lucy.

"We used to work together, before she went into TV." Paul nodded. I could feel myself blushing. Here we were, two mute people, staring at each other.

"Hey, where's my drink?" Adam came up from behind, put his arm around me, and gave me a kiss on the head.

Paul smiled and walked away.

"What's up?" Adam said.

"I was in the middle of meeting someone," I said. "Thank you very much."

"What kind of salutation is that?" Adam said. "Hi, Adam, I'm still waiting for your drink. Hi, Adam, it's nice to see you."

"Hi, Adam. I was interested in that guy."

"Thanks a lot," Adam said. "What am I? Chopped liver?"

Just then Lucy came shimmying up and grabbed Adam by the hand, dragging him off to the dance floor. They were doing the bump, and I wandered off to the bathroom with my drink. I could feel that familiar itch in my chest. The Anxiety. I locked the door and looked in the mirror, just to make sure that I was still here.

Then I tried on some of Lucy's perfume and sat down on the toilet lid and sipped my drink until someone pounded on the door.

When I came downstairs, people were fluttering around, trying to find their designated person for midnight.

I went out on the porch to get some fresh air, and there was Paul, smoking a cigarette and sitting in one of Lucy's wicker chairs. My heart jumped into my throat.

"Hey, have a seat," he said. "It's kind of cold out. Want my jacket?"

"That's okay," I said. I had sat on a book, which I pulled out from under my butt as gracefully as I could.

"I sat on one, too," Paul said, and he smiled. "At least yours was a paperback. Here, take my jacket," he said again, and he handed it to me.

The counselor had told me that you should never refuse

help when offered. If a man wanted to hold the door open for you, let him. If a man wanted to carry your books, let him. "Let someone help you," she had said. "It's a connection. You don't have to act so independent all the time."

"But I thought I was working on being independent," I had said to her.

"We *were* working on that," she had said. "Now we're working on this."

I took Paul's wool jacket and put it around my shoulders. It was warm and seemed to have been infused with some kind of pungent men's cologne. It made me a little lightheaded.

"So, are you here with that guy?" Paul said. "The tall guy with the red hair?"

"Oh, no," I said. "I mean, yes. He's just a friend." The same thing I had been saying over and over, all through college, and after college, at every holiday party and couples shower when neither of us had a date. "We just came here together."

Paul nodded. "You have good hair," he said.

"Thank you," I said. Oh great. He was gay.

"A bunch of women in there were looking at your hair and talking about it."

"Well, that's nice," I said.

"I thought you'd want to know," he said, taking a big drag on his cigarette. "Isn't that the kind of thing women want to know?"

Maybe he just had sisters.

It turned out that Paul had gone to college with Lucy. "Oh, you're Paul Miller. The media critic, right? I thought you looked familiar. I've read your column. I'm kind of a television fan, myself." *Wow. Yay! Someone who watched television.*

"I'm really not," Paul started laughing. "I used to be. When it becomes a job, it's not as much fun. You have to watch every dumb thing that's out there."

"Well, you're much cuter than your picture," I blurted out.

Under the holiday lights strung along the top of Lucy's screened-in porch, I could see Paul's face turning red. "Thanks," he said.

"I meant that as a compliment," I said.

We were sitting outside when the clock hit midnight. I was hoping he would kiss me. So *this* is what it was like to meet someone you were sure you wanted to kiss. He had these nice laugh lines around his lips. Instead he looked at me and smiled, raised his glass to toast, and said, "It's nice to meet you, Shannon Olson."

His breath produced a frost that hung in the air between us.

"You ditched me," Adam said. "You totally ditched me. Where did you go? The ball drops and Lucy's making out with the Amway guy."

"I was on the porch with Paul."

"I was on the porch with Paul," said Adam. "I was *on the porch* with Paul. That's great. Friends don't ditch friends on New Year's Eve. A room full of kissing people and I don't know any-body."

If I had been standing there, what would we have done?

"You were dancing with Lucy," I said. "You looked like you were having fun."

"She's kind of a maniac," Adam said, rubbing his hip. "She's a little bit much for me. I think I pulled something."

Though I couldn't explain why, I felt strangely relieved that Adam's brief interest in Lucy had passed.

"So where is Mr. Fabulous?"

"He left. He had to leave. He said he was going out of town tomorrow. He asked me if I'd like to have coffee sometime. When he gets back."

Adam was surveying the bacchanal before us. The hors d'oeuvres table had been devastated. All that was left were a few flakes of smoked salmon scattered across the tablecloth, an olive, and a couple of smashed crackers. People were making out on the couch and on the living-room dance floor. A few people had taken bottles of Cuervo from the bar and were dancing around, offering shots straight from the bottle.

"So, Shanny," Adam said, putting his arm around me. "Happy New Year! What are you looking forward to in the New Year?" A nice, brotherly question, followed by a kiss on top of the head.

"I have no idea," I said. I should know. I should have some goal, but the question froze me completely. This was one of the things that I should have an answer for, if I was going to change my life, if I was going to get out there, as Dr. Douglas kept saying, and explore life in its rich variety. Last time, I think he had compared it to an aquarium filled with beautiful tropical fish. "Maybe entertaining in my new apartment," I said. Entertaining in my new apartment seemed good, manageable, although I would have to buy some more furniture. I had put a couch on credit, but still lacked a kitchen table and chairs. Maybe I could serve sushi and we could all sit on the floor. (Like I knew how to make sushi.) Then I realized I was being impolite in not asking Adam the same question. This was another thing I was working on in group therapy. Reciprocity. "What about you?"

"I'm not sure," he said. "I think I'd like to find a new job. I'm in the mood for change," he said. "I'm still working on it." He smiled at me and gave me a big squeeze.

The more I thought about it, Adam really *hadn't* dated anyone in a long time.

He used to tell me about his dates, women he had crushes on. There had been a woman who worked in marketing at his company, and he thought she was attractive. They had gone on a couple of dates and he was getting excited about perhaps taking her as his date to the annual company picnic. Then he had seen her apartment. It was a complete disaster area and was decorated mostly in velour and leopard prints. There were scented candles in every nook and cranny. Plus, she had cats.

He thought that because their tastes were completely incompatible, they would be incompatible in even more significant ways down the line.

Adam was a minimalist.

He brought me to the picnic instead.

So there was the fact that he hadn't really mentioned anyone in a while. And he didn't seem all that interested in hearing about my dating life, either.

And then I thought about an afternoon in the summer. Adam and I had gone out for brunch on a rainy Sunday. Afterward, he'd come back to my apartment, my old apartment, and stretched out on my bed, my brand-new bed, which my mother believed was going to be my carnal undoing, and closed his eyes. I went into the living room. After a minute or two, he had sighed loudly and said, "Yep. This feels good. What's this music you've got on?"

"Miles Davis," I said.

"Miles Davis," he said. "That's nice, Shanny. Do you mind if I fall asleep for a few minutes?"

I had said that I didn't mind, but the truth was, I felt kind of funny about having him in my bedroom, though I couldn't say why.

"I can move over if you want to take a nap, too," he said.

"That's okay," I had said. I went into the kitchen and read the paper while Adam slept.

Chapter 16

"You know," says the counselor, "you two sound an awful lot alike."

"Who? Me and Adam?"

"Who else do you know who can dismiss someone so easily, for such a flimsy reason?"

"Me?"

"You," says the counselor. "I mean, come on. He didn't like her *couch*? Maybe you and Adam could help *each other* here. Encourage each other not to be so judgmental."

I don't know what to say. I feel the same way about chrome as Adam does about leopard prints. And Dr. Douglas had agreed with me about that afternoon in the summer. It was weird; there was something *off* about it, Adam offering to move over in the bed. But the counselor had said, *He's your friend. So he takes a nap at your house. Big deal.*

"Your *job,* as a single thirty-something," she continues now, "is to be out there dating, seeing what's out there, getting a sense of what works."

"That's my job?"

"That's your job."

"Can I go on unemployment?"

"I think you're both scared," the counselor says, taking a swig of Mountain Dew. "You and Adam."

"You do?"

"Yep. That's what I think," she says.

"Scared of what?"

"You tell me," she says.

I sit there, staring at her. She takes another swig of pop.

"Of you?" I offer. Sometimes I like Dr. Douglas better than the counselor. The counselor has a habit of challenging me on everything.

She rolls her eyes. "How's that calendar going?" she asks.

I pull out the calendar, on which I've recorded brief notes and my own little collection of created holidays. The Feast of the General Panic. All Singles Eve. Long Lunch Observed (Canada). I haven't really kept at it.

"Has that been helpful for you?" asks the counselor. "With your anxiety around Adam?"

I look at my notes: "Help." "Nice phone call." "Would I be restless?"

"This just doesn't seem like something I'm ever going to figure out," I say.

I hadn't heard from Ian for a couple of months. I had canceled our second date, and then we'd rescheduled to go see a Chagall exhibit at the Minneapolis Institute of Arts.

It hadn't gone very well. We met at the museum in the early afternoon and wandered through the exhibit together, saying almost nothing.

"Hey, that train's upside down," Ian had said. "And running backward."

"I like the floating chicken," I had said.

It had gone pretty much like that, with an awkward goodbye and a kiss on the cheek at the end.

But he'd left me a voice mail this week to see what I'd been up to, and asked if I wanted to go out for drinks.

"I think you should try going out with him one more time," says Dana, shaking her potato-chip bag for crumbs.

"Really?" I say. "I don't know. He's nice, I guess. I just don't feel any chemistry. And that second date. That was bad."

"You should never go to a museum on a date," Dr. Douglas jumps in. "Unless you've been dating someone for a long time."

"Why is that?" says Harvey. "I take a lot of my dates to the Art Institute."

Eileen snorts.

"What was that all about?" Harvey snaps. "I think it's a civilized thing to do. And it's inexpensive."

Eileen rolls her eyes.

"What is your problem?" Harvey says.

"It's just so *you*," she says. "Civilized. Inexpensive. With your little healthy sandwiches. Do you bring along sandwiches?"

"You're saying I'm cheap," says Harvey. "You're saying I'm a cheap Jew. Well you're a ladder-climbing Protestant."

"Oh, my God, that's so not what I'm saying," Eileen says.

"I really resent that," says Harvey. "That's unconscionable."

"That's not what I'm saying," says Eileen. "I'm Episcopalian."

Harvey's face is bright red. "Then what exactly is it that you *think* you're saying?"

"It's just, have you ever taken a woman out for a nice dinner? Do you ever ask her what *she* wants?"

"The women I go out with enjoy the arts."

"Let's finish with Shannon first," says Dr. Douglas. "The reason you should never go to a museum on an early date is this, and, Harvey, you might learn something here: When you're wandering through the museum, you're engaging with the artwork, not with each other. Or you're doing a half-assed job of both. Going to the museum is fine when you've been dating for a while and you're comfortable ignoring each other, and then you can talk later about what you've experienced. Art can stir up a lot for us; it can requisition deep, emotional responses." Dr. Douglas makes it sound like it involved a purchase order. "But if you're on a first or second date, you're not really interacting directly with the other person."

"See?" says Eileen. "That's what I meant."

"So maybe it's worth going out with this guy one more time," says Dr. Douglas.

"I kind of met someone else who I kind of like," I say. "At a party."

"Well, then, you can go out with him, too," says the counselor. "See, this is what you should be doing. This is what we talked about. Seeing what's out there."

"But I've been doing that for years now," I protest, and they ignore me.

"Okay, are you ready to move on?" Dr. Douglas asks me and nods. This is what they always ask when they're sick of dealing with your issue, when it seems like they've helped you all they can and there are more pressing dramas in the queue.

In the group-therapy triage, you've been bandaged and sent back out to the front lines.

"Ready," I say, even though I wish we could talk about me all night, until all of my problems are solved.

★　　★　　★

When I get home that night, there's another voice-mail message from Ian, wanting to know where I am, if I went out of town, wanting to know if I'd like to go to the Godard retrospective coming up at the Walker Art Center.

And a message from my mom, wondering why I hadn't called "all week." It is Wednesday, and I had seen her on Sunday night, when I had done three loads of laundry at their house. "Um, I'm worried about you," my mother said, which I know meant that she was bored.

There is a message from Adam, wondering what I am up to, how the apartment is looking, if I want him to come over and put shelves up or alphabetize my CDs.

There is still no message from Paul.

We're not allowed to drink after group because it interferes with our processing of the evening's events, of the powerful dramas that can take place on the microcosmic stage that is group therapy. Group is like Greek theater that way. Whatever you do in life, you're bound to repeat in group, eventually. And the things the other group members do are bound to relate to your own experience, or to provoke in you some unhealthy behavioral pattern, and to eventually stir up some projective trauma of archetypal significance.

Dr. Douglas had already pointed out on a number of occasions, for example, certain conversational behaviors I had that prevented me from connecting well with other people. "You assume you know what other people are thinking, without really asking them," he had said, for instance.

Thinking I understood him perfectly, I had nodded and neglected to ask him for an example.

"See? You just did it," he said. "You don't really know what I'm talking about, do you?"

"I thought it would come to me later," I had said.

So we aren't allowed to drink twelve hours before group or twelve hours after group, which sucks because usually after group there's nothing I'd like better than a beer.

Tonight I have a headache, so I pop a couple of Advils and make a frozen pizza. I've forgotten to tape *Oprah,* so I turn on *Frasier* reruns.

In the middle of the night, I woke up to a flapping, some kind of flutter.

I had fallen asleep on the couch watching *Frasier,* and at some point I had woken up, turned off the television, wandered into the bedroom, dropped all my clothes next to the bed, and crawled under the covers.

Flap, flap, flap.

Shit. A bat. I saw the outline of its wings. I sunk deeper under the covers, barely peering out.

Flap, flap, flap. From the window, across the room, and into the closet, whose warped door wouldn't close, and so I left it always gaping open.

What was I supposed to do? *I'm nude. I'm defenseless.*

Flap flap. Across the room to the window, and back again, into the closet.

I looked at the clock. It was 4 A.M. Then I turned on the lamp on my nightstand. Maybe the light would freak the bat out and he'd stay where he was. I scrambled out of bed and made a dash for the bathroom, slammed the door, and put on my bathrobe.

Victory!

Now what was I supposed to do? I was trapped in the bathroom.

I sat on the edge of the tub. Now what? I couldn't sit in here all night.

I opened the bathroom door and peered out.

The bat had gone into the living room.

I made a dash for the bedroom, slammed the door, and shoved dirty clothes under the crack.

Okay.

I put on a pair of sweatpants and a sweatshirt. My glasses, fortunately, were on the dresser. But there was no phone in the bedroom.

Crap. This was one of those times when you really wished you had a boyfriend. Or a roommate. Lucy had had a bat in her house once, which had shown up during a dinner party, and we'd all helped to get it outside.

It was easier to be brave when you weren't alone.

I could stay in the bedroom all night, but then, in the morning, I wouldn't know where the bat had gone. Maybe it would be hiding out in some cupboard in the kitchen.

Using a pillow as a shield, I emerged into the living room. The bat was swooshing around; it came toward the pillow, and then went back to a window, settling himself on the screen.

If I could just close the window, the bat would be stuck between the screen and the glass. How that would solve things, I wasn't sure, but at least he wouldn't be flying around the living room.

He was hanging on the screen, up underneath the glass. If I could sneak over and close the window in one fluid motion, I would have him.

Hiding mostly behind my pillow, I leaned over, reached for the top of the windowsill, started to pull down, and the bat came flapping out right at me.

"Ah! Ah!" I screamed and jumped, knocking over my CD player and some plants. I grabbed my cell phone, and went running out of my apartment into the hallway.

Maybe if I left the door open, the bat would come out into the hallway.

I propped the door open with a shoe and hid around the corner with my cell phone in hand.

Who could I call?

My first thought was the counselor. She was the person I always called when I was having a breakdown. But I couldn't call her at 4 A.M. because of a *bat*.

Dr. Douglas had wisely never given me his home phone number.

This was instructive. I had no *real* emergency people, only the ones I paid for advice.

Lucy lived only a mile from me, but I didn't want to call her this late. Although she often couldn't sleep, this was precisely why I didn't want to call her. If she was finally getting some sleep, I didn't want to wake her up.

Ellie lived over an hour away.

I didn't know any of my neighbors well enough to wake them up. And it was disturbing that with all the commotion I was making, they hadn't come to see what was going on, anyway.

Just then, the bat came flying out through my doorway and glided up the hall.

I darted back into my apartment, slammed the door, deadbolted it, and threw the chain on.

Now it was in the hall.

But what if it came back in? How had it gotten in here in the first place? I shoved some towels around the door.

My heart was thumping against my chest wall like Robert Bly at a men's retreat, pounding his warrior drums. I called my dad on the line his patients use for emergency calls.

"Dad? Dad? I have a bat."

"A what?"

"A bat. There was a bat in my apartment."

"Where is it now?"

"Now it's in the hallway. What should I do?"

"Go to bed."

"But now it's stuck in the hallway." I looked out the peephole and could see the bat sailing around. "Do I need to go back out and try to shoo it out of the building?"

"I don't think so, dear. I think you should go to bed and call your caretaker in the morning."

"What if it comes back in here?"

"I don't think he's that fond of you," my dad said. "I'm sure he's got plenty of other places to go."

I sat on the couch. How was I supposed to fall asleep?

Adam had helped me trap mice in my first apartment after college. He had even pulled a dead and bloated one up from behind the stove (which had made me throw up), and disposed of it for me. But I hadn't seen him since New Year's Eve; he'd left me a couple of messages and I hadn't called him back, because when he'd called he'd been on a speakerphone, which bugged me. Was it fair to call him for something like this, this early in the morning?

"I'll be right over," Adam offered, before I even asked.

He brought a tennis racket and some doughnuts. He inspected the hallway thoroughly; he even shook the curtains on the tall windows on the landing to see if the bat was hanging in them.

"I don't know, Shan," he said. "I don't see him."

"Maybe we should leave the fire doors open, so he can go out into the stairwell, just in case."

Which is what we did.

By then it was 6 A.M. I made coffee and we flipped on the early morning news.

"Do you still like doughnuts?" Adam said, offering me the box.

"I do," I said.

Adam looked over at me and smiled. I could never tell what he was thinking. He was just sitting there, smiling at me. I snapped my head to observe the TV. Then he put his arm around me and drew me in to him, resting his cheek on the top of my head.

"Shan," he said, with a kind of grandmotherly warmth, "you still like doughnuts." Still, there he was with his arm around me. What *was* he thinking?

I sat there diagonally, my back stiff, my heartbeat that of a tiny animal—furious, insistent palpitations—looking at the weather forecast. It was supposed to snow. Today's high would be twenty-two degrees. Tomorrow, there was also a chance of snow. In terms of snow, we were down two inches from last year. Would there be more snow this weekend? Let's look at a satellite picture.

"Do you want more coffee?" I said.

"Okay, so we're back to square one," says the counselor. "So what happens if you picture you and Adam together?"

"I don't know," I say. "Actually, I kind of start to panic. I get that panicky feeling. But he's so *nice*. And reliable. And maybe that's what I've been missing."

"Is that what you want?" she asks. "Nice and reliable?"

"It does make him sound like a car, doesn't it?" I say.

The counselor nods and pops open a Mountain Dew.

"But he's filled out since college," I say. "He looks different. Less like a really tall little brother."

"Yes, we've been over this," she says. "How do you feel about kissing him? Are you attracted to him?"

"I don't know," I say. "Does that even matter?"

"Well, people get married for all kinds of reasons," says the counselor, "but I would think that for you, it would matter."

"He has nice lips. He has very soft hands," I say.

"Okay," she says. "Let's try it again. Close your eyes and picture kissing him."

I try, but I shiver as though I've been slurping raw eggs.

"I can't," I say. "I mean, maybe. I don't know. Maybe it's one of those things where, like Dr. Douglas says, 'You don't know until you go.'"

"Maybe," says the counselor. "Or maybe it's just not right."

"Or maybe I'm crazy," I say.

"Or maybe he feels safe and familiar."

"Maybe you should talk to him," says Dr. Douglas at our session later that week. "Maybe you should confront him and see what he says."

"What do I say?"

"I don't know. Ask him if he's ever thought about the two of you dating."

"I'm not *sure* I'd want to date him. It's just that, I don't know. Things seem different than they used to. Maybe it's just me."

"You won't figure it out by not doing anything," says Dr. Douglas.

I can feel panic welling up in me just thinking about it.

"Do you know how hard it is for me to do something like that? This is Minnesota. No one has those conversations."

I am waiting for a piece of advice from the animal kingdom. Something along the lines of what he said last week about how male fiddler crabs wave a claw around to attract females. What point was that supposed to illuminate again?

"Have a glass of wine first." Dr. Douglas shrugs.

I called Adam the next day.

"Hey," I said. "I just wanted to thank you again for coming over on bat detail."

"No problem," Adam said.

"Can I buy you dinner tonight or something as a thank-you?"

"You don't have to do that," Adam said, which is what I knew he would say.

"How about that Chinese place in your neighborhood?"

"I've actually got a date," Adam said.

"A date? Really?" That was a surprise.

"Yeah, it's this woman from church."

"Oh," I said. "Do you go to church a lot?"

"Yeah, I started going again a couple years ago."

"Is it someone you like?" I said.

"We'll see," said Adam. "She seems nice. She's pretty."

"Oh. Well, good," I said. Maybe that answered that question. "Some other time, then."

Chapter 17

"Hey." Paul called me out of the blue at work. "I've been thinking about you."

I had almost forgotten about him and it took me a while to recognize his voice. "Thinking about me," I said, trying to buy time until I figured out it was him. "Really?"

"Yeah, but I was out of town longer than I thought I would be."

"Business?"

"Sort of," he said. "I was in Los Angeles."

"How was it?"

"Great," he said. "I've got friends there, so I stayed a little longer. Do you want to meet for a drink tonight? I could pick you up at work."

I should play hard to get, act like I'm on deadline, pretend I have other plans. "Sure," I said.

There was something about Paul that I found reassuring. His voice. The laugh lines on the side of his mouth. His little round glasses. I couldn't say what, exactly. He seemed safe, and at the same time he was sexy, self-confident. He had nice forearms.

He told me stories about Lucy in college. Something about running across campus in her underwear, which didn't surprise me.

"But you guys never dated?"

"Nah," said Paul. "You know, sometimes you just have that friend from college and, you know, you're just friends. For whatever reason."

"That's like my friend Adam," I said. "From the party."

"Oh, right. The tall guy."

"I like your shirt," I said. He was wearing a blue broadcloth shirt that showed off his deltoids when he leaned over in his chair.

"Thanks," he said. "I got it in L.A."

I hadn't read some of the books that Paul talked about, novels and short stories about hunting and fishing, but instead of saying, "What *do* you read?" he poured me a little wine and said, instead, "What kinds of things are you interested in? Who do you like?" And then he smiled and looked into my eyes and waited. And when I told him my favorite author, he said, "I've heard she's terrific," which for some reason made me feel like I'd just won the lottery.

And it turned out that we had a lot of the same television vices.

"I don't know why," he said, "because I watch TV all day, and I've seen them all at least five times, but late at night I always watch those *Frasier* reruns."

And it turned out that we both had the same recurring dream, in which our contact lenses are too big for our eyes.

"I can't believe you have that same dream," I said. "I've never met anyone else who has that dream."

"I think mine's a frustration dream," he said. "Like, it just won't fit, and there's nothing I can do about it."

"In mine," I told him, "the more I rub it and put solution on it and try to get it to become smaller, the bigger it gets."

"Really?" he said, blushing.

"That sounds kind of sexual, doesn't it?" I said.

"Just a little."

I confessed to him that I had been trying to figure out what it meant by reading Carl Jung's *Man and His Symbols*.

"I read that the circle represents wholeness and enlightenment," I told Paul. "And so, what I think is that there's something right in front of me that I'm not seeing, that I'm not ready to see, or that I'm trying too hard to figure out. Or the contact would fit in my eye."

"That's interesting," Paul said, taking a sip of his wine.

"It's not. I'm a big fat nerd," I said.

"No, I really think it's interesting," he said.

"I think I'm just a hair away from self-actualization," I said, finishing off my wine.

"Really?" he said, and he started laughing. "You and Mother Teresa and Gandhi, huh?"

"I think it's happened," I reported gleefully to Dr. Douglas the following week. "I think that met-and-matched thing has finally happened."

"Really?" he said.

I told him about Paul. About the dimple in his chin, his laugh lines, the crease in his forehead. His appreciation of Henry Moore sculptures, the fat, stunted sensuousness of them. How he liked to go scuba diving, which I had never done, and how he thought that the fact that I used to drive a Delta '88 was funny and oddly appealing.

"Well, fantastic!" Dr. Douglas said. "Now all we have to do is make sure that you don't eat him after intercourse."

"What's that supposed to mean?" Sometimes Dr. Douglas's exuberance was irritating.

"I believe it's the female praying mantis," he said. "You know, who devours her lovers."

"I wasn't planning on devouring anybody," I said. I wondered what the counselor would think of this theory. My guess is that she would have found it distinctly antifeminist.

"Yes," said Dr. Douglas, "but you do get kind of bitchy when you get scared. I think that's what happened with your last boyfriend. Marino? Marcos? What was his name?"

"Michael."

"Yes. I think you get scared about being close to somebody, and you get bitey."

"I don't feel that way so far."

"How's the sex?"

"We've only been out for drinks once, and a movie and coffee."

"How's the chemistry?"

"I don't know. I mean, we haven't done anything."

"Nothing?"

"No. Is that odd? I keep hoping he might kiss me, but he hasn't."

"Usually you want to pulverize someone when he tries to kiss you."

"I know."

"So maybe it's not that bad that he hasn't. Maybe this guy's intuitive, to boot," said Dr. Douglas.

"Maybe," I said. "Maybe *I'll* just kiss *him*."

★   ★   ★

I called Lucy the next day from work.

"What do you know about Paul?" I said.

"What do you mean, what do I know about Paul?" Lucy asked.

"I kind of like him."

"Paul?" she said. "I thought he had a girlfriend."

"Really? He's never mentioned a girlfriend," I said. I felt my heart sink a little. "We went out last week. We're supposed to go out tomorrow night."

"I thought he was engaged, actually," Lucy said. "He's had this long-distance thing going on. But I haven't talked to him in a while."

"He hasn't mentioned her."

"She's supposed to be moving here pretty soon. I *thought*," said Lucy. "Maybe they broke up."

What was it that Dr. Douglas had said? *You need to leave the nest and explore the richness of life,* or some such thing? So far life had proven to be a big, fat, artery-clogging vat of hollandaise sauce.

It couldn't be true that Paul was seeing someone else. He would have said something.

"I'll ask around," said Lucy, "if you want. And see what I come up with."

I called my mom that night to see if I could come out on Sunday and do laundry.

"I'm sorry," I said. "I woke you up."

"We were sleeping," my mother said, in the clipped way you'd be rude to a Jehovah's Witness who came to your door at dinner.

"I'm sorry," I said. "I'll talk to you tomorrow. I thought you'd still be up."

"No," she said. "Your father isn't feeling well. He's got a cold."

"That's too bad."

"And I'm getting up early for my stress-management retreat," she said.

"I forgot about that," I said.

My mother had signed up for a community education class about stress management and finding spirituality and peace in your daily life. The teacher was making them read a thick book called *Thriving in Chaos,* which was about living life fully, baptizing yourself in the mess of it, and Flo was having trouble keeping up with the reading. I was having trouble remembering the title of the book and kept calling it *The Big Disaster of Life.* In addition to the reading, the instructor was having them meditate for an hour a day, do yoga for an hour a day, and write their thoughts about their progress.

"I can't keep up with all of it," Flo said. "He's stressing me out." She didn't want to go to the retreat, she had told me earlier. "He's too intense. He's really bugging me."

So tonight, when I woke her up, she said, "So, was there anything in particular?"

"I didn't think there *had* to be," I said dramatically. "You've changed. You never send flowers anymore. We never go *out.*"

The truth was, even though I was trying to keep things from my mother, I missed her. It was like we were going through a kind of puberty, which my mom pronounced "poohberty," and our new relationship didn't fit in our old clothes. Seemingly overnight we had become gangly and awkward.

"I'd like to go back to bed," Flo said.

"I was thinking of coming out on Sunday to do laundry."

"Big surprise," said Flo. "See you then." And she hung up.

*   *   *

Paul and I met Saturday night at the Dakota Bar and Grill to listen to some jazz. I had been excited when he asked me to go, because I'd never met anyone else under the age of sixty who liked bossa nova music. But now I felt kind of funny. What if he did have a girlfriend? He wouldn't do something like that, I didn't think. But maybe he just thought of me as a friend; he hadn't tried to kiss me or anything. But it really seemed, when I was around him, that he was sort of attracted to me. But then again, what did I know? The way my dating life was going, I was clearly no expert on alchemy.

We had ordered beer and buffalo wings, and were sitting near the back, in the general-admission area. The woman at the table next to us was bouncing her head violently with the bass, and every once in a while would let out a joyous whoop, then close her eyes and bounce again. Then yell, "Yeah!"

"There are arguments to be made for listening to jazz at home," Paul whispered to me, nodding his head in the direction of the woman.

I had just taken a sip of my beer and choked on it laughing.

It was true. The guy sitting with the whooping woman had his eyes closed and was drumming his fingers on his head.

Paul patted me on the back. "Are you okay?"

"Fine," I said. It is hard to describe how nice it felt to have his hand on my back. I looked over at the couple. She was bouncing. He was drumming. "I bet they have really weird sex."

Paul's face turned red. "I hate to say it, but I was thinking the same thing."

"I bet they have a lot of cats."

"Or maybe a ferret." Paul shivered. He bobbed his head a little and then let out a big whoop. "When in Rome," he said, grabbing a buffalo wing.

"I'd give that a five-point-seven," I said. "Six for the dismount."

Since we got there, the band had been playing particularly buoyant songs; now they slid into a glassy version of "The Girl from Ipanema."

"I actually think the band is really good," Paul said. "Don't you?"

"I do," I said. It had been a long time since I'd been out with someone who I so definitely wanted to kiss. Tonight again I could see the outline of muscles through his shirt; it was a torture. "You have sauce on your chin."

"Where?" Paul said.

His chin was so nice. Everything about him was so nice. I leaned over and rubbed the sauce off with my napkin.

"Thanks," he said, looking at me and then down at his sauce-covered hands. "I'm a mess."

I handed him my napkin. Something was wrong here. Usually, by now, if someone asked me out a few times, something would have happened. Although it was true that if McDonald's gave frequent-flyer miles I could fly to Tahiti, I still thought I looked *okay*. The triathlon coach had, after all, grabbed me by the back of my head. Right? Right. Paul was wiping off his hands and smiling at me.

"I do like the band," I said.

Paul nodded.

"Do you have—" I started to say, and then stopped. "So what do you do when you're in L.A.?"

"What do I do?" he said. He shifted in his chair and began tapping his foot, jiggling his leg.

"I don't know," I said. "What do you like to do when you're there? Or is it all business?"

"It's some business," he said, looking off at the band. His leg was jiggling faster.

"I really like L.A.," I said. "I've been there a couple of times for work. You know, I didn't think the traffic was *that* bad. But maybe I just hit it at the right time." I was blabbing.

Paul looked back at me. "There's something I should tell you, but I'm not sure how to say it. I really like you. And I don't meet people that often who I like as much as you."

I suddenly felt sort of peptic, my whole body churning.

"I . . . ," he continued. "But I have a girlfriend. We're engaged, actually."

I didn't know what to say. I wanted to wring his neck as much as I wanted to rip all his clothes off.

"We got engaged right before I met you. We've been going out for a long time and it was time. I mean, we'd been talking about it for a long time. She lives in L.A. I just thought . . . ," he said. "I just thought you and I had a really great connection. I'm sorry. I didn't know what to do."

"Telling me might have helped," I squeaked out. I was trying not to cry.

"I just kept thinking," Paul said. "I'm sorry. You know. Why didn't I meet this person sooner? Like five years ago. Three years ago."

I thought back to what I was like three years ago. I was a basket case, still hoping Michael would come home, but because of that, I was also much thinner. But also, again, a basket case.

"I don't think you would have liked me three years ago," I said.

"I am pretty sure," said Paul, "that I would have."

The bossa nova music was starting to make everything sort of surreal, bouncy, and odd.

"You really could have told me this earlier," I said. Though, when I thought about it, he hadn't done anything really *wrong*. He hadn't made any kind of a move on me, at all.

"I know," he said. "Maybe I'm nervous about getting married. I mean, you always wonder, just a little bit, if it's the right thing, and, I mean, it is. I know it is. It's just. I'm sorry."

He was staring at me now and I didn't know what to say. Even though he was sitting right there, I felt so incredibly *alone*.

"Do you think . . . ," he said. "Would you want to be friends? I'd still like to hang out with you."

The thing was, it had taken all of my willpower to use a napkin and not to *lick* the sauce off his chin. It wasn't fair. He would have the best of both worlds. The girlfriend, fiancée, in Los Angeles, who was probably really tiny and had cool clothes, and me, the buddy-pal to hang out with. I wouldn't want to hear him talk about his girlfriend. I would be constantly staring at his back muscles and feeling sad.

"The thing is," I said, "I'd be wanting to have sex with you all the time."

Paul smiled and then looked at the floor.

"I just think," I said, "that might be really hard for me."

"So what's new?" my mom asks as I'm dumping my laundry on the floor the next day.

"Not much," I say. "Just work."

"Any hot dates?" she says.

"No."

"Are you sure?"

"Yes, I'm sure," I say.

"Has your bat returned?" she asks. "You were so worried that he would come back for you."

"I think he's found someone new," I say. "How was your meditation day?"

"Well, we weren't allowed to talk all day," she says, and then she goes on in some detail about the sandwich she ate at lunchtime. It was made with whole-grain bread, hummus, and mixed greens and sprouts and turkey and some kind of gourmet mustard.

"That's a lot on one sandwich," I say. "Could you talk during lunch?"

"Well, you shouldn't talk with your mouth full anyway," Flo says. "But no." She had sat under a tree and watched a bee, and some little kids in the nearby wading pool, and a seagull that was eating potato chips.

"What's a seagull doing in Minneapolis?" I say.

"I don't know," she says.

"So you were quiet all day?"

"We did guided meditation," she says.

"So the *guide* got to talk," I say. "Isn't that just the way. The guide always gets to talk."

Flo starts laughing and comes over to hug me. "I like you," she says, gripping my shoulder to pull me in for a big kiss on the cheek. At some point in the past few years, my mother started kissing us the same way our grandmother—her mother—used to. These big, noisy, suction-cup kisses. Even though my mother insists that she's done everything humanly possible to avoid becoming her mother, she seems, from what I can tell, more and more to be turning into her.

"My daughter!" she says. "I love you. My sweet little sweetpea!"

"Thank you," I say, and I kind of move away. I'm not sure why. I wasn't in the mood to be anyone's sweet little sweetpea, I guess.

"Oh," my mom says, "I don't get anything in return? How about 'I love you, too, Mother?'"

"I love you, too, Mother," I say, putting laundry detergent in the washing machine.

"Well, I shouldn't have to *drag* it out of you," she says. "What about all of those years of changing diapers? Isn't anybody around here grateful for anything I've done?"

"Thank you, Mother," I say, looking in the cupboard for fabric softener. "You'll notice I don't wear diapers anymore."

"Well, you'll notice I don't do your laundry anymore, either," she says. "And maybe I won't let you come here anymore and do that, either," she concludes.

And she goes off to the back room of the basement, where she keeps two floor-to-ceiling storage shelves packed with canned soups, sauces, vegetables, and fruits, plus jars of relish, pickles, and beets. There's a can of oysters on those shelves from the 1960s. And there are cans of Campbell's Soup whose labeling I recognize from the seventies, when they first came out with "Soup for One." When the idea of catering to a single person, who would eat alone night after night, was a revolutionary one.

I can hear my mom clanging around, lifting cans and juice jars out of their brown-paper grocery bags on the floor, moving things around on the shelves to make room for the new food.

I had recently told my mother that a food expert on the *To-day* show had said that canned food should be eaten within a few months of buying it.

"Oh, it shouldn't, either," my mother had said. "People are so fussy about things these days. It's antibacterial this and that. We used to cut all of the mold and rotten parts out of everything. And eat around it. We kept what was good."

It struck me at the time as a metaphor for marriage. My parents' generation ignored what was rotten. Mine threw out the whole fruit.

If you considered that half of all marriages now end in divorce, and probably half the women I knew who *stayed* married said that they often still wished they were single, that added up to a seventy-five percent failure rate, of sorts. Why *did* I want to get married? Except the same people who said that marriage was hard work and that it would be nice to be single didn't actually want to *be* single and dating. So, there was that. But I knew a couple of women at work who had had affairs, who were emotionally lonely in their marriages, and who said it was worse to be *with* someone and be lonely than to be alone.

Which led to the question What is marriage? What are we supposed to expect? Are there more divorces now simply because they're easier to get? And back when they weren't, did you just learn to live with less? Did you resign yourself to your lot? Was it like wartime? Here was your marriage. You got your ration and that was that. You were married in the same way that you participated in the drives for paper and tin, because you wanted to do your part.

Now there were so many options. You didn't have to sacrifice. Now you could shop online.

Last week, Flo had said, "Doesn't anybody work anymore? Boy, back in my day, you wouldn't be—what did you call it, 'on the Web'?—at work."

"You had a watercooler," I said. "Now people take their breaks online."

"People put in a hard day's work back then," she said.

"Work is less tangible now," I said, explaining to her that much of what my company sells is ether. "We sell brand images. It's not something that goes by on the assembly line. It's an idea. And you have to see what other sorts of ideas are out there."

"I have an idea that you all spend a lot of time *wasting* time," my mom had said.

While I am tossing a load in the dryer, I hear a big rip, and then the clunk of toppled cans tumbling out of the grocery bag, and then "Shit!"

"Are you okay?" I say. "Do you want some help?"

"I'm fine," Flo says from the back room. "Just the usual messes I'm used to dealing with. On my own."

"Doesn't she think I already feel like enough of a loser for not having my own laundry machines?" I say to the counselor. "If I want to do laundry at my building, I have to go up and down four flights of stairs every time I change a load. And half the time, by the time I get down there, someone has butted in line ahead of me."

"You don't have to justify it to me," says the counselor. "I love it when my kids come over."

"Well, see, that's the thing," I say. "I actually like seeing my parents. And if I don't come over, she says things like, 'Oh, I know. It's fun to be free and single and you've got your own things going on. Who wants to spend time with the parents?' But when I do come over, they both basically ignore me, or she gets mad at me for not being fun anymore. She keeps telling me I'm no fun anymore. That I don't have fun stories. It's a catch-twenty-two. She wants to have me around, but on her terms. If I don't tell her everything, she gets upset. If I tell her too much, I feel like I don't have my own life. Sometimes I feel like I'm her ambassador. Someone she's sent out into the world to represent her, and I'm expected to come back and report."

"See, now," says the counselor, readjusting herself in her chair to sit up and lean forward, "*this* is your spiritual journey. We're all on one, and this is yours. Learning how to claim your own life. To claim your boundaries. *To claim yourself.*"

"That makes me sound like a little plot of land," I say.

"Well," she says. "it's like that."

"I'm a pioneer."

"You are, indeed."

"Homesteading my own life."

"You got it," she says, and she hands me a cookie.

"I just really liked Paul," I say.

"I know you did, honey," says the counselor. "But, you know, I'm proud of you. You got out there. You made a con-nection. And you took care of yourself."

"I just think it would have been hard to see him all of the time."

"Probably," she says. "Maybe you'll be friends someday. Maybe when you meet somebody, you could all go out as couples."

"Ha," I say. "Right."

I just kept picturing the bar that night. The bouncy lady. The energetic band. The buffalo wings. Paul saying, "You're fun. I don't know. I like you, a lot. I don't meet people all that often who I feel that way about."

The sad part was, neither did I.

Chapter 18

"Have you even called Ian back?" Ellie said. "Why don't you give him one more chance? At least you know he doesn't have a fiancée. I don't think. Well, whatever," she said. "Just go out with him again. He was nice. Didn't you think he was nice?"

Ian and I agreed to meet at Emily's Wine Bar for drinks and appetizers before the last film in the Godard festival. Maybe something would click this time. Three's a charm. He was cute. He was smart. He didn't mind subtitles. Adam wouldn't go to a movie with subtitles. Michael wouldn't either, when I thought about it. Paul would. But Paul wasn't an option. Ian and I had similar interests, except for misogynistic literature. And camping. But so far he had been nice. He smoked considerately, never blowing it in my face. Ian dressed well. He had a gentle voice. And he seemed to like me. There was a lot to be said for that.

Was I making myself lonely for no reason?

I had a late-afternoon haircut appointment in the same neighborhood where we were supposed to meet, and I needed to kill about an hour before our date. I browsed in the bookstore next to Emily's and got depressed by all the things I hadn't taken the time to read because I'd been too busy watching *Blind Date, Frasier* reruns, and taped episodes of *Oprah* late at night. Maybe that was another thing that had to go. The television. But those were my people, my everyday company. People should not live alone. In Italy. Or anywhere.

I looked at shoes in the shop across the street. The ones I liked were $195. I went to the bar early and ordered a glass of merlot.

When Ian got there, the sun was beginning to set, glazing the shop windows across the street orange, and I was on my second glass of wine.

"Hey, I like your haircut," Ian said, spreading his leather jacket across the back of the chair and pulling his cigarettes out of the front pocket. "Want one?" he said, sitting down.

"Sure," I said.

"I thought you didn't smoke," he said. "I was just being polite." That's when I noticed what nice dimples he had when he smiled. Maybe I had missed other things about him, too.

"I feel like smoking today," I said.

"Okay," he said. "Why?"

"I just do. How was your day, dear?" I said.

"You're in a funny mood," he said. There were those dimples again. "You know, actually, it was great. We just signed Barry Chavez. Have you read his stuff? I'm such a fan. And I get to work on his new book. It's the first big name I've edited, and normally I think I'd be terrified, but I think we're really simpatico, you know?"

I told Ian about a couple of the books I'd worked on as a graduate research assistant. The professor I was working for was putting together these collections of feminist essays on literature and poetics. The essays had titles like "Ode to a Grecian Yearning: Sexual Longing and the Other." And "Stand by Your Mann." I couldn't understand what half of them were about, which actually made me a fairly good copy editor. I could read for typos without absorbing any content. Except that some of the essays incorporated Old English spellings, which were a nightmare for the spell checker. And the contributors would call me, panicking, at all hours, needing to make small changes: "On line sixteen of footnote seventy-two, I think it should say 'neither Smith nor Browne *demures* on this point; though I am *grateful* to both for their groundbreaking readings of stanzas three and four, I must hold fast in believing that the image of woman here represented in the mist rising off the moors undermines . . . blah, blah." Their sentences made my grammar checker go crazy, and some of the contributors were still using five-inch floppies and such ancient computer programs that I would have to type their essays from scratch.

Ian was laughing at me.

"What? What?"

"It's just that, the other times we've been out, you've never talked this much. I *knew* you were holding back. I knew it," he said, blowing smoke out of the corner of his mouth. "I was beginning to think you didn't like me at all."

"It's not that," I said. What should I say? "It's just, I guess I'm shy."

"You don't seem shy," he said.

"I guess I'm drunk," I said.

"Maybe that's it," he said, handing me another cigarette. He got the waitress's attention and ordered us two more glasses of wine.

By the time we'd finished our third glass, we'd also finished off Ian's cigarettes. We wandered down to a little mom-and-pop store on the corner and Ian bought a pack of unfiltered Camels.

"I thought you smoked Marlboros," I said.

"That was when I was trying to quit. I've given up." He looked down at his watch. "We missed the movie. It's such a nice night. Let's walk down to Bar-T."

Bar-T was a Southwest-themed bar with tall cowhide stools and horns on the walls. We ordered a couple of margaritas and some nachos, and Ian leaned in to light my cigarette.

"I don't think I'm going to feel very good tomorrow," I said. The bar was loud and smoky and lit with shifting green and purple lights and an occasional strobe light burst. "Ian, I'm seeing two of you," I said. I was beginning to slur my words. "Do you have an evil twin?"

"You're so different tonight," Ian said. He was beginning to slur, too, and it came out sounding more like *show different*. Then he took my hand and kind of started to caress it. It was loud in the bar. He leaned in but kept shouting. "You know, my friends told me to stay away from you. They were like, 'That girl sounds like a bitch! She's totally leading you on.'" He smiled and patted my knee.

The counselor once told me that if anyone ever called me a bitch, I should say, *Thank you for noticing!* It meant I was independent, not afraid to take care of myself. But it really didn't feel like a compliment, and so instead I said, "What's that supposed to mean?"

"I don't know. You know, I asked you out that one time and you said you were working late. And then I don't hear from you for *forever*. And after the Chagall exhibit, you had to go off to do laundry. *Laundry?* I mean, I don't know. Isn't that the same kind of thing as washing your hair?"

"I don't stick my hair in the washing machine."

"Come on, you know what I mean."

"Why are you telling me this?"

"I don't know," he said. The lights in the bar were pulsing and Ian's head was bobbing slightly. He took my hand again. "It's just that girls usually practically jump in my lap."

"Like little frogs?"

"I don't normally have any trouble with women. Like, they come and find me."

"Are some of them watching us now?" I said, scanning the bar.

"I'm serious," he said.

I didn't know what I was supposed to say about that. "Maybe I'm just more guarded," I said. Maybe he wasn't so polite after all. Maybe the real Ian came out after a few margaritas. *Bitch,* indeed.

"Maybe that's what I like about you," Ian said. "You're full of secrets." And he leaned in and kissed me. "See? We should have done that a long time ago. I'll be right back."

And then he jumped off his cowhide bar stool and walked past me, and as he passed, he grabbed my ass and squeezed it.

"It was so weird," I said to Ellie. "There I was on my little cowhide bar stool. I felt like I'd been branded. He just grabbed and *squeezed.* 'You're *full* of *secrets.*' *Squeeze.* Like an orange. Were the secrets going to come squirting out? I thought people stopped doing that in the seventies. I felt like I was on a bad *Love Boat* episode."

"Were there good episodes?"

"You know what I mean."

"You know, he was probably so drunk, he doesn't even remember doing it," Ellie said. "But I'm sorry. I thought you guys might hit it off."

★   ★   ★

I called my brother and told him about my date. Even though my brother had been married for almost ten years, he was still usually good about offering reassuring stories from what he called his "Frozen Burrito Days." Now, he and his wife cooked dinner together every night.

"I don't know," my brother said. "My experience of dating was that women were usually really timid and cautious, probably because of things like that, right, being grabbed at all the time, and that the best thing to do was to back off a little and let them set the pace."

He called it his "Bunny Theory." Not all, but a lot of women were like rabbits: nervous because they had so often and so aggressively been pursued; and the best thing to do was to set the carrot in the grass and wait quietly. If they were interested, they'd come and check it out.

"I guess as an image that could be misinterpreted," he said.

"Right," I said. "But I get it."

Anyway, it seemed to him that instead of being patient, most guys would see the bunny in the grass and go, "BUNNY!" and start chasing after it, which was the cause of the whole problem in the first place.

"So, I just need to find the guy who won't shout 'BUNNY,'" I said.

"It's a theory," said my brother.

Chapter 19

"The thing is," says Dr. Douglas, "you demonize the guys you go out with. You make them seem absolutely retarded or vile. You don't need to do that to reject them. You get to make a choice about whether or not you want to see someone again, and they don't have to have horns coming out of their head for you to say no. People are flawed."

"I just feel like I've had one weird dating experience too many," I say. "I mean, I know I'm supposed to be out there enjoying life in its *complexity,* running around in the maze with all the other rats, but it's, I don't know. It's disappointing."

"Well, you know what?" says Dr. Douglas. "You're not perfect, either. I mean, that guy Paul? Clearly he liked you, but he must also have decided that you weren't quite right for him, either. Or he'd already chosen someone else and he wasn't going to take a risk and do anything about it. But I'll bet he's not wandering around telling everyone what a nut you are."

"He probably is," I say. I'm not in the mood to be challenged today.

"I'm just saying, it's all a matter of perspective," says Dr. Douglas, dumping so much artificial creamer into his coffee that it looks like he is trying to fill a quarry.

"Do you know that stuff's flammable?" I say.

"Okay," he says, "you're sharing your anger."

"No, it really is flammable," I say.

"Really?"

"Uh-huh."

"Good thing I don't smoke," says Dr. Douglas. He laughs a little and snorts. "So what do you think about all that?"

"I, um. I don't know." Dr. Douglas is stirring his coffee fervently and waiting for me to reply. His enormous blue eyes make me want to be honest, even when I don't want to admit that I'm wrong. "I suppose it's like great literature, right? 'Everyone is complicated. No one is entirely evil. Many sides to one story.'"

"You get to make choices about how you want to spend your time, who you want to be with. You have a way of attracting these three-legged dogs," he says. "And then hating them for being flawed."

I wonder if Dr. Douglas has flipped from Animal Planet over to the Family Channel and stumbled across *Old Yeller.*

"But I don't seek them out," I say. "I think a lot of the time the three-legged dogs approach me. I'm just standing there and the three-legged dog comes stumbling up."

"Right," says Dr. Douglas. "But they approach everyone. You just keep standing there. It's like, at a bar, there's always some guy who's going to hit on every woman there, until someone says hello to him. Right? He'll start at one end of the bar and work his way up. And every time he gets blown off, he just moves on. He'll stop when he's got someone's attention."

"And I'm where the three-legged dog stops?"

"Right," says Dr. Douglas. "To someone else, he might have four legs, for all we know. He might be the best dog in the world, the best companion. But for you, he's not, and you stay when you've already figured out that you don't want to be there."

"Right," I say. "Okay."

"And what does that remind you of?" Dr. Douglas gives a little nod of encouragement, like a friendly goat, butting the air.

"I don't know."

"It's what you do with your mom," he says. "You get tired of your mom's shenanigans, like at that, what was it? The Mary Chapin Carpenter concert? But you hang in there anyway. Way past the point that other people would."

I was supposed to go to the concert, which was being held in a big casino on an Indian reservation near Chaska, with Lucy. But Lucy got sick and so at the last minute I asked my mother if she'd like to go.

I was still pissed off at Paul for failing to mention his fiancée, and when Mary Chapin started singing, "He Thinks He'll Keep Her," I leaned over and said, "Mom, listen. This is a great 'fuck-you to marriage' song."

Somewhere in the middle of it, when Mary was singing about the stay-at-home wife with three kids who finally leaves her husband and joins the corporate world, where she'll actually get paid for her work, but only minimum wage, my mother leaned over and said, "You know, maybe you don't understand that I like my life."

After the concert, my mother and I went into one of the

casino's casual food-court areas for a snack. While I dunked chicken fingers in honey-mustard sauce and Flo licked her twist cone, I said, "I didn't mean to say anything about you, Mom. I like the song because it reminds me that I'm going to have to take care of myself. That I won't necessarily be able to rely on someone else. Maybe it's good to just stay single."

My mother had just nodded and licked her cone.

"I don't trust men," I told her. "You know, even the best ones will fuck you over. Or wind up doing something weird."

"You know," she blurted, "I don't know where you get your bad attitude, or what *I* would call stinkin' thinkin', but I really am tired of feeling discounted and taken for granted. And I think that if you would just take charge of your life and make better choices about what you buy and what you choose to in-vest your energy in, you would find yourself in a better place and not be having these feelings about being insignificant and alone and then you might actually find someone. You know, maybe you *feel* bad because you *feel bad about yourself.* I mean, you have been thinner, like you've said before, that's true. I mean, you said it first; you've been going to McDonald's. But that's a matter of cutting back on what you eat, like your sister has done, and exercising."

I felt for a moment like I was sitting at the U.N. and some-one was speaking Japanese in one ear, Russian in the other, with a little something Middle Eastern coming from a nearby table.

I had complained that my clothes were getting tight, but where had all of the rest of this come from?

Still holding her cone in the air, my mom went on to say, "I know I for one get really tired of being alone and feeling like I'm not valued. You know, being the wife who sits at home all the time. I'm almost always alone. And your father's just gallop-ing around, saving lives, saving the world, expecting me to be there." My mom dabbed an eye with her napkin.

I wished she would tell a friend these things and not me. I wished she would tell all of these things to a *therapist* and not me.

"Mom," I said, "I don't want to talk about Dad."

"Well, cripes," she said. "That's right. I keep forgetting. I can't talk about anything. Am I supposed to be quiet all the time? Maybe I'll just put a sign in the yard, MOTHER FOR SALE, CHEAP," she said, taking a big lick of her ice cream.

At that moment, I felt like a little kid sitting in a booster chair. The world around me was out of control and I was too small to get myself unstrapped.

"I'm just asking you not to criticize Dad around me," I said. "In the same way that if Dad criticized you, I'd ask him not to."

"Well, your father—" Flo said, and then stopped. "*My husband* has really disappointed me."

"Nice," I said. "Nice loophole." Which made her start laughing. "Did you think you were going to get away with that?"

"I thought it was worth a shot," she said. She finally hit the cone and took a big, awkward, crunchy bite out of it. "I just want you to know all the things no one ever told me. No one ever told me that relationships weren't perfect. My mother made my father sound like he walked on air. I'm a big believer," she said, "in communication."

"As long as you're hooked in to your mom, thinking about what she wants, you're not going to be able to give that energy to someone else," says Dr. Douglas, "which works out great for your mom. And for your dad, because he can keep doing what he likes to do. As long as you're triangulated in there, it keeps your parents from focusing on their marriage. And it keeps you from establishing the next generation. And," he says, "it keeps you from being a mother and giving that same energy to a new life and to the next generation. Your mother is like a spider, devouring her own eggs for nourishment."

I really should order cable.

"It's shortsighted," he continues. "It's immediate. It's protein. But then, that's the end of the line. No next generation."

It's Just So Exciting
to Have a Frog

Part 3

Chapter 20

"What is the Upper Level Bonus?" Adam said, looking with great intensity at his Yahtzee card.

"That's if you get at least three of everything on the top half."

"Is that hard?"

"You kind of have to decide if you're going to focus on that, or on the things on the bottom."

"What do *you* do?" Adam asked.

"My theory is that the top opens the bottom."

"The top opens the bottom."

"I've never heard that," Ellie said. "That's why you always win."

"Sweet," said David. "I'm going to remember that."

"The top opens the bottom," Adam repeated. "What does that mean?"

"I'd take care of the top first, unless you get lucky bottom rolls."

"Lucky bottom rolls? That sounds like a British pastry," Adam said, which made me spit out part of my drink.

"Roll the dice, Grasshopper," I said.

He rolled. The dice tumbled across the table and came to a stop, staring up at him like a group of crossed eyes.

"You could go for a small straight," I said.

"What is that again?"

"Four dice in a row. Like one, two, three, four. Or you could go for full house. You have twos and threes."

"And why would I do that?"

"A full house is good for points."

"I thought I was supposed to work on the top."

"This looks more like a lucky bottom roll, to me," I said. "Either way, you only need one thing of something else. You either need another two, or another three. Or, if you go for a small straight, you already have the one. You would just need a four."

"I'd do the full house," Ellie said. "Personally."

"I'd do your threes," said David, who was sitting next to me and jiggling his leg under the table, getting restless for his turn.

"This is complicated," said Adam. "I thought this was a game of chance."

"This is where you are wrong, Grasshopper."

"Stop calling me Grasshopper."

"Fine."

"So now what do I do?" Adam said.

"You're on your own."

Adam picked up two dice and rolled a four and a five.

"Son of a bitch," I said.

"What? Is that good?"

"You got a large straight."

"Is that good? Where is that on the card?"

"It's the next hardest thing to get, besides Yahtzee. It earns the most points, besides Yahtzee."

"Tee hee!" Adam said, looking on his card and scribbling in his score. "Now, why didn't you tell me I could go for *that*? You said *small* straight."

"Because the large straight hardly ever happens when you're trying. Things never line up like that. It happens by accident."

"I like this game," Adam said.

"Well," Ellie said, cupping the dice and shaking them in her hand. "Now is as good a time as any, I suppose. I have gathered you all together"—she looked at me and then at Adam. She was still shaking the dice—"in the presence of God and Yahtzee and whatever to tell you that I'm pregnant."

"I knew it!" I said. It was late spring, Ellie's favorite time of year, the time of year she called "Gin and Tonicky Time," and she had made them for Adam and me, while she, I had noticed, was drinking ginger ale. "David, did you know about this?" I said.

"This is the first I'm hearing of it!" he said.

"You must be shocked," I said.

"I don't even know who this woman is," he said, taking the dice away from Ellie. "Hurry up, Madge. If you're not going, I'm going."

"We wanted you two to be the first to know," she said. "After our parents and brothers and sisters and grandparents and cousins."

"So basically, you're telling us last," I said.

"Basically," Ellie said. "Sorry about that."

"Well, congratulations," Adam said. He patted Ellie delicately on the arm.

"How far along?" I asked.

"Just over three months," Ellie said. "I have a ways to go."

"I *thought* something was up when you poured a ginger ale," I said.

"Thank you for noticing," said Ellie, beaming at me. We were always pleased when we noticed some small detail about the other, because in this busy world, who had time for that anymore?

"And do you have names?" said Adam.

"We're actually thinking Adam, maybe," said David.

"If it's a girl," I said.

"Ha, ha," said Adam, and he punched me on the arm. "I think Adam is a fine choice."

"And Shannon if it's a girl?" I said.

Ellie scrunched up her face.

"Sorry," she said. "It's just that neither one of us has an ounce of Irish in us. Or really anywhere in the family. It's just not a good Scandinavian name. And, you know, that's our heritage, for better or worse. We want to honor it. Uff Dah," she said, raising her ginger-ale glass.

"Is *Adam* Scandinavian?"

"My grandfather was named Adam," said David. "We're also maybe thinking Thor."

"Well, that's great," Adam said. He looked at me. His face was flushed. Then he looked down at the table.

Ellie and David had gone to bed, and Adam and I were sitting in the blue-white light of late-night cable, the fish bubbling in the background. "So, Shan," Adam said. "Weird, huh?"

"What?"

"Ellie being pregnant. We're the last of the people with no kids."

"You knew it was coming," I said. "Eventually."

"I suppose," he said. "Everyone's having kids, Shan, except

you and me." He scratched his head and picked the remote off the floor by the couch.

What did he mean by that? Did he think of us having kids? "I think they'd been trying ever since they got married," I said, staring at the TV.

Then I looked over at Adam, his long legs spread across the couch. He was flipping the channels. Maybe this was the time for that conversation Dr. Douglas had suggested. Maybe I should see what Adam had been thinking. I'd been drinking. Adam had been drinking.

"Do you ever . . . ?" I began. Was this really such a good idea? Although maybe a heart-to-heart talk might be good for us. "Oh, never mind."

"No, what?" he said.

I thought of Dr. Douglas, nodding at me in encouragement. "Do you ever think about the two of us going out?" I said.

"Well, it's not like it never occurred to me," Adam said. He was still sitting in a recumbent position, and he reached a long arm over to the coffee table for his gin and tonic and looked back at the TV. His nonchalance was bugging me, because I, for one, was sick of living in life's Switzerland. Not committed to anything or anyone. Things should go one way or the other.

"I guess I kind of thought . . . ," I said. What should I say? I thought about Adam putting his arm around me all the time. How he would simply smile at me sometimes for no reason. How he had said, last time we met to go out for dinner, that I looked like "a hottie." I was thinking how his face had looked flushed after Ellie announced her pregnancy. Maybe he was getting anxious about being alone, too, not having a family. "Well, I've been thinking that maybe you're attracted to me," I said.

Adam had begun taking a sip of his drink and sprayed it back in his glass. "Oh, my God. Get over yourself!" he said. He was guffawing.

"Well, I—" I said. Clearly this was not going as I had envisioned. "You don't have to laugh *so* hard. I just . . . We've always been such good friends. And I just started thinking. How come we've never gone out?" Adam was looking at me blankly. "Maybe I wonder if I'm attracted to you sometimes," I said. I had been warming my feet with a macramé blanket, and now I pulled it up around my shoulders.

Although it wasn't much, I had just managed to extend myself further than I ever had.

Adam muted the TV and was quiet for a few seconds. The aquarium bubbled.

I looked over at the fish, who looked constantly surprised. One was sucking on the glass.

"I kind of think," he said, and he scratched his head again. "It's like *Seinfeld*. It's like Jerry and Elaine. I wouldn't want to jeopardize our friendship. I mean, *we have this,*" he said. "We can talk. I wouldn't want to lose *this.*" He was quoting from *Seinfeld*.

He turned back to the TV and turned the volume up.

"I suppose," I said. But what was *this*? What did he think it *was*? I certainly didn't know anymore. And if we were such great friends, why didn't he have more to say about it? Whatever it was? How could he address and dismiss the complications of our friendship by quoting from television?

For some reason, I thought of the street where I grew up. Our street was as wide as a landing strip, and at the end of it, a gravel road about a quarter-mile long led to the crumbled stone wall of an old barn, an abandoned silo, rolling hills, and, beyond them, a ravine. At the top of the first hill was Farmer Twiggy's windmill, which creaked in all seasons, making its rusty rounds, echoing over the hills and into the sprawling ravine.

Adam's flat declaration was like that windmill, whose rotations were ultimately pointless, whose hollow creaking always reminded us that we lived in the middle of nowhere.

Was it really that easy for him? *We're friends?* Was it really so cut-and-dried?

Did he not remember that Jerry and Elaine used to go out? I felt as cold and lonely as a cornfield in winter.

And though I wished he had said something more, I no longer wanted to talk about it. Maybe I was afraid of what he would say. Maybe I was afraid of what I would find in myself.

The next morning, Adam woke me up by bringing a glass of orange juice into my room and setting it on my nightstand. "Rise and shine, Shanny," he said. I had been completely out of it. Doing the thing I do best. The blessed denial of sleeping.

"It's a bright new day," he said, and then he went off to take a shower.

"Sleep okay?" Ellie asked when I wandered downstairs for coffee.

"Uh-huh."

"You have no idea how much willpower it's taking me," she said, "to make this coffee for you and not drink any."

"Thank you," I said. "I do appreciate it. I don't know if I could handle nine months of no coffee."

"Did you stay in your own bed last night?" Ellie said, and started giggling.

"That's not funny," I said.

"Sorry," she said, still visibly pleased with herself.

Adam wandered into the kitchen, freshly showered and smelling of aftershave. He put an arm around me and jiggled me a little, which bothered me because I was still in my flannel pajamas and had no bra on. "Good morning, everybody!" he said, and asked Ellie where the coffee cups were.

Why was he so cheerful? *Monsieur Laissez-Faire?*

Obviously nothing about our relationship puzzled Adam.

Nothing about our talk last night had bothered him. It had all bounced off the surface, like skipping stones.

We have this. And that's all there was to it.

What was it like to be that way? I wished I didn't feel so conflicted. How can you hang out with someone for years? Make cookies together? Go skiing? Go to dinner? Watch everyone else get married? And not think *anything*?

"What did you guys do last night?" Ellie asked.

"We watched TV." Adam looked at me and smiled. "Nothing much on. Do you want help with breakfast?" he said to Ellie.

I felt so vulnerable for having said anything, and he seemed, well, *fine*.

"You can help with pancakes," Ellie said. "Shan, will you be in charge of sausage?"

"Sure," I said.

"I was thinking that *sausage* was probably your specialty," Ellie said, winking at me dramatically.

"Ha, ha." Did married people forget what it was like to be single?

"Hey," Ellie said to Adam, "do you want to go to church with me?"

"Sure," Adam said. "Can we make it on time if we make breakfast? Shan, do you need to get back early?"

"No," I said. "Not really."

"David won't want to go," Ellie said. "He's still sleeping. Do you mind hanging out here?"

"I'm fine," I said. "I'll read the paper. Keep an eye on the sausages."

Adam and I drove back into the cities together without saying much of anything. He was singing along with *Achtung Baby* and I stared out the window, mostly, at the strip malls and office parks along the way. Who came up with the term *office park*?

As if the buildings had sprouted up naturally. As if there were slides to go down and an abundance of greenery. Bears picking through the trash.

I wished I could feel some relief about having said something to Adam. The issue should be resolved now. Right? He only thought of us as friends and that should settle that. I was free to go forward without conflict. I was free to grieve with and for the lone honker.

Adam was not my backup person, was not someone who'd been there all along, waiting, right in front of me.

I could go forward now, that was the thing. "You don't know until you go," Dr. Douglas had said. Well, the thing was, now I knew.

But it didn't feel like it. Like I knew anything. Should I have pressed him on it? Said, "Well, how come it's so easy for you?"

The thing was, maybe I didn't want to be any more vulnerable than I already felt. And what if we did date and it was a disaster? Or what if we got married and we hated each other? And could I even trust my own judgment? I thought Paul might be the right one for me and I was wrong about him; he was already spoken for. Maybe I was just afraid to be close to someone I knew really well.

I wished I had one of my emergency anxiety pills with me, different from my maintenance dose of Calmzene. After taking the emergency pill, I was not to operate heavy machinery.

"So, Shan," Adam said, "busy week coming up?"

"Probably," I said.

"Me, too," he said.

"Do you like your job?" he said.

"Yeah," I said. "It's all right."

If he wasn't going to bring it up, I didn't feel like bringing it up again.

"What about last night?" I blurted anyway, surprising myself.

"What do you mean?"

"Did our talk weird you out at all?" I said.

"No," Adam said. "What do you mean?"

"I don't know," I said. "About us dating. Not dating."

"I just think we have such a great friendship," he said. He didn't say anything for a minute. "Do you feel funny about it?"

"Sort of."

Adam took one hand off the wheel and scratched his head. He turned the car stereo down. "I mean, it's not like I never thought about it," he said. "But then I just think, you know, if you're thinking endgame, there'd be all kinds of things to think about. You know. Religion. Different religions. And stuff."

"Oh," I said. That hadn't actually occurred to me. I thought of Catholicism like having asthma. There was nothing you could do about it. Didn't everyone think of their religion that way? It was like having a disease or a birth defect, something you inherited. You just managed it.

Church was a place that was just always *there,* though you didn't visit it as often as you knew you should. Like grandparents.

Of all of the reasons for Adam and me not to date, that one hadn't occurred to me. As much as I liked to bitch about the Lutherans, I didn't think of Adam as *Lutheran.* I thought of him as Adam.

My mother had been raised in the most strict Lutheran synod, whose teachings she had happily abandoned when she left home. When she and my father got married, she didn't convert, but she came to church every week.

"You know," Adam said.

"Yeah."

We rode in silence for a while and passed an old mayonnaise factory. On top of the building there was a huge jar of spinning mayonnaise. I had passed that thing a million times since I was little. Why did it suddenly seem to represent something about my life?

"So that's what I think, Shanny," Adam said. "Everything okay?"

"Sure," I said. There was something about him referring to me in the diminutive that was just now starting to bug me. I was sick of feeling small. "You have a crack in your windshield," I said. I hadn't noticed it the day before.

"Yeah," Adam said, glancing at the crack and then looking back to the road. "I don't know how that got there."

Chapter 21

"It just sounds like he kind of bugs you," says Louise.

"The way you've always talked about him," says Harvey, "it almost sounds like you're siblings. You get so irritated with him, but it's like you're stuck together."

"See, that's the problem," I say. "We've known each other so long. But I was thinking, on the other hand, isn't it better, maybe, to develop a relationship with someone you know? Rather than trying to meet someone out of the blue?"

"I suppose my ex-wife and I had a similar relationship," Harvey says.

"Are you actually attracted to him?" Eileen asks.

"I don't know. When we were in college, I never thought of him that way. I was always in love with men who didn't even know I was alive. Like Greg Louganis. But now, well, his butt's kind of filled out. He looks more like a man."

"Hmmmm," says Eileen. "Because I've been on a couple of dates now with a guy who's really nice, but I can't tell if I want to kiss him. And maybe it's just because I'm out of practice."

"Did you have the feeling that he's attracted to you?" says Dana.

"I don't know," I say. "He's really private about stuff like that. He could be thinking any number of things and not tell anyone. I *thought* he was attracted to me. He's very touchy-feely around me, in a way that he isn't around Ellie. But I guess he's not. I guess that's that. But it still feels weird. Maybe I'm just mad because I always thought he'd be there as a backup. You know. I thought if I wanted him I could have him. And I guess that's not true."

"Yes," says Dr. Douglas. "You know, more and more I believe that this is really about something else. You can be pretty critical of him, and he's just a regular guy. I think this is about something bigger."

"Like what?"

"Well, that's what we've got to figure out."

Chapter 22

Tonight, my mother calls and says, "I have to tell you about our domestic adventure."

"What did you do now?" I ask.

Last week, she had started a fire in the microwave by trying to thaw some frozen spinach. It was the kind that comes wrapped in one of those silver boxes. *"I didn't know that was foil!"* she had said. *"Who knew frozen things could catch fire?"*

"Well, your dad and I got home from that wake on Sunday night—you know, Fritz Schmidt died, he used to bring us raspberries—and your dad was going downstairs, and all of the sudden I heard this shriek, and I thought, 'My gosh, I'm going to find your dad passed out at the bottom of the stairs.' So I go over there, and he's standing in the middle of the staircase, and there's a little frog, coming up the stairs."

"A frog?"

"And your dad had his hands cupped, to grab it, and he got it, and then he goes and puts it out in the garage."

"Why the garage? Is he trying to kill it with fumes?"

"Oh, I didn't even think of that. Your father didn't want the frog to spend the night outside, because it's still pretty cold at night and I think the sudden warm weather during the day has them all confused. Although I think the little frog could have figured out a place to go, you know, to burrow into like they do in the winter."

"It's cold in the garage. Why didn't dad just put the frog in a little pan of water or something and let it loose in the morning?"

"I don't know. The garage made sense at the time. We were just so pleased," she says. "The frog had all its legs and nothing funny. No malformations. Nothing mutant. Which I think speaks well for the quality of life in Chaska."

"Oh, of course," I say.

"So then we're wondering, 'How in the world could a frog get in here?' Because, you know, we've struggled with bats and mice, but we've pretty much got that taken care of. So we figured that, you know, I'd had that rubber plant outside during the day, and I brought it in, and, you know, it's a little tree frog, with suckers, so we think that he rode in on the rubber plant, which is all the way in the other corner of the basement now. So he made quite a long journey over to the staircase."

"I think it's funny that he was trying to go out the front door."

"He's a very smart frog, apparently."

"And quite a hopper, to get up those stairs."

"Well, so, today, your father asked me to leave the garage door open all day so he could hop out."

"I hope he got out."

"Yah," says Flo. "I've been walking around so carefully in the garage today, and not parking the car in there, of course. It's just so exciting," she adds, "to have a frog."

More and more, I think, I wouldn't mind if that was all the excitement I had in my life. If I were with the right person—not living alone—an evening spent helping a frog escape would be fine with me.

There was something nice about these shared moments of domestic management. Over the years, my mom and dad had spent countless evenings with their heads stuck up in some crawl space, searching with a flashlight for the dead field mouse that was making that awful smell. And to me they always seemed strangely happy when they were doing it.

I tell Flo about this weird new guy at work who keeps coming to my office and making small talk on his way to the copy machine. And then in meetings, he's always talking over me, talking really fast about nothing, and interrupting me during presentations. "He's a little creep," I tell Flo, "and he won't shut up and he's going to drive me crazy."

"You need to find ways not to let people like that run you over," says Flo. "To get him out of your office faster. You know, you can interrupt him in meetings with funny things like, *Okay, we've heard you, I think.*"

"That's not funny," I say.

"It is if you say it right," says Flo.

I'm getting a headache now and want to get off the phone.

"Well, how was your time at Ellie's?"

"It was fine," I say.

"What's new with her?" asks Flo.

"Not much," I say. "Oh, she's pregnant." I'd been so busy since then thinking about my conversation with Adam that I'd almost forgotten Ellie's news.

"Well, that's kind of big," says Flo. "You weren't going to tell me? How far along is she?"

"A little over three months."

"Okay," says Flo. "Well, say," she says, "I know what I was going to ask you. You've seemed kind of preoccupied lately. And I'm wondering if you have a lot on your mind, or if you're just pulling away from me, which I know you're kind of doing. I mean, *I know that*. But if you're doing that then I'd just kind of like to know about it."

"I had a deadline yesterday when you called. I thought we were having a nice conversation, Mom."

"Well, I just know that you'd rather be anywhere else in the world than near me right now, and that's okay."

"Mother, stop it."

"No, no. That's okay. I just would appreciate it, if you're pulling away, if you'd announce it, so that I know what's going on."

"Mom, I don't think people announce these things."

"They do if they're considerate people who care about someone and who care to communicate."

"Mom, we're not married!"

"Who said we were?" she says. "I'm not even attracted to you. I'm already married."

"Mom, you know, sometimes you do cross a line into my privacy, and then, you're right, I don't share as much with you." I was doing my best to stay contained.

"Okay, now, *thank you!*" she says. "Thank you. Because that is exactly what I needed to know. That's what I want to know. Then I can understand what's going on."

"Mom, this is one of those times when you're crossing the line. Needing me to announce when I'm backing off is another example of crossing the line."

"No, it's not. It's communication."

"It's control," I say. "You need to control everything."

"You mean *you* need to control everything?" asks Flo. "Um, are you sure you're not projecting that?"

"No," I say. "It seems like you do. By needing to know everything."

"I just need to know what's going on with you."

"No, you don't."

"Well, excuse me for caring. Excuse me for being a mother."

"Mom, when you cross the line, I'll try to tell you."

"Thank you. Thank you. That's what I need."

"I'm going to go now. I need to get off the phone."

"Okay," she says.

"I think you did pretty well with that," says the counselor. "I'm incredibly proud of you."

"Really?"

"Oh, my goodness, yes," she says, offering me a Mountain Dew. "A couple of years ago, all your mother had to do was look at you funny and you'd cave. And if she criticized your outfit or your hair, you'd be devastated for a week."

"I'm glad you're keeping track of all of this," I say, opening my soda. "Because I still feel like a little kid. I feel like a little kid, divorcing my mom."

"No," says the counselor. "See, now that's where you're wrong. We never really get to divorce our parents."

"Well, God knows if we got divorced she'd still find a way to have custody of me."

"What you're working on here," says the counselor, "is *emancipation*. And that's different. And this is part of your spiritual journey."

I had forgotten about my spiritual journey.

"You're learning to emancipate," the counselor continues, and then she burps. "Excuse me. This Mountain Dew makes my stomach crazy, but I do love it. You're learning to be your own person," she goes on, "so that you *can* have a relationship with your mother *as your own person*. You get to set limits. You get to decide what's right for you. What you want out of life. You get to join the larger community."

Chapter 23

Adam called me after work and asked if he could come over to my neighborhood for dinner.

I hadn't talked to him since we'd been to Ellie's, and I wasn't sure I wanted to see him. Adam and I often went weeks without talking—we just got busy doing other things—but after our car ride home, I kept thinking about what Dr. Douglas had said about my mother. *It's immediate. It's protein. But then, no next generation.*

Maybe it really was time for me to stop hanging around with Adam. The more time I spent with Adam, the less likely it was that I'd meet someone else. *No next generation.* People thought we were a couple. Although maybe it was only my conflict. Adam was my friend. Only wanted to be my friend. Why couldn't I just deal with that?

"What's the occasion?" I said.

"No occasion," he said. "I just thought it would be fun to have dinner in your neighborhood. And I haven't seen your apartment in a while."

"I'm not sure it looks all that different than when you last saw it," I said.

"How about that Italian place?" Adam said.

I had been about to go to McDonald's. "Okay," I said.

The Italian restaurant was set up like a cafeteria. You'd go up and order your food; they'd give you your drinks. If you had something hot, that required preparation, they'd bring it over to you. Adam and I both ordered the spaghetti.

"What else can I get for you today?" the server asked me.

"A lot of wine," I said.

"House red?" she said.

"Sounds good," I said.

"And these are together?" the server asked, looking at Adam.

"Separate," I said.

Adam hadn't heard her. "Hey, look," he said, pointing to a sign on the counter. "Unlimited refills on the house wine. You can't beat that. I'll have the house red, too."

Adam had two glasses before our spaghetti came and his tongue started to turn purple. I was actually sticking to one glass because I had an early meeting the next day.

"This is a great deal," he said. "This is how everything should be. It's kind of European. Gracious. Generous. The Europeans know how to host, how to entertain. They don't count up every little thing on the menu and then split the bill in six different directions. Someone will just graciously take the bill while no one is looking. It's so civilized."

This irritated me, because in all the time Adam and I had been friends, he had never picked up the bill and he made a lot more money than I did. We always split everything.

"If they do it while no one is looking, then how do they know if it's been done?" I said. "Maybe Europeans are constantly leaving unpaid restaurant bills. Sneaking out."

"It's just very deft," said Adam.

"I don't think I could afford to be European," I said.

"I would like to go to Scandinavia again," Adam said. "And you know where I would really like to go? To Iceland. In the summer. I've just read about all the cool things you can do there. These really cool hikes and beautiful little villages. And the sun stays up half the night."

"Then you should go," I said. "Definitely."

"Would you ever want to do something like that?"

"Maybe," I said, but I was thinking, *I want to do something like that with a boyfriend.* I didn't want to spend my life tethered to Adam like a couple of mittens. It was time for me to move on. "I don't think I could afford it right now."

"I need someone to go with," Adam said.

"Too bad Ellie's pregnant. Otherwise she'd have the time," I said. "And the money."

"I might get more wine," Adam said, looking over at the counter.

"Go on one of those singles trips," I said. "A woman at work met her husband on one of those. She went on a hiking trip in the Sierras."

"I don't know if those are really for me."

"I'd go on one if I could afford it," I said. "I want to go on a kayaking trip."

"Oh, I'd do that," Adam said. "I'd do that with you."

Why did Adam want to go on vacation with me? Why didn't he mind hanging out with me and not meeting anybody new? I just kind of looked at him, and then looked off into a corner of the restaurant where a couple my parents' age was sitting, eating in silence. None of this seemed to be at all complicated for Adam, and that was irritating.

"So, Shan," said Adam, "what's new in your world? Ellie said you've been busy."

"Yeah, I have. And no one has shown up to clean my apartment lately," I said. "Which is frustrating."

"Did you hire someone?" asked Adam.

"No," I said. "Maybe that's the problem. What's new with you?"

"Nothing new," he said. "So, you've got everything in your apartment done?"

"Except for the paperwork. I'm still trying to organize all of that crap. It's in a closet."

"You know what," said Adam, "if you want, I'll go through all your paperwork and sort it for you into categories and clip it into three-ring binders. I took a few days off work once and did that, and it took a while, but I have to say, it was very satisfying." He took a big sip of wine. "I think it's easier if someone does it for you. It goes faster when it's not your stuff."

"It's really nice of you to offer," I said, "but I have so much paperwork. There's no way I could ask you to do that." In truth, I didn't want Adam going through my personal stuff the way Flo would, organizing my life for me. When I lived at home, she always seemed to know exactly how many pairs of socks and underwear I had. How many pairs of jeans and how many T-shirts. If anyone was ever going to organize my life, it should be me.

"I really don't mind," he said. "I hate to say it, but that kind of thing is fun for me."

"Thanks," I said, "but God only knows what's in those

piles. I've got all of these articles that my mom has been sending me since the eighties. Things about AIDS and stress management that she sent me in college." I had trouble simply throwing them away because I kept thinking that somewhere in that pile maybe there was something that might actually change my life.

"Well, let me know if you change your mind," Adam said, extending his hand over to my side of the table and taking my fingers. "I like you. You're just so *you*."

What was with him tonight?

"Whatever happened with that woman from church that you went out with?" I said. I had forgotten all about it, for some reason, until now.

"Huh? Oh, that was months ago. Didn't work out. I thought she was kind of needy. Here comes the spaghetti," he said. "I'm going to get more wine. Do you want some?"

By the time dinner was over, Adam didn't think he should drive home right away. "Could I just come over for a while and crash at your place?" he said.

"Sure," I said. I didn't want him to drive home drunk, but I really wanted to watch *Frasier* and to be alone. Adam's ebullience was bugging me.

I flipped on the TV and went into the kitchen to make some coffee for Adam, who grabbed a pillow and plopped down on the floor in front of my couch.

"While you're in there, can I have a glass of Rieeeeeesling and some quesadillas?" Adam said. He was giggling to himself.

"Don't you want to sit on some furniture?" I said. "You can sit on the couch."

"I'm fine," Adam said, flipping channels. "The apartment looks good, Shan." Channel surfing didn't take long at my place, since I didn't have cable, and I could hear Adam cycling through the same shows. *"Dateline,"* he said. "Why do women love Stone Phillips?"

"I don't love Stone Phillips."

Adam had given up on the TV and was flipping through the catalogs and magazines on my floor; then he began sifting through the things I had dumped out of my purse that morning when I was trying to find my keys, announcing each object as he picked it up.

"Lipstick!"

"Rouge! Is that rouge? What the ladies call *rouge*?"

"Receipt, receipt, receipt."

I sat on the couch behind him and was trying to watch *Dateline* when Adam flung a tampon over his shoulder and it hit me on the eyebrow.

"Tampon! Incoming."

"Why don't we call Ellie?" I said, tired of him tossing around my personal things. "Let's call her and see what she's up to."

"Alrighty," Adam said, leafing through magazines.

I got up to grab the phone, and as I did, Adam reached up and squeezed my butt. "Hey, baby, baby, baby," he said, and then he made a whoopee-cushion noise.

"What are you doing?" I said. "Knock it off, Adam."

Adam grabbed for me again, giggling, and I whacked him on the head with the J. Crew catalog that was on my table. *"Stop it,"* I said, and I meant it.

He thought it was funny and grabbed my butt again.

I stuck the phone into his outstretched palm. "Here. *You* call Ellie." I went to check on the coffee.

"I don't have her number," Adam said. "What's her number?"

I recited the number from the kitchen.

Maybe he'd had more wine than I thought.

I got out cups and some milk. I dug a box of cookies out of the cupboard; maybe they would soak up the alcohol.

When I came back in to the living room, Adam had fallen asleep on the floor.

I covered him with a blanket and went to bed.

In what seemed like the middle of the night, from a deep sleep, I heard a rustling. My eyes flew open, and my heart hit my throat. *Shit a bat oh shit!*

"Morning, Shanny," Adam said. He had climbed into bed with me and was resting his head on a pillow.

"What are you doing?" I looked at the clock. It was 6 A.M.

"Rise and shine," he said, and he reached over and shook my shoulder. "It's a bright new day." His lips were still purple. "Well, I guess it's not bright yet."

"Jesus, you scared the crap out of me." I scrambled out of bed and went into the bathroom.

"Do you want to go out for breakfast?" Adam shouted from the bedroom. "Can I take a shower here and just go straight to work? No, wait," he said. He was half talking to me, half talking to himself. "Never mind. I left my briefcase at home. Do you want to just go to the coffee shop and get some coffee? Do you have time for that?"

"No," I said. "I've got a meeting." This was true, but it wasn't why I wanted to skip coffee.

"Okay," Adam said. "Well then, I'm just going to hit the road."

"Okay," I shouted through the closed door.

I looked at myself in the mirror. I needed to say something to Adam. Okay, he was kind of drunk last night, but he'd crossed a line. Why did he think he could say with complete nonchalance, "I wouldn't want to ruin *this,*" and then grab my butt? And if Adam wasn't attracted to me at all, then what was he doing? It was so juvenile. How could he be so clueless? I expected more from Adam. I thought he knew me better than that.

"I'm going to let myself out," he shouted.

"Right."

Maybe Adam was conflicted and didn't even know it. He never grabbed Ellie. He never grabbed anybody. Whatever was going on, I was sick of dealing with it.

"Thanks for dinner," he shouted.

I heard the door close behind him and I came out of the bathroom to make coffee. I sat on the couch for a while, just staring out the window.

When I left around 8 A.M., there was a tour bus idling outside the building and a group of Elderhostel participants staring out at me from behind the tinted glass.

"He grabbed your butt?" says Harvey, swallowing a bite of his sandwich.

"I thought you guys were just friends," says Dana, setting her potato-chip bag on the floor. "Isn't that what he said when you asked him?"

"So, is this the same guy you had margaritas with?" asks Wayne. "You went out with him *again*?" Wayne was in therapy for narcissism, and had trouble keeping any of our stories straight.

"No, this is my friend Adam," I say.

"So, you're going out with *him* now?" says Wayne.

"That's the point," I say. "We're not."

"But you slept with him?" says Wayne.

"Pay attention, Wayne," I say.

"Now what do you do?" asks Dana.

"I think I'd be kind of mad," says Eileen.

"You would?"

"Yes, I would. I mean, didn't he tell you to get over your-self?"

"Pretty much," I say.

"I think you might have had that one coming," says Dr. Douglas, and he starts laughing. "Sorry," he says, and keeps gig-gling.

I give him a dirty look.

"Do you think if you were really, really attracted to him, you might have liked it?" asks Wayne.

"So, do you think he was just really drunk?" says Eileen.

"Probably," I say. "But it makes me mad. He said he wasn't attracted to me."

"Maybe he's secretly in love with you!" Eileen says.

"He said he didn't want to ruin your friendship," says Dr. Douglas, ignoring Eileen.

"Well, he was pretty clear that he didn't want to go out with me. He acted like it was no big deal."

"To him," says Dr. Douglas.

"In general," I say.

"I'd be pissed," says Eileen.

"Yeah?"

"Sure. It's disrespectful. Of where you are. The place you're in. I'd feel disrespected," she corrects herself to incorporate the first-person pronoun, because we are always supposed to speak from our own perspective and not make generalizations.

"I just thought that of all the guys I knew, Adam would be the last person to do something like that. I mean, it's not *that* big of a deal. But on the other hand, I felt like, I don't know."

I thought about my brother's theory on dating. Of all of the men I knew, Adam was the last I'd expect to be running up to me shouting "BUNNY!"

"The two of you have known each other a long time," says the counselor.

"Adam always knew everything about me," I say.

"Exactly," she says.

"At least, he used to," I say. Maybe Adam was like the microwave I'd gotten rid of, with which I'd had a flawed intimacy. Why keep something with so many kinks and quirks when you could find something that would work fine, without all the problems? "I think it's time for me to make room for someone else."

"I think that's a good idea." Dr. Douglas nods.

Is Anyone Fond of
Canadian Bacon?

Part 4

Chapter 24

I hadn't seen Georgia since she was born, and now here she was, fifteen months old, this whole little person, fighting her fellow toddlers for toys. I was staying for a long weekend and went to Georgia's Friday play group. A room full of squirrelly kids, diaper bags, Elmo dolls, and reproductive women. And they were all so thin, from chasing after their children.

I felt suddenly masculine, like Janet Reno. Large by comparison, independent, and yet still attached to my mother.

"Don't be afraid to say no to her," my sister says when we're back home in her living room.

I have let Georgia eat some Gardetto snack mix, and also play in her yogurt.

"In the long run, it's better for her to have some limitations," says my sister.

"But I'm popular right *now*," I say, while Georgia digs around in her Yo-Baby yogurt cup with her entire hand. She smiles and reaches up to me for a hug. I have strawberry yogurt in my hair and all over my shirt.

"Heh," my niece smiles at me, baring her four tiny teeth, which resemble little chalk stubs. She sticks her hand back in the cup and holds a finger covered in yogurt in front of my lips. She wants me to lick it off her hands. I think she has me mixed up with the family dog.

Then she drops her spoon and says, "Ow." Every time she drops something, she says, "Ow."

My sister has been trying to teach her to stay away from the oven by saying, "Hot, hot, hot." Now, every time Georgia is asked to stay away from something, like a plant, she shakes her head and says, "Hot, hot, hot," sighs, and walks away.

Greta is talking about how one of the women in her mommies group found a crack in her diaphragm and was worried that she'd get pregnant again. And then she had to go through the whole thing in her head: Am I ready? Am I not ready? Can I handle another one of these energetic little people? So when she found out she wasn't pregnant, she went on the Pill right away. "I'm glad *I'm* on the Pill," says my sister. "I just felt like, when I was breast-feeding, my hormones were so out of whack. I was just at the mercy of my hormones."

"You seemed normal," I say.

"It was an illusion," my sister says.

"Your mom is magical," I say to Georgia, who nods and points at the dog. "I'd like to go off the Pill," I say. "I've been on the Pill for over ten years, and most of the time for no reason. Except for keeping my face clear and for cramps. And for helping me to act normal."

"Then I don't think it's working," my sister says.

"Har, har. But then," I continue, "you have no sex drive. I went on the Pill to have sex, and then, once you're on it, you don't even want sex."

"If you went off the Pill, you'd be scooting around on the carpeting like a dog."

"That's probably true."

"Where'd Georgia go?" my sister says.

"She's in the living room. Getting the dog leash out again."

George wanders over to me with the dog's leash draped around her neck like a stole and hands me the owner's end. I take it and ask, "Do you want to play puppy?"

George sticks her tongue out and pants.

"Come here, puppy," I say, and I begin to lead her into the living room. "Come on, good puppy," and she follows me.

George is the one who came up with the puppy game. She walked up to me yesterday with the leash around her neck and handed me one end. When I took it and asked her if she was a puppy, she started to giggle.

"Do you think it's demeaning?" I had asked my sister.

"She thinks it's funny," Greta had said. "Think about it. The dog is her older sibling. She wants to be like the dog."

"That's true."

"And remember what happened when Mom told Peter to stop being a lion," my sister said.

"It's the shame of her maternal career."

On our brother's first day of kindergarten, he had gone underneath a table and roared at the other children. "Come out from there," my mother had said. "You're a little boy now, not a lion. Be a little boy."

Now Flo says she feels terrible about it. "That was his way of coping with something that was scary to him," she says. "I feel awful."

"Good puppy," I say, leading Georgia down the hallway. "Come on." And she follows me into the kitchen, where Shasta discovers that her leash is being used for play and tries to take it back.

"Do you want to give Shasta a biscuit?" I say to Georgia as the leash is being tangled around both of us. She nods. We give Shasta a biscuit. "Okay, here's *your* puppy treat," I say to Georgia, and I give her a little bit of a doughnut.

She points at the dog.

"No, Peanut," I say. "That's your treat."

She nods and goes "Ummm" and sits in my lap on the kitchen floor to finish the rest of her doughnut. She sings a little and swings her feet. She takes one of my fingers and swings my hand around while she hums and eats.

I picture myself twenty years from now. Georgia will be in college. She won't be wrapping her little arms around me anymore, or wanting me to read her stories. She will have her own life. And I will be thrilled with any time that she wants to spend with me.

I will be like my mother.

After a while, Georgia gets up and starts sifting through the Sunday circulars, which have been tossed near the garbage can. She hands me a coupon book and sits back down in my lap. This is her signal that she wants me to read to her.

"Chicken drummies," I recite. "Five ninety-nine."

"Betty?" she says, pointing. It took my sister a few weeks, but she finally figured out that "Betty" was Georgia's way of saying, "What is it? What's it doing?" Earlier today, she had pointed in a picture book to a little boy dressed as a king and said, "Betty?"

"Ham," I say.

"Betty?" she says, pointing at something new.

"Irish Spring deodorant soap," I say. "Three for one ninety-nine."

"Ooooh," she says. She gets up suddenly and grabs Shasta's leash, drapes it around her neck again, and goes into the living room.

I watch Georgia toddle around the house with the leash around her neck and I think of the little fox in *Le Petit Prince,* who wanted to be tamed.

He wanted to belong to someone, which makes sense to me.

Then she comes back into the kitchen, walks over to the oven, and says, "Hot, hot, hot," even though it's not on.

"I have two messages from Adam," I say to the counselor, "and I haven't called him back yet."

"It's okay to tell him you're mad at him. It's okay to tell him that you're uncomfortable."

"Maybe I'm overreacting," I say. "But I'm mad. And I don't want to talk to him. And I don't want to be around him anymore." Dr. Douglas had said he thought it was fine if I told Adam that I didn't want to see him.

"Because you had a fantasy," says the counselor. "You had a fantasy about him being the right one and it seems like it's not going to work."

The counselor believed that this was the root of my anger: anytime my fantasies about life didn't match up with reality, which was most of the time. Which meant I was angry a lot. Which the counselor had once said could be a gift.

Hey! I was gifted.

"Maybe that's it," I say.

Ellie and I were at the outlet mall, shopping for baby clothes, and I was sifting through footed pajamas. Little warm things with giraffes and elephants on them. Ellie was looking at tiny hats for newborns.

"Adam, um, I don't know what to call it," I said. "Made a pass at me, I guess."

"I'm not that surprised. It's about time something happened with the two of you," Ellie said.

"It wasn't really like that," I said. "He just grabbed my butt."

"What?"

"Just kind of grabbed it. I think he was drunk."

"Adam? Drunk?"

"It was weird."

"Was he kidding? I'm sure he was just joking around."

"He tried to grab me a couple of times. And then he jumped in my bed in the morning."

Ellie looked at me and raised an eyebrow.

"He fell asleep on the living-room floor," I said, and she nodded. "Or passed out. It was weird. I haven't talked to him. I don't want to talk to him."

"It really doesn't sound like that big of a deal," Ellie said. "I'm sure he just thought he was being funny."

"Easy for you to say. You're married."

"What's that supposed to mean?"

"It's no big deal to you. You're in the safety zone."

"It's really not like that," she said. "Actually, I suppose it's always nice to be able to flash the ring when you need to."

"Thanks a lot."

"I wouldn't worry about it," she said. "Are you still staying for dinner?"

"Yeah, isn't David camping?"

"Well, yes," she said. "But I also invited Adam."

"Maybe I'll just go home."

"It'll be fine," Ellie said.

★ ★ ★

Adam's car was in the driveway when we pulled up. He had let himself in and was sitting on the couch, doing a crossword puzzle.

"Hey," he said. He got up and gave us each a quick hug, then sat back down again. "How's it going? How was Portland?"

"Good," said Ellie.

"Fine," I said.

"Can I help with anything?" Adam offered. "Groceries?"

"We're fine," Ellie said. "You sit. Say, did you find anyone to go to that couple's shower with you next weekend?"

I knew what Ellie was trying to do.

"No," said Adam, "I didn't. Shan, do you want to go? I tried calling you."

"I'm busy next weekend," I said, which wasn't true.

"Oh," he said. "Maybe I'll go alone. It's at the 510."

Crap. I would have liked to have gone there. But I wasn't about to play buddy-buddy date night.

"Some other time," he said.

"How was the play last night?" Ellie asked Adam, and then she instructed me to put the soda in the hall closet.

Adam had gone to see *Who's Afraid of Virginia Woolf?* with a woman from work. *She* had asked *him* out, he made a point of saying, and he wasn't too sure that he was interested.

He thought the play was pretty long. Too long, probably, and that all the tension and the yelling was a lot to handle. The cruelty was too much.

"It was a game they had," I said, "a way of staying together."

"That's true," Adam said. "I guess we were both tired." He went back to his crossword puzzle.

Ellie and I were getting out the ingredients for homemade pizza, and I started telling her about my happy-hour date that week. A woman from work had set me up with her brother, who had worn an Izod shirt and a jeans jacket, both with the collar turned up, like in the eighties. And his hair was feathered. I knew it was small of me, but I couldn't help but think that it was a bad sign. Two decades had passed and he hadn't noticed. If you were dating him, you might have to tap-dance to get his attention, didn't she think?

"Doesn't sound like the right guy for you," Ellie said, flattening out the premade dough we'd bought.

"Not that I'm one to talk, but two decades behind? He looked like he was in Loverboy," I said. "Oh, God. I'm an asshole."

"We've all been there," Ellie said. "Glad I'm not anymore. Hand me the sauce, would you?"

"What are you talking about?" Adam murmured from the couch in the next room.

"What did he look like, otherwise?" Ellie asked.

"He was actually good-looking," I said. I explained that he had these birdlike yellow-green eyes that were kind of beautiful and scary at the same time. They made him look predatory. And he was a little shorter than I am. "I wish I didn't have a problem with that, but I don't like feeling like an Amazon."

"What are you guys talking about?" Adam said louder.

I heard Adam, but I didn't feel like answering. I didn't feel like sharing anything about my dating life, even though I knew, at the same time, that I was talking loudly enough for him to hear parts of our conversation. Ellie wasn't answering him, either, but it wasn't her story.

"That's the thing about David," Ellie whispered. "I love that he's a good half-foot taller than me. And he's all worried lately about the spare tire he's growing, but I say, bring it on. I like that he's bigger than me," she said, sprinkling cheese across the pizza.

Adam had given up on us and was working his puzzle.

"Why didn't you say something to him?" says Dr. Douglas.

"I don't know. I just left after dinner. Ellie didn't seem to think the whole thing was that big of a big deal."

"Who's Ellie again?"

"We all went to college together."

"He doesn't lean on Ellie," says Dr. Douglas.

"What would I even say?"

"You claim the tension between you," says Dr. Douglas. "You say, 'Look, I think there's been this sexual tension between us, and I'm getting mixed messages from you.' Adam's been pressing on you for years like a point guard. Using you instead of forcing himself to meet new people and struggle in new relationships. He gets a little affection. He doesn't have to commit. He doesn't have to invest himself or stick his neck out and ask someone out. You've relied on Adam, too."

I wonder if Dr. Douglas has switched from Animal Planet to ESPN.

"I still feel jealous when I think about him finding someone else," I say.

"You've known Adam a long time," says Dr. Douglas. "And your love life isn't so great right now."

"Duh," I say, and Dr. Douglas starts laughing. "I mean, I don't think it's my imagination that things are like this."

"If you don't feel comfortable, that's real," says Dr. Douglas. "And I think we have some evidence that he has some sort of conflicting feelings."

"So now what do I do?"

"Ask him to dinner."

"And then say, 'Hi, now that you've selected your entrée, I don't think our friendship is working'?"

"Then just ask him out for a drink. You tell him that until he's out there dating someone or developing relationships with other women, you need to move on and not be a surrogate date for him. Not be the person he feels like he can grab. Why don't you ask the group for advice next week?" says Dr. Douglas. "It would help you to keep bringing these things into the group."

"It really *doesn't* seem like a conversation to have over the phone," I say.

"I think it would be good," Dr. Douglas says, "for you to draw that boundary."

I am just leaving the office for group the next week when the phone rings. I don't want to answer it, I shouldn't answer it, but it might be the printing quote I've been waiting for all day. It's Adam. His voice is kind of quiet, weak and shaky.

"Hey, Shan, what's up?"

I really don't want to miss group, and I haven't had a chance to ask their advice yet about how to talk to him. Did Ellie say something to him?

"I'm running late," I say. "For group. Can I call you when I get home?"

"Yeah. Sure," says Adam.

He really sounds bad. "Are you okay?" I say, cradling the phone with my shoulder, shutting down my computer with one hand, and digging around in my purse for my keys with the other.

"Yeah," he says. "Yeah. It's something. But it can wait."

Group was starting in ten minutes and last week Dr. Douglas had given us a speech because people kept coming in late.

"You're sure you don't mind?" I say, finally locating my keys. Why did I say that when I really needed to get out of here? This was my whole problem. Establishing what I needed. Why did I answer the phone? Why is he calling me at work? He never calls me at work.

"That's fine," he says.

I walked in late, to Dr. Douglas's disapproving look.

Eileen was talking about how she'd suddenly become depressed and was having trouble leaving the house. Louise talked again about ordering too much takeout and then said she thought she'd been engaging in bad self-talk. Harvey talked about synagogue, and a woman he kept seeing whom he found particularly attractive. Wayne was cheating on his girlfriend but refused to call it that, because he thought this new person might actually be his soul mate, even though she was his girlfriend's sister.

"Shannon," said Dr. Douglas, "didn't you have something that you wanted to talk about tonight? Didn't you want some advice from the group?"

"I did," I said. "I need to talk to Adam and I wanted advice. But then he called me right before I left the office. And said something was wrong."

"Well, of course something's *wrong*," said Eileen. "*Duh*. Men."

"No, I mean, it sounded like something was really wrong."

"What do you think it is?" asked Dr. Douglas. "Did he tell you?"

"No," I said. "I told him I was late for group."

"You set a boundary," said Dr. Douglas. "About your time."

"I guess," I said.

What do you say when your friend tells you that he has cancer?

I call Adam when I get home from group. "They found some tumors," Adam says. "In my head, and in my lungs, and in my liver. I was watching this spot, this spot on my skin, all year, but I never went in until now."

Adam is the healthiest person I know. He is a runner and he swims. He is in excellent shape. He rarely has more than one drink. He's never smoked. He eats Ry-Krisps with cottage cheese as a snack. He watches his fat intake even though he doesn't need to.

The cancer was like an unattended stove, burbling and simmering, and under the surface, on the cellular level, it had suddenly spilled over.

"I'm just . . . I'm just . . . ," he says. "I'm kicking myself for not going in until now. If I had gone in earlier . . ." He stops himself.

"Don't do that to yourself," I say.

"I know," he says, "it's not helpful."

"Now what do you do?" I ask him. "How do you feel?"

"I *feel* fine," he says. "I go in for more tests tomorrow."

"We'll get through this," I say. Why did I say that? What had I done for anyone lately? "You'll be okay."

"Oh, my God. Oh, my God," my mom says when I call her. "Oh, my God. Oh, why?" And she begins to sob. "What is he going to do?"

"He starts radiation next week."

"What do they say? What are his chances?"

"He won't say. He doesn't want to talk about it. He says he feels hopeful."

"Right before his thirty-fourth birthday," says Ellie. "He's thirty-three. He's like Jesus. He is. Adam's not like the rest of us. He's always been mild. Always patient. Always thinking of others."

I'm not sure why, but I had forgotten how religious Ellie could be. Perhaps my college friends saved their most religious selves for when I wasn't around.

"The only reason Adam ever remembers your birthday is because I remind him," I say. Did we have to make him a martyr immediately?

"I know," she says. "But Adam's different. He's not driven the way the rest of us are to create a mess of his life. He's always been so moderate." That was true. Adam was the only person I knew who actually followed standard medical opinion about not popping your zits. "And now at thirty-three he's facing his own mortality. He's like Jesus," Ellie says again. "He's like Jesus."

Chapter 25

Adam's old roommate Karl called me.

"Shan," he said, "I think you need to get over there and put your arm around Adam. Put your arm around Adam and just let him break down."

I tried to picture myself doing that, the weight of Adam's grief coming down on me, his arms around me, his sobbing body, like a condemned building, imploding, collapsing in on itself, on me, and it gave me an instant panic attack. "Could you hold on a second?" I said to Karl, and I went to the bathroom to get a glass of water and one of my emergency anxiety pills. "I'm sorry," I said when I got back on the phone, "but why should I be the one to do that?"

"Because Adam's always relied on you. And he's alone."

"His parents are with him. His older sisters are coming, aren't they?"

"That's not the same," said Karl. "I mean, I've been over there, talking about it with him, but that's not the same, either. If something like this happened to me, I'd have Jennifer. But Adam doesn't have anyone, a girlfriend, a wife, someone he can share everything with, the stuff he can't tell his parents."

"But doesn't he tell you that stuff? You guys have always been close."

"You're the person he's always told everything to," Karl said.

Was I really? I felt like I barely knew him anymore.

"He needs someone that he can really break down with," said Karl.

"Did he say that? Because he said he felt fine," I said.

"I just think he needs this," said Karl. "He doesn't have a, you know, a partner. And you're the closest."

"I don't know," I said. I didn't know if I could actually handle it. If the ship were going down, could I handle being the life raft? Adam's pretend girlfriend? Adam's pretend wife? "He says he feels optimistic."

"And maybe he'll be the miracle. We're all praying that he'll be the miracle. And I have faith that he might be. And so does Adam. But the fact is, Shan, he's heard some terrible news. My friend Steve is a neurosurgeon," said Karl. "He says he's guessing that they gave Adam two months."

How did this happen?

Ellie and I drank like we just got out on parole. At least until she got pregnant.

Lucy smoked at least a pack a day and her idea of outdoor exercise was to walk down to the local coffee shop and get a latte, and then browse in the Smith & Hawken garden store next door.

The designers at work went to happy hour three nights a week and chain-smoked and then went dancing and drinking and smoking pot all night. Of course, they were in their twenties and were slightly more resilient.

But really, my arteries were probably lined with Mc-Nuggets.

Adam never did any of these things.

Some of Adam's Lutheran friends from work, and from his neighborhood, formed a prayer circle. His mom formed a prayer circle with her friends, too, to send healing prayers and energy to Adam.

I had never heard of this. In the Catholic church where I grew up, coming out of our shameful personal silences to shake a shy peace with one another during Mass took all the energy we had.

Adam's mother encouraged all of his friends to come to the prayer circle, but I didn't think I'd do well with all that earnestness.

"I'm sorry," I said to Adam on the phone. "That's just not my thing."

"I know it's not," Adam said.

"I'm thinking about you in my own way," I said.

"I know you are," Adam said.

"How's it going?"

"I just started my treatments," he said. "And I'm pretty tired. But otherwise I'm okay. Gotta stay positive."

I did not offer to come over.

"Why don't you come out on Sunday and go to church with me?" asks my dad. "I think a little church might be exactly what you need at a time like this."

"Are you going to Our Lady of Sorrow?"

"I'm afraid that's all I'll have time for," he says. "I'm on call."

"It's not exactly uplifting."

"Oh, come on. They're trying. They've got new music. It's a little slice of your past," he says. "A little church will cure what ails you."

I wished that were true, but church always seemed, instead, to be a thing I had to recover from.

It was complicated. There was something oddly comforting about the guilt I'd grown up with, the shame. Being told every week that you were innately flawed and probably going to hell. It gave you something to aspire to. There was nowhere to go but up. It followed the psychology of abuse; if it was what you knew, it was hard to leave, even if it didn't feel very good.

I felt a kinship with the Catholics I'd grown up with; we had that common subtext. And I liked the musty scent of our old church, mothballs and candle wax. But going to church was like dating; I was always hopeful when I entered. *Maybe today God will speak to me. Maybe today my soul will open up in a blast of light. I will feel the revelation. The warmth and wisdom of the universe will open itself up to me, a blossom in springtime.* And then an hour later, I always left with no new clarity and the remnants of a rice wafer still stuck to the roof of my mouth.

But who knew? Maybe this would be the time that church made me feel better. Maybe this would be the day that the weight of being alive would be lifted.

"Can we go to Embers afterward?" I say.

And if not, there would be pancakes.

"If I don't get called to the hospital," my dad says.

Our Lady of Sorrow had a new priest, who spoke really slowly, leading us through the Lord's Prayer as if he were driving a school bus, stopping at the end of every block and making us stop behind him.

"Our Father," says the priest.

"Our Father," we all say.

Pause.

"Who art."

"Who art."

"In heaven."

"In heaven."

And so on.

"I think he thinks that we need to absorb the meaning," my dad whispers.

"I think I want to kill him," I say.

Today the priest is all decked out in gold and announces that, because it is some kind of special Feast of Something or Another, we are going on a journey. The altar boys are holding a kind of canopy over him, red silk with gold trim, and the priest is holding what appears to me to be some kind of gigantic magic wand—this long gold thing with a gold star on the end that looks like it's from the Louis XIV collection.

We follow him out of the church and down the stairs, a school of shuffling fish, past the play yard for the elementary school, down the block past Pizza Hut, past Embers, around the corner past the new brew pub and the video store, singing "We Shall Overcome."

"What *is* this?" I whisper to my dad.

"I think it's some kind of throwback to the Crusades," he says.

"Are we going to pillage Embers?"

"I don't have any idea," my dad says as we file back into the church.

When the choir breaks into "Soon and very soon, we will meet the Lord," I start crying, despite myself, and quickly dab my eyes with my sleeve, hoping no one will notice.

My dad is singing along. I never sing in church because I

have a voice like ice cracking on the lakes in January, hollow and sharp, both contracting and trying to make more room for itself, but I try to squeak out a few lines.

"I don't think I'll go back there again," I say when we get back to the house. "That priest is a patriarchal control freak."

"Who's that?" says Flo. "Did you go to Embers?"

After we all left home, my mom stopped going to Our Lady of Sorrow with my father every week, calling it "uninspiring," though she probably would have liked going to brunch with us today.

"I still don't quite understand what that little march was all about," says my dad. "I'll have to call Bill and see if he remembers why they do that."

"What is with that magic wand?" I say.

"It's not a magic wand."

"A scepter."

"It's not that, either. The host was in there," my dad says. "What do they call it? They put the host in there. I think it starts with an 'm.'"

"Microwave?" says my mom, and we both burst out laughing.

"It's not *microwave*," says my dad. "Flo, we're going to the driving range. Would you like to come and hit a bucket?"

"No," she says, "no, thank you. I'm going to stay here and plant."

I wish church had made me feel better, had solved something, and I suppose I am angry that it hasn't. I expect church, I guess, to function like an ambulance. In an emergency, it should come and rescue me.

Though I never admit it to anyone, I believe in God. Or perhaps, having grown up listening to punishing homilies every week, I am afraid *not* to believe in God. I like to believe, at least, in the idea of God, of something larger, something like the collective unconscious, some greater force that leaned, ultimately, toward benevolence. The idea of Jesus is comforting. Someone who could be so forgiving and kind, who existed without judgment.

Though after church, I never feel connected to anything much. I usually feel more alone than I had when I got there.

"I suppose you're used to it, huh?" I say to my dad as we walk out to the range with our buckets and our clubs. "People who might die. You see it all the time at work."

"Sure," my dad says, surveying the range. "You're just getting older. This is when life starts to change. And when you're really old like me, you're used to it."

"Well, it sucks," I say. "It doesn't make any sense."

"It never does," my dad says, stretching his arms out and doing a few deep knee bends.

"Dad, would it be true that the doctors only gave Adam about two months to live? That there's only, like, a two percent chance that he'll survive this?"

"I'm afraid that's probably true," my dad says, getting out his driver. "Melanoma spreads like wildfire. Did Adam tell you that?"

"No. Someone else did. Adam doesn't want to talk about it."

"Well, who knows?" says my dad. "Maybe Adam will be one of the lucky ones."

"Adam thinks he will be," I say. "He's feeling really optimistic."

"Well, that's good," says my dad. He hits a wayward shot that bounces off a nearby tree. "Your friend's got a tough road ahead."

When we get back to the house, my dad asks if I want a drink.

"What are you having?"

"I think I'll make a little vodka and tonic," he says. "Hey, when you're an athlete, you've got to keep up your strength."

"Then I'll have the same."

"Why don't you go see if your mother wants anything?"

"She didn't go golfing today. How come she gets a sports drink?"

"She's one of our sponsors," my dad says. He picks up a can of Planter's nuts and shakes them in my face, then tears the vacuum seal off, which makes a big swishing noise. He offers me some nuts. "We were saving these for when your boyfriend came over, but the expiration date was coming up." He barely makes it through his joke without laughing.

"Jerk." I punch him in the arm.

Flo is out on the deck, sitting next to a big pot of hibiscus that she's replanting. She can sit in the most impossible positions for hours. Now she's sitting on one leg, with the other kind of flopped off behind her and to the side.

"What yoga position is that?" I ask.

"The one I happen to be in," she says.

"Do you want a drink?"

"What kind?"

"Whatever you want. Dad's pouring drinks."

"Yah," she says. "I'd like a Canadian Club with some Sprite."

I go tell my dad what she wants and I bring it to her.

"Just set it over here," she says, motioning with a hand spade.

"We were thinking of ordering a pizza. What do you think of that?"

"I certainly don't feel like cooking."

"What would you want on it? What about pineapple and Canadian bacon?"

"I'm not fond of Canadian bacon," Flo says.

"Is anyone *fond* of Canadian bacon?" I say.

"It's the polite way to say something," says Flo. "When we grew up, we were taught to be polite."

"It's just pizza. I don't think the Canadian bacon will feel bad if you don't choose it."

She gives me her new, forced celebrity smile, which is the facial-muscular equivalent of *I used to like you when you were small, but now I'm just tolerating you because we're related.*

"Which ingredients would you be fond of?" I say.

"I don't care," says Flo, going back to shoving dirt into a new pot.

"How about olives and green peppers? And mushrooms?" I say, thinking that she likes vegetables.

"That's fine," she says. "Your dad will want meat."

"Sausage?"

"Sure," says Flo. She readjusts her legs and grunts a little, and knocks over her drink with her foot. "Oh, shit."

"Hey, Dad," I shout into the house, "Mom drank her drink already and we need another one!"

"Already?" my dad says.

"I didn't, either," my mom shouts.

I look over at her. A few ice cubes have skidded across the deck and landed underneath her butt, which is sort of propped up because she's sitting on one leg.

"You know," I say, "if you sit on those ice cubes long enough, they'll hatch and they'll imprint on you. And they'll follow you everywhere. Until they melt, of course."

"Go get my drink," says Flo.

"I thought you were raised to be polite."

By the time I get Flo's drink, she's in the bathroom, rummaging through the drawers, setting old makeup and lotions on the counter. I tell her that when I was bored at work the other day, I came up with an idea for a cable show called *Flotastic!* and wouldn't she like to star in that? Every week, she'd go to

Target and browse the aisles to different music tracks. Barry Manilow's "Could It Be Magic," for instance. Or Prince's "Get Off."

"I don't think that sounds very funny," says Flo.

"You haven't heard the music," I say.

"Who would watch it?"

"I don't know. People with nothing else to do."

"Like you?" says Flo.

"Hey," I say, "I work hard."

"I think this is another one of those 'poking fun at Mother' type things," she says.

In truth, this is the only kind of truce I know how to offer. The kind where I am her funny daughter again. The one she used to like being around, until I established *boundaries*.

"Every week there would be a segment where you'd get to talk about something that interests you, or teach the audience something new. That segment would be called 'FloTivities.'"

Flo is ignoring me now, burying her head in the bathroom cupboard, pulling out various bottles of lotion to consolidate, digging around in the old nail-polish bottles, opening them to see how thick and pasty they are.

"What do you think about that?" I say.

"Not much."

"Why are you mad at me?"

"Did it ever occur to you that I'm just busy?" says Flo. "That I'm trying to get a few things done? The world does not revolve around you, you know."

I go downstairs and check my laundry.

At dinner, my mom asks how Adam is doing.

"I haven't seen him yet," I say. "They hardly ever answer the phone."

"Who's that? His parents are there?" she says.

"Uh-huh." I pick some of the green pepper off my piece of pizza and put it on her plate. "They were only supposed to put this on half."

"Well, how is he doing?"

"Karl said the treatments seem to be working."

My mom nods and takes a bite of her pizza.

"Karl seems to think that I should go over there and be Adam's surrogate girlfriend."

"Adam's been a very special friend to you over the years," my mother says sharply, through a mouthful of pizza. It was the same thing the counselor had said.

"Before he started his radiation treatments, he had his sperm frozen. That's what Karl said."

"Why does Karl know all this?" my mom says.

"I don't know. Maybe Adam feels comfortable saying it to a guy. He had his sperm frozen so that he could still have a family. Radiation can ruin your chances."

"And I suppose you think he wants to have a family with you? Um, I think you need to get over yourself," my mom says.

"Isn't that what Adam said to you when you asked him why the two of you don't go out?" my dad says, and he starts laughing. "*Get over yourself?*"

"Pretty much," I say. I had told my dad that story while we were golfing.

"What's that about?" my mom says, looking irritated. "I don't think I know about that."

"But things have been different," I say. "They've been weird. And Karl keeps telling me to go over there. And saying things like, 'Adam really wishes he had a girlfriend, someone to help him through, someone to give him hope for a future.' Who knows what Adam is thinking at a time like this?"

"I'm not sure what you're getting at," my dad says. "He's your friend, isn't he?"

That was a question I didn't know how to answer.

"Um, I'll say it again," my mom says. "I think you need to get over yourself."

And she takes a big bite of pizza and keeps her eyes on the stretching string of cheese as she pulls the slice away.

"We are all always dying," says Dr. Douglas. "That's the thing to remember. You could go at any moment. Some people just have the luxury of knowing when." As if dying were like a cruise or a big fur coat.

"That's true," I say.

"And we don't know that Adam will die. He may survive this. And regardless, he's here now. And like all of us, he's imperfect. He's the same person you've always known."

"Right," I say. "But Ellie keeps comparing him to Jesus. And Karl keeps saying that Adam's thinking about having a family, and he wishes he had a woman in his life. He's making me nervous. And they both keep telling me that I should go over there."

"What if it were you? What would you want from Adam?" Dr. Douglas says, with an exasperated sigh. Today he is wearing a teal sweater, and the color of his eyes has changed again to match it. I wonder what his wife likes best about him. What they do around the house. If she helped him pick out the sweater.

"I guess I'd just want him to be the way he always was."

"Did you ever say anything to Adam about what happened between you?"

"No," I say.

"So, maybe now is a good time," says Dr. Douglas.

"It kind of seems beside the point now," I say.

"I don't think it's ever beside the point. I know I'm not a typical Minnesotan that way. But maybe that's where some of your confusion and your anger and reluctance are coming from," says Dr. Douglas. "I think you were pretty mad at Adam for his awkward advance. For not being the person who could be both your lover and your friend. For kind of missing the boat. For being such a presence in your life but not what you're looking for."

"Maybe," I say. "That's a lot to think about."

"Adam needs people around him who can support him right now," says Dr. Douglas. "You either need to work this through so you can support him, or you need to stay away."

I hadn't been able to work it through so far; why would I be able to now?

I chose to stay mostly away.

Chapter 26

The Dalai Lama's speaking engagements on the University of Minnesota campus had immediately sold out to people on private invitation lists. But the rest of us could see his lecture on closed-circuit television, on a huge screen in the women's athletic complex.

"Mom, do you want to see the Dalai Lama?" I had said when I called her from work.

"Yes! Oh, yes!" she had said. "I would love to. Now, *that* would be something to tell my spiritual group about." My mother's disappointment with both Protestantism and Catholicism had led her to join a spiritual group—a group of women in their fifties and sixties who met once every three weeks at 7:30 A.M. to discuss readings they'd assigned themselves, books

on the topic of women and spirituality, the problems of organized religion, the goddess within, and so forth. Mostly, from
what I could tell, they ate mini-muffins and bitched about their
husbands.

"I thought you might want to go," I said.

We sat in the women's gymnasium with hundreds of people, trying to hear His Holiness the Dalai Lama over the hum of the bad
sound system.

"There are a lot of Tibetan people here, I think," said Flo.

"I think you're right," I whispered.

"In what appears to be the traditional dress. Do you want a
cough drop?" my mother said, digging around in her purse.

"No," I whispered.

She began unwrapping her cough drop with a loud, uncer-
emonious crinkling.

Someone down the aisle shot my mom a look.

Earlier, a group of monks had chanted to welcome the
Dalai Lama and my mother had exclaimed, loudly, "What a fas-
cinating sound! It's like that Australian instrument. The creepy
one."

"The didgeridoo," I had whispered.

She had hummed a little out loud in imitation.

"Use your indoor voice," I had said to her, and she nudged
me hard with her elbow.

Then they'd escorted the Dalai Lama in and he'd sat cross-
legged on a platform with some pillows and started joking with
the audience about his English not being very good. "Now, my
translator take over for me," he said, and started laughing wildly.
I liked him. He rearranged his robe and nodded and rocked a little while the translator spoke.

"He's so fidgety," my mother said. "Look at him. He rocks
and rocks and fidgets. It's like he has ADD."

"I like that he's fidgety," I whispered, thinking he was a restless soul like everyone else, not perfect or pious, and that the fact that he had trouble sitting still, like I do, was a comfort. I thought he seemed divine in his humanness.

The Dalai Lama said some prayers and then began a lesson in the tenets of Buddhism, the twelve links of dependent origination.

My mother began to look around and stare at members of the audience. I was having a flashback to the only time that I had taken my family to the St. Olaf Christmas concert. We had been seated high up in the bleachers, and my mother had spent half the concert playing with the fur coat of the woman ahead of us. Rubbing the fur up, and then smoothing the fur down to keep herself entertained.

The Dalai Lama explained to us that from contact comes feeling. From feeling comes craving. From craving comes grasping. That man, if he did not grasp, would be freed, would not come into existence.

"Do you want a butterscotch candy?" my mother said, nudging me.

"No," I whispered in what I hoped was a harsh tone.

The Dalai Lama then read in broken English from the pamphlet we'd all received on the way in. "Thus," he said, "this entire mass of suffering comes into being."

"I thought this would be more interesting," my mother whispered.

"He's explaining the human condition," I whispered back.

"These bleachers are hard," she said. "I'm uncomfortable."

"You're missing the point," I whispered. "From feeling comes craving."

"I don't have any more feeling," she said, readjusting her position in the bleachers. "I don't like sitting this way. My legs are going numb."

Existence is suffering, the Dalai Lama said. From feeling

comes craving, he repeated. From craving comes grasping. Man, in craving, suffers.

If man could let go of want, the Dalai Lama explained, he would be free.

My mother liked to say sometimes that long ago, she had learned not to expect anything from anybody. That other people couldn't make you happy, and that she had learned she could depend on herself, and in the end, only on herself.

I never believed her.

"I can't make you happy or unhappy," she would say to me sometimes when I was a teenager and we were fighting. "You're in charge of your feelings."

It was a particular bit of seventies pop-psych rhetoric that annoyed the shit out of me. I was a teenager. Clearly, I was not in charge of my feelings.

And so, most of the time, I would go storming off to my room.

"From existence comes birth, old age and death and misery and suffering and grief," the Dalai Lama read. "Confusion and agitation. The root of cyclic existence is action. Therefore," he read, and the translator translated, "the wise one does not act."

Chapter 27

"I want you to promise me," says the counselor, "that as long as Adam is alive, you'll call at least once a week, and you'll go over there at least once a week."

"I think he's doing pretty well, actually," I say. "Ellie says he's really hopeful."

Ellie had told me that Adam's treatments were going better than expected. At least, that's what Karl had told her. Whenever she called Adam's house, she said, she got the answering machine. She and David had been there once, to check in on Adam, but he was sleeping. And most of the time, she said, she felt too tired and too big to go anywhere. She still had morning sickness.

"And what if he wants a massage?" I say. "What if he wants me to rub his feet?"

"Why would you even think that?" the counselor says.

"Because that's what his mom does. That's what his sisters do. I don't know what to talk about with him. I'm not one of the prayer circle people. I don't want to go over there and mess things up with my bad energy."

"I think you're just scared," says the counselor. "And you can handle it. You don't have to stay long. You can visit for ten minutes and then go. You just make the connection, and then you can go. I promise," she says, "that you'll be glad you did it. You go as an *old* friend. You leave all of your conflict at the door, and you go as an old friend. *I want you to do this.* Okay?"

Of all of the Skinnerian behavioral changes she's assigned me over the years—getting up at 7 A.M. every day including Sundays, joining Toastmasters, cutting up my credit cards—this is the only one that I accept.

"Okay," I say.

"You'll do that?" she says. "You'll *promise?*"

"Yes," I say. *I promise.*

"I promise you," she says, "no matter what happens with Adam, you will not regret going over there every week."

"Okay." We nod at each other in silence.

I went to visit Adam one evening after work. He was supposed to go in for a treatment early that afternoon, and should have been home resting, but when I got there at 5:30 P.M., no one was home.

Ellie had said that Adam had been forgetting things lately. He would double- and triple-book himself, forget other dates and appointments. He might have forgotten that he'd told me to come over. Perhaps he'd told me the wrong time. Or maybe he and his parents had stopped somewhere on their way home.

I parked on the street and waited for a while in my car. It was raining lightly, and the drops were staying intact on my windshield.

After half an hour, I was about to leave when Adam's car pulled up. His father was driving and his mother was in back. Adam was in the passenger seat. By the slump of his shoulders, I could tell that his hands were resting in his lap. His head was bent forward and Adam, who normally had excellent posture, looked like he was about eight years old, being driven home from an unsuccessful piano recital, having flubbed the notes.

I got out of my car and waved to them.

Adam kept walking into the house, went straight in, his head lowered and bent a little to one side. It looked a little swollen to me, and his hair was falling out in patches.

"He has a headache," his mom said.

"Hello," said Adam's father as he followed Adam into the house, shortening his long gait to stay behind Adam.

I didn't know if I should stay. Maybe Adam hadn't even told them I was coming over. Had forgotten entirely.

"Why don't you come in and we can fix dinner together?" Adam's mom said to me, so I followed her into the house.

Adam had the same bad habit that I did of sharing his personal life with his mother. I wondered what sorts of things he'd told her about me. If she knew about the time that I'd taken my bra off and waved it around outside the sunroof of Adam's car as we sped down the freeway? I was grateful that she didn't ask where I'd been all these weeks.

Adam had passed out in the recliner right by the door. His father was sitting on the couch reading the paper.

Adam's mom and I went into the kitchen. I put some water

on for tea, because she thought that Adam might like some when he woke up. I was happy to have a small job to keep me busy. The air in the house was stale and still; it smelled of sadness. Adam's mother pulled the herbal tea bags out and we began scrounging around in the fridge, in the cupboards for food.

"Adam says you've been very busy at work this year," she said.

"Yes," I said.

We found onions, tomato sauce, pasta, a little garlic.

"I think we need red wine," she said.

"Why don't I go to the liquor store?" I said.

"That's an excellent idea," Adam's mother said.

"Get something red and cheap to put in the sauce," she said. "And another bottle to drink. And would you mind picking up some more scotch?"

By the time dinner was ready, Adam was awake and his headache was gone. He picked at his spaghetti and poured himself a glass of red wine.

Adam's mom was on her second glass of scotch and her first glass of red wine, drinking both at the same time. I was on my second glass of wine. Adam sipped a little of his wine, but set it back on the table. His father was quietly twirling spaghetti.

"So, when will you get to see your niece again?" Adam's mom said.

"I was just out there," I said. "A couple of months ago." I wondered what Adam was thinking about kids and if I should talk about Georgia.

"How exciting," she said. "And what do you think of Portland?"

"It's gorgeous," I said. "It's so green. I'd like to go back for Thanksgiving, maybe."

"I've always wanted to see Portland," Adam said. "I'd like to go out there with you when I'm feeling better. I'm going to plan on that." Adam nodded.

"Sure," I said.

Adam's mother gave me a pointed look.

"What?" Adam said. "Don't do that."

"You don't know if you'll be in any shape to do that."

"That's negative and that's not what I need to hear right now," Adam said.

"Okay," said his mother, looking down at her plate.

"Did I tell you that Ellie threw up in Marshall Field's last week?" I said.

"Really?" said Adam, and his face seemed to brighten.

"Yeah," I said. "She's still puking every morning, and she knew she shouldn't have gone over there, but they were having a thirteen-hour sale."

Adam's mom smiled at me; her eyes looked a little watery. Maybe it wasn't good to bring up children.

After dinner, Adam went to lie down again. He crossed his arms over his chest and fell asleep in his recliner.

Who knew what he was really thinking? Whatever it was, he clearly didn't have the energy to talk about it.

"Thank you for coming over," Adam's mom said, giving me a hug when I left. "You act normal, and that's nice. You bring the real world into our home."

No one had ever thanked me for acting normal. Maybe it was the scotch.

Chapter 28

There were so many questions I wanted to ask Adam, but there never seemed to be a good time. What if you die? What if you get better? What are you glad you've done? What would you do differently?

Adam would never say how he was feeling or what he was thinking. And each time I asked him how the treatments were going, he would say, "Fine."

There were weeks when Adam didn't want visitors and weeks when only the answering machine picked up. Mostly, when I went over there, I talked to Adam's parents. Adam was usually tired and quiet. And sometimes Adam's mom and I would just eat cookies and have tea, or look through catalogs and magazines together while Adam rested.

He had finished radiation and a round of chemotherapy. He had lost all of his hair, and until recently, his entire head had been swollen. Now he was starting to look more like himself again. His weight was good. His hair was growing back in a soft auburn fuzz, completely different than his original color.

"Adam is so *positive*," I say. "I don't understand it. It's kind of frustrating."

"How else is he supposed to be?" asks the counselor.

"I don't know. I'd like to have a real conversation. About what's going on. About what might happen."

"Why would you have that *now*?" she asks. "I think you're projecting what *you'd* be thinking onto Adam."

"You do?"

"Yes, I do," she says. "You'd be thinking, *Why me? Why me?* And you'd be complaining about it, *loudly,* I think." She starts laughing. "And you'd want everyone to listen."

"You're probably right," I say. "Ellie doesn't seem to want to talk about it at all."

"I wouldn't either if I were almost nine months pregnant," she says.

"I just wish I knew what he was thinking."

"If he wants to tell you something," she says, "he will."

Chapter 29

"Have you spoken with Adam lately?" I asked Ellie.

"I saw him a couple months ago, but we've been pretty busy getting ready for the baby."

"No one's answering at his house. I mean, even the answering machine isn't coming on," I said.

"That's weird," she said.

"Has he talked with you at all about what's going on with him? Like what he's thinking about?"

"No," said Ellie. "He doesn't seem to want to. I take my cues from Adam."

"No one's answered there for a couple of weeks."

Karl didn't know where Adam was, either.

"Let's talk tonight about the things that make us feel connected," the counselor says. "That's why we're all here, in this group. We're looking for ways to connect better with other people. So how do you do that for yourself? What makes you feel connected and not alone?"

"Ordering takeout," says Louise. "They know my order by heart."

"Listening to Barry Manilow," says Dana.

"I don't feel alone when I'm with my girlfriend," says Wayne.

"Which one?" says Eileen.

Clearly we are all in trouble.

"What about you, Shannon?" asks Dr. Douglas.

"Can we come back to me?" I say.

"I like spending Sunday nights with my friend Sally," says Eileen. "We watch movies and eat popcorn. That's when I feel most connected."

"I go bowling with a group from my synagogue," says Harvey. "I like to do things where there's some kind of equalizing factor, and pretty much everyone is bad at bowling. Or at least not very good at it. You would all be welcome to join us, by the way. Anyway, that's when I feel most connected," he says. "That's when I feel most like a child of God."

Later that week, Ellie had a little girl, Ingrid.

I brought her flowers in the hospital, and Ellie and I watched *Wheel of Fortune* while David went out for sandwiches. I held tiny, sleeping Ingrid.

None of us yet knew where Adam had gone.

Children of God Go Bowling

Part 5

Chapter 30

Adam is lying in his recliner, explaining to me the principles of Qigong and healing meditation, which he'd spent a month practicing in Florida, which is why no one had been answering at his house. He had just decided one day to go, and he left with his parents, not telling anyone except the neighbor, who'd been keeping an eye on the house, bringing in the mail.

He learned, he said, that he was responsible for his cancer. That he had created it and could therefore divest himself of it. Which seems to me like telling a colonized people that they had brought the colonizers into their country, that they had wished to be invaded.

He learned that cancerous cells are all always popping up

but that the body normally takes care of them. That usually the cancer patient has experienced some kind of emotional trauma in the year or two preceding the illness. Something that has weakened the immune system.

"Do you think that's true?" I ask.

"Well, yeah," Adam says. "My new job. And, well, yeah."

Becoming healthy again is a matter of realigning your *chi,* rebuilding your thinking, worming your way out from underneath the stultifying weight of concrete, your old way of doing things, your old approach to life. Learning to be peaceful.

"For instance," he says, "right now I was able to go away in my mind with a single image in front of me, and that's relaxing. That helps."

"What was your image?" I ask.

"A napkin," says Adam. "I let my mind float around, and then I was able to see very clearly in front of me, a napkin." Adam smiles and closes his eyes again.

I put my feet up on the ottoman and watch Adam, his eyes closed, beginning to snore softly. His mouth slightly open, pulling at his gaunt face. He'd lost weight at the meditation center. When I had seen him before he left, he looked relatively normal; his hair had grown back in and his coloring was good.

But at the center, he had not been allowed to take any of his medication. And they had fasted, and then gradually reintroduced foods. "Everything I've had since then has been the best ever," Adam had said. "The best lobster. The best almonds. The best ice cream."

Now he is thin and jaundiced. But he seems happy.

"He looked fine before he left," Ellie seethed on the phone. "I know he needs this, I know it makes him feel better. But it makes me so angry."

The doctors felt, Karl told us, that they had done all they

could with radiation and chemotherapy. Adam wasn't eligible for other experimental treatments; his cancer had spread too far. They had made some progress, but it would all come back.

"I guess this is Adam's last hope," I said.

"I know that," Ellie said. "But it seems like too little, too late." In a way, none of it seemed real.

"Does Adam talk to you at all about dying?" I asked her. All this time, I had believed, in some way, in Adam's optimism. As befuddling as his positive approach was to me (a way of thinking I'd always equated with denial), it was the one thing that made me believe he might actually make it through all of this.

And with his meditation practice, Adam still seemed hopeful. Maybe this eleventh-hour intervention would work. But his body told another story. He had begun to look old.

"No," she said. "He doesn't want to talk about it."

"It seems like if he doesn't bring it up, we shouldn't bring it up," I said.

"I'm still taking my cues from Adam," Ellie said.

"He still wants to go to Portland with me," I said.

A few years ago, I had visited my sister in Portland during the winter, and one afternoon we had gone up to Mount Hood to go snowshoeing.

We parked next to the trailhead, put our snowshoes on, and led Shasta across a narrow bridge above a rushing mountain stream. We crunched our way up a series of switchbacks for about an hour, while Shasta kept stepping on the back of my snowshoes, bouncing ahead of us, and then getting behind me again to mess up my stride.

We were moving up and up through thick trees and then, seemingly out of nowhere, there was a clearing and bright sun.

"Sun!" my sister said with an exhausted sigh. "It's about damn time." It had been gray and rainy in Portland all winter.

We sat down in a curvy drift of snow, on the shore of a small, frozen, snow-covered lake.

"You wouldn't even know this was a lake if you'd never been here before," I said.

"Nope," she said.

"It could just be a clearing."

"I want to see how those people get across," my sister said, pointing to the other side of the lake, where a group of three people and two German shepherds were moving tentatively through the drifts.

"Are they on the ice?"

"No," Greta said. "There's a little strip of land over there between the lake and a marsh. I want to see how they do before we go over there."

"We could always just go back the way we came," I said.

"I like doing a loop," my sister said. "They seem fine."

She put her backpack behind her and leaned back on it, closing her eyes to sun herself in her snowsuit and hat.

While my sister was resting, another group came out of the woods and trudged behind us. They got part of the way around the edge of the powdery clearing and then stopped to sit, too, even though they'd walked into the shade.

"It's amazing," I said to my half-asleep sister. "People will even sit by the *idea* of water."

"Um-hmmm," she murmured.

"Why is that?" I said, though she didn't respond. "It's not even sunny over there." Here we all were, I thought, keeping some kind of vigil.

I made some snowballs for Shasta and tossed them into nearby drifts. Shasta went bounding after them and then dug frantically where they'd landed. Not being able to tell the formed snow from the powder, she kept completely obliterating the thing that she was looking for.

★　　★　　★

Maybe I had been digging too hard, I thought now, ruining things by picking at them.

Maybe the secret to life was that simple.

The frozen lake of life.

It would thaw in the spring. And it would freeze again.

And that was that. You just had to be patient. And have faith that underneath the frozen snow, something was living. That what you couldn't see had its own sense and would emerge.

Chapter 31

On an unusually warm fall weekend a bunch of the guys from Adam's company came over to his place to do yard work; they raked leaves and mowed the lawn. They painted Adam's fence, a project he had wanted to do himself that summer.

His mother had cut some watermelon squares for Adam, a food the meditation center had recommended, and placed them on the patio table. Adam sat outside for about five minutes to oversee the painting and then got too cold. His face was ashen and severe, the skin of his lips stretched tight across his bones and teeth. While his hair, eyebrows, and eyelashes had begun to grow back thick and soft, the rest of him was disappearing.

Adam and his mom and I went inside while the guys kept painting. Adam lowered himself into his recliner and laid his arms gently on the rests. He was wearing a long-sleeved T-shirt and it was hanging off the bones of his shoulders the way that the skin stretches over a starving calf's backside. His stomach was distended and he had trouble getting comfortable. A few days ago, he had been rushed to the hospital. They'd taken ten liters of fluid out of him, which had left him weak.

"You probably lose a lot of protein," I said, "when they do that. I bet that makes it even more tiring."

"That's true," he said. "It does. How'd you know that?"

"I asked my dad about it," I said.

Adam nodded and closed his eyes, and his mom and I spent the next half hour talking about where you could buy pants if you have any hips at all.

From his half-sleep, Adam murmured something about the Lands' End Web site and how you could order custom clothing.

I told Adam's mom about a business dinner the week before. I had spilled merlot all over the client and was beginning to think that soon I would be working at Arby's.

"You're too hard on yourself," Adam mumbled. "You have interesting experiences."

"I guess public embarrassment is interesting," I said. "They're sending me to Phoenix to meet with a new client, so I guess I'm not getting fired yet."

"See?" Adam said, with his eyes still closed. "You get to do new things."

After a while, Adam wandered upstairs to lie down, and I started to go outside to help paint, but as I was making my way through the kitchen, Adam's mother stopped me and handed me a Tupperware container full of ice chips.

"Could you please bring these upstairs?" she said.

"Sure," I said, and made my way upstairs with the little container.

Adam was lying on his side, covered by a sheet and thin blanket.

"How are you doing?" I said.

"I got a little tired being outside," he said, "but otherwise, this has been a pretty good day."

Adam was everything I'm not. Understated. Patient. Grateful.

"Where would you like these?" I said, holding up the ice chips. "On the nightstand?"

"Sure," said Adam. He sat up a little and rearranged the pillows behind his head.

"Can I help you?"

"I'm okay," he said.

I looked at the pictures in Adam's room. Photos of family vacations. A skiing trip with Karl. An old photo of us when we went out for Adam's birthday. In the last few years, we hadn't done anything to celebrate our birthdays. Maybe a beer a few months after the fact.

"This is my suction machine," Adam said, draping one long arm over the machine by his bed. "It's really nice," he said. The machine was to help Adam with the spit that built up when he tried to eat, even a Popsicle. It was a big contraption for the little it did. "When I'm better," Adam said, "I'd still like to go to a movie."

"Okay," I said. There was a brief silence in which we both stared off at nothing in particular. "I'm sorry this is happening to you," I finally said. "I'm sorry you have to go through this."

"Well, whatever," Adam said, looking off at a corner of the room.

I felt stupid. Although the counselor would tell me that stupid isn't a feeling.

"I guess that's the understatement of the year."

"Right," Adam said.

"You've been a really good friend to me," I said.

Adam just nodded. Then he held his open palm out to me, and I took it.

"Can I talk to you about something?" I said. "It's kind of

hard for me to say. And so, if you don't want to talk about it, just tell me. Okay?"

Adam nodded.

I said that I thought, in the last couple of years, there'd been some odd tensions in our friendship, being the last two single people and all, and that I didn't think I'd always handled it very well, and I was sorry about that, and that I'd felt like I'd needed to keep a distance until I figured out what it meant. For me, I added.

"Being the last two single people is hard," Adam said, nodding. "But nothing to get upset about. I mean, things are a certain way and then they change. You get older and things change. And then you get sick and certain doors close. And we've talked about religion, and language." I wasn't sure quite what he meant. "And then, I just wouldn't ever want you to feel badly about yourself," Adam said. "I mean, you do so many things so well. You really do. I just think you're great and I wouldn't ever want you to feel badly about yourself. Or to think that I thought badly about you."

"I never thought you thought badly of me," I said.

"I just think, you know, you get older and things change, then things happen and then windows close," Adam said again, and stopped. "Could you say more about what you meant? About tension?"

"I just sort of thought, well, that there were a few times in the last few years when I wondered if maybe you were attracted to me, although you said you weren't. I mean, I know you said that, but I didn't know what I thought about that. So I've sort of been staying away until I could figure it out. I mean, I'd wondered why we didn't date, and then I finally came to the conclusion that maybe we've just been good friends for such a long time. It would be like kissing your cousin."

"Oh," said Adam. "This is a lot to take in right now."

"I'm sorry," I said.

He rubbed his hand over his forehead and covered his eyes for a second. "Well, I just really appreciate that you're willing to talk so openly about this," he said. He lifted his hand from his eyes. "And if you ever do want to talk about it, openly, just let me know. And I'd be happy to talk about it."

"Okay," I said.

Adam grabbed my hand again and gave it a squeeze, and we sat for a while. I looked around at the walls, at the pictures. "Your room looks nice," I said.

"Thanks," he said. "You know, you don't need to stay up here if you don't want to."

"I guess I should do a little painting."

"I'm going to close my eyes," Adam said.

Through the window screen I could hear the guys downstairs talking while they worked.

"I'll go downstairs and start doing some damage to your fence," I said. "Lowering the property value with my painting skills." It was a dumb thing to say. I just couldn't think of anything else.

"You're so hard on yourself," Adam said. "Don't do that."

"I was just kidding," I said.

We finished the fence just as dark clouds and a strong wind were moving in. The guys went upstairs to say good-bye to Adam while his mom gathered things for me from Adam's garden. Pumpkins and the last of the squash. Apples from his tree.

"Thank you for coming over," she said. "Maybe we could have lunch some time."

"That would be nice," I said.

I wondered how much she knew about Adam's love life. Who he was interested in. What he told her about his crushes and occasional dates, what he revealed to her about his secret longings. I wondered what he revealed to himself. If any of us know what we really want, or if we want what we think we should, and talk our hearts into it.

I went upstairs with my bag of groceries to say good-bye. The guys were just on their way out the bedroom door, telling Adam they'd call him during the week.

"I'm going to go, too," I said. "It's starting to rain really hard outside." I wondered why I'd said "outside" when that part was obvious.

"Okay," said Adam, sitting up in bed a little.

"Don't sit up," I said.

"It's okay," he said. "So, are you going to go to Portland again?"

"I'm not sure when I'll go," I said.

"I'll go with you when I'm better," Adam said. "I'd like to meet your niece."

"Sure," I said.

Adam extended his arms for a hug and lifted his lips up to my face.

I turned, instead, without even thinking, so that his kiss landed on my cheek.

He put his arms around me, and so I put a hand gently on one shoulder, the other on his back. I could feel the line of his spine, and a lump next to it the size of an egg, arching below the skin. Adam's body had become like a bed of rocks, uninhabitable. He couldn't get comfortable. Couldn't lie on his side or his back without having to shift every few minutes.

"I'll talk to you this week," I said.

"Okay," he said. And he took my fingers gently, kissed the back of my hand, and laid his cheek there.

And I thought that in that moment, perhaps he had forgiven me everything.

★ ★ ★

You so want to ask the person who is dying, *What was your favorite place to be? What are your best memories?* If I were dying, I think I might try to remember smells. Lilacs and fresh-cut grass. Garlic and tomato sauce and basil and rosemary. Chocolate-chip cookies.

I wanted to ask Adam, *So, who am I to you? A sister? A friend?*

But those aren't the kind of conversations that Adam wanted to have, because it meant admitting that he was leaving us.

So you are left in the end with this kind of sign language. An interpretive gesture.

A body comes out of seemingly nowhere, grows out of a single cell. Becomes bigger than the sum of its parts, a spirit, a friend, someone you depend on.

Then you watch it decay and shrink. A body with cancer harbors hidden, furious life, taking everything in its path, taking on a life of its own, before the person inside of that body can leave.

"It sounds like you and Adam made a kind of peace," said the counselor. "I think there was some acknowledgment on both sides that you didn't know what to do with each other. How did that feel? That moment of connection?"

"It was nice," I said. "We hadn't had that in a long time."

The next time I went to see Adam, he was too weak to open his eyes.

"Shannon is here, Adam," his mother announced, standing in the doorway of his bedroom.

He remained motionless under the covers, except for one hand, which he extended. I reached out and took his hand lightly, and he drew my fingers to his lips.

And then he let them go.

When I found out that Adam had died, I cried for two hours in the counselor's office. She let me stay longer, because I was the last appointment.

That tiny office, with its pink walls, the same walls I'd been staring at for eight years, was the only place I really felt like I could break down.

Over the years, I had always been surprised, once I sat down with the counselor in that familiar furniture, by the things that had been going on inside me. They emerged like cicadas after a long sleep. Who knew they were there? They had been so quiet and now appeared with such noisy insistence.

"You loved your friend," the counselor said. "And the two of you had grown apart in certain ways." She handed me more Kleenex and I nodded. "That happens, sweetie. Friendships change. People move on. That's normal. And the two of you had different fantasies about what you wanted. You were both distracting yourselves with those fantasies. But no matter what happened between you, you will always have memories of that early friendship."

I told the counselor about how Adam and I used to go cross-country skiing together in Carver Park. We'd each bring a cold beer and tuck it in our jacket pockets; when we were hot from skiing, we would stop and sit on a tree stump, and watch the wind blow across the fields, and drink our beer and listen to the dried weeds scratch the snow.

Chapter 32

At Adam's burial, everyone else cried so hard that their faces were streaked and red. I had been driving with my mom, and had wound up at the end of a long line of cars, one of the last people to arrive at the burial service.

By the time we parked and walked up, the pastor had begun the burial rites, and we were so far away that I couldn't see what he was doing and could barely hear him. But I could tell by the bursts of grief from the front that he had blessed the grave, could hear from a communal sob that Adam's parents and his sisters had laid flowers over his marker.

"Why are you holding up so well?" my mother said to me sharply, dabbing her eyes with Kleenex.

★   ★   ★

After the funeral, we all went to a big hall where Lutheran women were putting out ham sandwiches, potato salad, and chocolate cake. There were poster boards up around the dining room with pictures of Adam organized by category. Adam with his friends from business school. Adam with his family. Adam skiing with the guys. Adam with his friends from college.

There's me, fat from eating too many doughnuts and draped across Adam's lap. Adam is holding a bunch of grapes over my open mouth. There's Adam and me in Ellie's kitchen, trying to make stir-fry. There's Adam and me, shoveling my car out of the snow.

Afterward, we were all invited back to Adam's house.

On the way there, I stopped at the liquor store and bought the ingredients for vodka and tonics, and a bottle of whiskey. At every Irish-Catholic wake and funeral that I have been to, you cry at the funeral, and then you go back to the house, get drunk, and curse the son of a bitch who died, leaving you all behind with the memory of his imperfections. And with each curse, with every story, the dead become more sainted.

I walked into Adam's house without knocking. In the living room, a couple of people I didn't know were silently looking through a photo album. Most everyone was quietly sipping chardonnay and drinking Diet Coke. I walked back to the kitchen and dumped my bag of booze, ice, and lemons on the kitchen counter.

"About time you got here, Olson," said Matthew. "So anyway," he said and turned back to our friend Mike, "we got in at a really good time. I could give you his number if you want it. Great guy."

"Where's Ellie?"

"I think Ellie decided to go straight home."

"Why?"

"She has a long drive."

"Where's Karl?"

"His wife wasn't feeling well. He took her home."

I looked around for more of our friends from school. Irene Larsen. Thor Gunderson. They'd been at the funeral. Jeanne Carlson.

"Where is everybody?"

"I think a few people are still on the way," said Matthew. "I think some people just wanted to be alone. Or they needed to take their kids home."

I went over to the counter where I'd left my bag of booze and started pouring myself a glass of whiskey.

"Maybe Lutherans grieve differently," says the counselor.

"Maybe," I say. "No one was drinking. No one was telling stories. No one was telling bad jokes. Maybe people were just so stunned that they didn't know what to do."

"It's different when someone young dies," says the counselor.

"I guess a lot of us didn't really believe he was gone. It's like he suddenly disappeared. All the time that Adam was sick, you knew somewhere in the back of your mind that this was probably the end. But Adam never talked about leaving. At least not with me. He always talked about what he wanted to do next, when he was better."

The thing was, maybe I hadn't cried at Adam's funeral—maybe I was holding up so well, as my mother put it—because I hadn't yet figured out just what it was that I had lost.

★　　★　　★

"I don't get the part about religion," Dr. Douglas says. "When Adam said, 'We've talked about religion.' What was that?"

"He mentioned it that one time in the car," I say. "But I guess I never realized how religious Adam was until the eulogy. The Lutherans at St. Olaf kind of looked down on Catholics, I think. At least that's what I noticed. Like we were a little dirty. Drive-thru confession. Too much drinking."

"Oh, right," says Dr. Douglas. "I've noticed that, too. I went to a Lutheran school, too. I was raised Lutheran."

"I don't think Catholics take themselves as seriously as Lutherans do. We know we're flawed and we just want to get by with a little bit of humility."

"The pastors' kids at my school drank like maniacs," says Dr. Douglas.

"Mine, too," I say. "Yet they could still quote Bible passages, and identify religious symbolism and allegory in Italian painting, so somehow that made them better than everyone. It drove me nuts."

"Catholics and Jews have more in common," says Dr. Douglas. "Psychologically."

"I was thinking that, too."

"The guilt thing. The shame."

"The thing I don't get about what Adam said is this 'we've talked about language' thing. I don't know what that meant."

"Well, you do have quite a potty mouth," Dr. Douglas says.

"That's true."

"Don't get me wrong, I think it's delightful. It's just not very Midwestern."

"Adam did want a nice Lutheran wife, I think," I say.

"So you know that?"

"Yeah, I think that's true."

"I'm guessing," says Dr. Douglas, "that Adam had a system of checks and balances in his head. About what he wanted and didn't want. And you had some pluses behind your name, the things he liked about you, and some minuses, whatever didn't work out with the rest of the dream."

"I guess that's true," I say. "I guess I had the same thing. But the thing that bugs me is that, as long as I knew him, he had crushes on all of these nice Protestant women, women from church, or a woman who worked at the Scandinavian bakery, and I don't think he ever made a single move on any of them. Adam told me he didn't want me to think he thought *badly* about me, but he must have in some way or he wouldn't have brought it up."

"Right," says Dr. Douglas. "I'd take it as a compliment from the universe. You're more fun. Maybe a little dangerous. That's kind of cool."

"I always thought that Madonna/whore thing was more for Catholic guys. That it was *their* hang-up."

"Oh, sex and shame," says Dr. Douglas. "That's sort of a universal entanglement."

Dr. Douglas had been a philosophy major, and usually let me run with my half-cocked theories like a kid with a balloon, but I knew that the counselor would tell me to stop obsessing and enjoy the moment of connection I'd had with Adam before he'd gone.

Which is why I also knew that I wouldn't tell her about my conversation with Dr. Douglas.

"What if one of Adam's stresses was me, his old friend, pulling away?" I say to Dr. Douglas, knowing that the counselor would have told me that *that* was my narcissism. My fantasy. A way of connecting with Adam.

"You know," says Dr. Douglas, "someone with cancer is going to be able to pinpoint a stressful event in the last two years. So is someone without cancer."

"Why do I feel so empty now?" I say, explaining how, at the funeral, everyone was crying, and I felt like a shallow pan, catching rainwater, except there were only tiny drips.

"I think you cared about Adam," he says. "I don't think you loved him the way you *thought* you should. You *thought* you should love him like a wife would. But you did love him. And that's where your anger came from, in the discrepancy. You were conflicted. And death, in someone young, usually leaves people not knowing what to think."

I nod and wait for more.

"Do you want some coffee?" Dr. Douglas says.

He gets up to pour us each a Styrofoam cup full. He sets the cups on the coffee table between us and goes back across the room for the creamer and some stir sticks.

"I think a lot of this has to do with your mother," he says.

"How's that?" I say.

"Creamer?" he says.

"Just a touch," I say. The only time I used creamer in my coffee was with Dr. Douglas. It was like having a special thing that you do with one parent. With the counselor, I drank Mountain Dew. With Dr. Douglas, I added creamer.

"I think when you were little, and you were sick with asthma, you lived with waiting. Waiting to get well, waiting for life to come back to you. And your life was your mother's primary responsibility. Soon, the two are inseparable. Your life; your mother's reason for being."

We had already talked about this. "I don't get what this has to do with Adam."

"Well, that's the great archetypal drama," concludes Dr. Douglas, leaning back in his chair. "The choice between security and a life. You depend on your mother to live," he says. "Or at least you think you have to, because that's the way it was when you were little. You feel smothered by her love and yet dependent. Then there's Adam. You knew him, what? Fifteen years? Well enough for him to become a screen for your projections. He loves you; you think you should marry him because he's nice, but where's the passion? Then you can't breathe; you feel trapped. There's not enough room for you to be you. For you to have a future. Who does that remind you of?"

"My mom."

"Exactly. Somewhere along the line, your relationship with Adam took on the archetypal drama that you're going to have to have with your mother. You rejected Adam in a way that you have not been able to with your mother."

Dr. Douglas is staring at me. He takes a sip of coffee. There he is, waiting for me to say something. I look up at the window. Dr. Douglas has a basement office whose view revealed only feet, the tires of parked cars, bumpers and plates, winter light, pale and thin.

"Couldn't you have pointed that out earlier?" I say.

If only there had been a satellite photo to show those things, the complex circuitry of mind and heart.

"I kind of did," he says. "But I don't think you were ready to hear it."

Chapter 33

"It's strange to have the holidays without Adam," says Ellie. "Remember those awful cookies you made last year?"

"They weren't that bad," I say. "Were they?"

"We used to have our little Christmas party," Ellie says. "We haven't done that in a long time."

"No, we haven't." I begin to tear up a little on the phone.

It's such a strange thing for someone just to be *gone*. And it doesn't take long before you begin to wonder if they were ever there. Or if they were a fantasy. Soon, all you're left with are the artifices of memory, *based* on something real, like a made-for-TV movie, or processed cheese.

"You know what Adam said to me before he died?" Ellie says. "He told me he'd been in love with me since freshman year in college. But I was always dating someone else. And then I got married, and you know the rest. Since *freshman year.*"

I took a course my freshman year called Freudian Psychology and Buddhism.

I can't remember now, for the life of me, what the two had in common. But the professor memorized all of our names and the town we'd grown up in. All seventy-five of us.

He would go around the classroom and ask a student his name, and the student would say, "Jim Thompson," and the professor would say, "Jim Thompson. Clara City." And he got it right, every time.

The professor talked about the Buddhist idea of letting new information settle into your mind.

He had managed to memorize our names and hometowns over the course of a month, gently letting the information find a home in his brain through association. He had let his mind wander until some connection had formed that prompted "Clara City" when "Jim Thompson" came up. So we learned about that.

And we learned something about the Buddhist notion of letting go, of experiencing something in the moment and then detaching from it.

What on earth did it all have to do with Freud? I can't remember.

The memory of that class floated to the surface now, like some migrating whale, getting air before diving under again.

In the same way that this new information had appeared, as if from nowhere, though it had been there all along. *Adam had loved Ellie? Why hadn't I made the connection myself?* Just deep enough to be out of reach.

Chapter 34

Tonight in group therapy we are helping Louise cut up her credit cards. One by one, she snips them into bits, her hands shaking, tears streaming down her face. "I won't be able to order takeout now," she says, sobbing. "I won't be able to buy presents for my family. I won't be able to go out to lunch."

"You can *make* presents," says the counselor. "You can pack a sandwich."

"Does anyone have any advice for Louise?" asks Dr. Douglas. He looks over at Harvey, who is eating one of his sprout sandwiches. "Harvey, maybe you can give Louise some sandwich ideas."

"I'd be happy to," Harvey says.

I have been restless all night. Earlier we had spent about half an hour talking about Wayne's new dog, which he didn't expect would *replace* his old dog, Jumpy, but with which he already felt a special bond. Harvey had talked for a long time about a theorem he'd been working on at home, in his spare time, that was puzzling him. Eileen had talked about a pose she was having difficulty perfecting. And now I was going to sit here and listen to *sandwich* ideas?

"Do we have to do that now?" I say, without really meaning to. It just sort of pops out.

Dr. Douglas looks at me, seemingly startled, as if a bee has just flown by. "I think that might be a way of supporting Louise," he says, "as she's making this lifestyle change."

"What's going on with you right now?" the counselor says, leaning in, looking patiently at me with her big brown eyes.

"What do you mean?"

"I mean, why did you just say that?" she asks matter-of-factly.

"I don't know. It just seems like a waste of time," I say. "We sit in here talking about sandwiches and dogs," I continue, surprising myself. I never say what I'm really thinking in group; it feels kind of good. "And maybe next week we can all learn how to knit. Wouldn't that be great? That's what I'm paying the big money for."

"Don't you think this group has supported you in the past?" asks the counselor. "When you've needed it?"

"It just seems like a waste of time," I say.

"You keep saying that. Waste of time. What does that mean?"

"I think it's like church," I say. "I'm starting to wonder why I even come here. We go through the motions. We hold hands. We say our things that we're supposed to say."

"Like what?" asks the counselor.

"Like, 'I can understand how that might make you feel,' because it's the nice thing to say." I cross my arms over my chest. I recross my legs. I am crying. Why am I crying?

"Don't you think the people in this group have been through some of the same things you've been through?"

"No, I don't," I say. "I don't know. I just don't think it's all that helpful. We're all supposed to sit around here and love each other and be nice and connect with everybody. You have all your theories about apes and salmon and tree frogs." I look at Dr. Douglas, whose gaze is like a snowbank, completely blank and unreadable. "And you"—I look at the counselor—"you let everybody blather on and on about anything and you don't seem at all bored. The two of you drive me crazy. Sitting up there on your fucking mountains, looking down on us and not bothering to offer anything helpful. And you never agree on anything." Something in my chest was loosening.

Louise is staring at me with wide eyes, still holding her scissors.

Pretty much everyone is staring at me. Except Harvey, who is trying to chew quietly.

"Why don't you just go back to what you were doing?" I say, looking over at one of the counselor's clocks, which were never right anyway.

"No," says the counselor, "let's finish talking about this. Why are we making you crazy?"

"Can't Louise just cut her fucking credit cards up and we can go *home*?"

Dr. Douglas is rubbing the beard he's been working on growing.

Louise starts to cry.

"I'm sorry, Louise. I'm sorry," I say. "It's just," and I began to really sob, and then a stream of dark words fly out of me like bats from a cave. "It's just so *fucking* pointless to be on this fucking planet where no one ever says what they're fucking thinking, waiting for something big to happen and it's empty and pointless and I come in here week after fucking week after week and I pay you to help me and you don't fucking do anything!

And it's too late to do anything about it." I am sort of curled in on myself and I feel Dana scoot closer to me on the couch and put her arm around me. And I lean into her and keep sobbing.

"It will be all right," she says. "You did the best you could. He knew you loved him. You did the best you could." She held on to me, and the room was quiet for what seemed like an eternity.

How had she known that? How had she known the perfect thing to say?

"Thank you," I say, and then I look up and notice that she is crying, too. "Why are you crying?"

"I felt the same way when my dad died," she says. "Except I only yelled at Dr. Douglas." She smiles and hands me a Kleenex.

I nod and blow my nose.

"I'm sorry about your friend," says Wayne.

"I miss him," I say. "I'm sorry, Louise." She had put her scissors down and is wiping her nose with her sleeve.

"It's okay," she says.

"No, you know. I have the same problem with my credit cards," I say.

"You do?"

"I do. I just never talk about it in here."

Sometimes the things you learn in therapy make sense, but you don't know how to absorb them.

And sometimes they sink like an anchor.

This is the thing I would realize later, and I would finally *know* it. That we were all just doing the best we could.

"This is about you," the counselor had said so many times, though I never really understood what she meant until now. "When *you* claim your independence, when *you* rely on your-

self, on your own sense of security, you won't have these conflicted feelings. It's not really about them; it's about *you*."

Adam had been my friend. My mother had her own life and
was fine with it.

"I'm really proud of you," the counselor says to me in our next
session. "You really let me have it."

"But it wasn't even about you," I say.

"I don't care," she says. "I'm just glad you did something.
You take care of yourself and I'll deal with it." She stops and
nods. "And your mom can deal with it, too. She's strong. The
two of you will be fine," she says. "Eventually."

Chapter 35

My mother and I are wandering through the Degas exhibit at the Minneapolis Institute of Arts with special headphones on, which means that we can't really talk. I make a mental note that this is a good togetherness activity; she can't probe me about my finances or my dating life.

"This is sensuous!" my mother exclaims, still wearing her headphones and standing before a portrait of horses and jockeys. She runs her finger in the air, mirroring the line of a horse's backside and legs. Her finger is about a centimeter, if that, from the oil, and I'm afraid that she's actually going to touch the painting, setting off the alarms.

"Mom, don't touch the paintings."

"I'm not touching anything. Look at that woman," my

mother says, pointing to another painting. "What a striking portrait! What a beautiful lady!" she announces to the gallery over her headphones.

A woman sitting at a table with a bouquet of flowers. The wife of one of Degas's friends. She looks strong, accomplished. The curator's card notes that Degas was criticized in his time for his treatment of women—that he didn't make them beautiful enough, but instead captured them in natural poses, the humility of everyday life.

"Stunning!" Flo says, moving along to another painting. "Let's see," she says, propping her bifocals on her nose. "She looks so angry. On the notes here it says he was painting his brother's mistress. She doesn't look like she could *have* a young lover. It says it's supposed to show something about her vulnerability. I think she looks bitchy," Flo concludes and moves on.

I stay behind to finish the curatorial comments, which note that Degas often painted a subject from life, then changed her name to something more generic, blurring the lines so that the person couldn't be said to be herself, was more of a type, represented something instead.

In the next painting, Degas had left behind his corrections. He'd moved furniture around and changed the angle of the woman's arm, edited her gesture until he felt he'd gotten it right. You could see each of his attempts before he felt he'd achieved the proper composition and balance. He hadn't bothered to paint over his errors.

I guess they weren't *errors;* they were just *tries.* And because he'd left all of the lines where he'd begun to draw the woman's arm and then changed his mind, it conveyed motion.

That was my favorite painting. I guess I liked the idea that, in painting this woman, he didn't mind people seeing that some trial and error had been involved.

That it was okay if you hadn't gotten it right the first time.

Chapter 36

"I was mad at Adam when he was alive," I tell the counselor, honking into a Kleenex, "for not being what I wanted him to be. Mr. Perfect. The One."

"You were mad at him for dying," she says. "That's what I think. He was one of your best friends, and even though you had grown apart, you counted on him being around for a long time. You never counted on him leaving. So you treated him like he was going to *live*. The way you always had. You stayed mad at him." She hands me another Kleenex. "You know," she says, "when my first husband had cancer, I was very angry. I thought he'd always be with me."

"I didn't know your first husband died of cancer," I say.

"Mhmm," she says. "That's why I made you go over there every week."

When Adam was dying, I tell the counselor, everyone started to treat him as if he were magical. They would go visit him and they would come away saying, *Talking with him is so amazing. He's just got such a great perspective.* And I would say, *Like what? What did you talk about? What did he say?* And they would say, *I don't know. I can't think of anything in particular. He's just got this amazing perspective.* People came away with his words as if with some dinosaur bone, an artifact whose placement and function in an actual body they did not understand.

People want the dying person to have amazing perspective. They want him to reveal secrets. When, in reality, we are all in the same kind of boat. The dying person just knows which particular boat he'll drift away on.

"I just wanted to know," I say now to the counselor, who hands me the whole Kleenex box, "what he would miss. I would miss how it feels to jump into a cold lake in the Boundary Waters after a day of paddling. I wanted to know if there were things like that for him."

When I'm better, Adam would say—and by that time, it had become clear to me that he would not ever be better, except by some miracle—*let's go see a movie.*

The problem is, the cancer patient has lost his appetite. And his body hurts too much to remember what it might have enjoyed. And there is this vague stirring, a misplaced libido, about which the patient can do nothing. Though it is the one thing that would ensure some kind of survival, the hope of continuation.

Who gets sick? I ask the counselor. Is it the people who are unhappy? The people with depressed immune systems? Is it just anyone? Is it someone, like my grandmother, who scrubbed everything so hard that eventually cancer spread through her body in that same way, cleaning everything in its path? I couldn't help but wonder if Adam got sick, like he'd learned at the Qigong center, because he'd needed to realign. But then again, we are all messed up in some way. And how could he possibly have done it in time to save himself? Did something in him give up? Hope is what gets us up in the morning. Hope that something in the day will reward us in some small way. And if not today, tomorrow. Had he lost faith in whatever vision he had had for his future?

Or was he being rewarded for his faith, as the eulogist had said, with a better life?

And was it true what Billy Joel said? That only the good die young?

"My great-aunt lived to be a hundred and one," I say to the counselor. "And she was such a bitch."

"God doesn't take the sour ones until they mellow out a little." She nods.

My mother had clipped an article about melanoma, which said there was a gene that indicated predisposition. Was that Adam's destiny, then? To leave us early, when we all thought he would be here longer than anyone?

When I'm better, let's go see a movie. Adam's optimism had driven me crazy because I thought it was denial.

But maybe, I think now, it was a code. It was code for *We used to have fun, and I wish we could go out and have fun again.*

And so perhaps what I thought was denial was an acknowledgment of our early friendship. I had been waiting, like everyone else, I suppose, for some kind of gestalt, an appraisal. *Here is what I liked and here is what I will miss and here's how I'd sum up my life. The end.*

I wasn't so different; I was waiting for something magical, too. A logical conclusion. And I missed it. Adam *did* tell me what he would miss. *When I'm better, let's go see a movie.* He would miss spending time with me. Why couldn't I have found a way to say it, too?

"I think you did," says the counselor. "I think the two of you reached an understanding."

"At Adam's funeral, the pastor talked about how, just before Adam died, they had recited Adam's favorite psalm together. I had no idea Adam *had* favorite psalms, let alone had them memorized."

"So you missed that about him," she says.

"I guess I did."

"We all have different experiences of one another," says the counselor. "That's part of the mystery of it."

Maybe that's why people love mystery shows. There's always a conclusion. In the end, they *always* tell you exactly what happened.

"Life isn't like that," says the counselor. "There are too many versions of every story. And in the end, most of us don't really know what we're doing or why we do what we do. We're just doing the best we can. And we just have to have faith."

"That doesn't seem good enough," I say. "Shouldn't there be more?"

"That's life," she says. "See, I think this is part of your journey. In the same way that learning to emancipate from your mother is. And emancipation means that you can have some *connection* to her and still be yourself. So that you're doing things because you want to do them. Not because your mom advised it or because you're rejecting her advice. You're acting from your center, as an adult."

"That's my journey?"

"That's part of it," says the counselor. "We're all here to learn. And we don't learn much. I mean, very few, if any of us, really change who we are. But we can learn about our behavior. We can modify some of the things that we do."

The counselor made spirituality sound like going through puberty. The unavoidable process of learning to be a less gawky, more graceful human being.

"And I think you were connected to Adam in a complicated way," she says. "You were connected not to *him,* as the friend that he has been to you, but to a fantasy about what he could be."

It was true. It was the same thing Adam might have been doing all along with Ellie.

I had been imagining my life in the future tense. I will have a husband. I will have children. I will have a house.

I had been missing what I have now.

And I had missed Adam.

Therapy was like church. It was the act of going, week after week. Not knowing what you were going to get out of it.

Faith was the act of showing up. Trying to move forward, glacial step by glacial step.

I called in sick the next morning and drove three hours to West Bend, Iowa, to the Grotto of the Holy Redemption. To the tinkling tackiness of it, thousands of tons of gems and stones, taking up an entire city block, nine separate grottos accumulating in one enormous shrine to the life of Jesus Christ. Marty had told me about it once, and shown me their Web site.

From a distance, it looked disappointingly brown, something like Disney's Magic Mountain. Up close, staircases wound up and around the grottos, every inch of which, inside and outside, were adorned with turquoise, gems, crystals, shells, agates, colored glass, stalagmites and stalactites from caves in the Dakotas, petrified sea urchins, starfish, fossils, corals, amber, quartz, fool's gold, onyx, and copper.

Across the street, the Grotto restaurant served sloppy joes and cold beer for $2.95.

I stopped first in the adjacent church to light a candle for Adam, and stayed to view the Christmas Chapel, a nativity decorated entirely with gems. Above the manger, where the baby Jesus sat in a bed of hay surrounded by a donkey and a cow, a 300-pound chunk of Brazilian amethyst had been settled into the wall.

Mary and Joseph were kneeling while tiny sheep looked on, tucked up on a terraced mountain of copper and quartz.

I pushed the button that offered information about the chapel, and a friendly voice that seemed to be coming out of the plaster donkey greeted me.

It explained where all of the gems had come from, how hard the priest who had built the Grotto had worked to create this celebration of Jesus' life. That Jesus, Mary and Joseph, and the donkey were not made of plaster, as I had thought, but of Italian marble.

Of the lambs, the donkey explained, the first was lost, forlorn because it lives in the world but does not know why. It does not know its purpose.

The second lamb represented hope. It, too, was lost and forlorn, but the good shepherd nearby would help him figure out where to go.

The third lamb was drinking from the stream of life. He had found life through faith and other sacraments.

The last lamb was in repose. He represented the religious person who contemplates the Christ child, the donkey said. The last lamb had found his purpose, and with it, peace and joy.

"Thank you for your kind attention," the donkey said. "God love and bless you all."

I left the church, its warm smell of wax from the hundreds of burning candles within it, and went out into the cold air to wander through the grottos.

I sat for a while in the Grotto of the Ten Commandments; in my mind, it was one of the prettiest ones, with a high, domed ceiling decorated with rose quartz.

There was a tablet with a passage from Matthew on it, and

if I were better with Roman numerals, or knew anything at all about the Bible, I could tell you which one it was. "Good Master," it read. "What Good Shall I Do That I May Have Life Everlasting?"

Before Adam died, his mother told me, he turned to her and said, "Is it okay if I go now? Have I done enough here?"

"It's okay," she said. "You have done enough."

And soon after, he stopped breathing.

"Just bumming around by yourself today, huh?" said the lady who served up my sloppy joe and pulled a cold Miller Lite out of the refrigerator.

"Yeah," I said.

"Well," she said. "Some days you just want to be alone."

But that was just it. More than ever before, I did not want to be.

Chapter 37

In the spring I joined Harvey's bowling league and quit group therapy. I had finally gotten to the point where Optional After-Group Hugs didn't frighten me, and I thought it was time, I told the counselor, for me to go out and try new things in the world instead of practicing them in a small, safe room.

It was true, what she and Dr. Douglas had been saying. I had not been going out to figure out what I wanted; I had only been complaining about what showed up.

I brought in a cake on my last night of group therapy and bawled my way through the good-byes. Especially when it came to Dr. Douglas. I wouldn't see him anymore. I would have to go out and find another nice guy to spend time with. He had been holding that place, too.

"But I'd still like to come and see you," I said to the counselor. "But maybe not as often."

"That's fine," she said. "Whatever works for you."

We had always been encouraged to socialize with one another outside of group, but one of the group rules had been that if we were with another group member in public and we ran into friends, we were not to say that we knew that person from group. It was a privacy issue, an issue of integrity.

Harvey introduced me to everyone as "someone I used to work with," which was true. The counselor always called our therapy "work." If you did the work, she said, you'd see the results of your therapy. You'd see it in a refashioned life. A sparkling life that would flow like a Bob Mackie gown. But you have to do the work, she would say.

I am on Harvey's team with two other women, Harvey's rabbi, and the rabbi's son, Eli, a guy around my age, with curly brown hair and big blue eyes. He just moved back here after living in Berkeley for ten years, his father told me. He was hoping Eli would meet other nice young people.

"Have you ever been to synagogue?" the rabbi asked me the first week.

"No," I said. "I'm sorry. I haven't. I was raised Catholic."

"It's not all that different," he said. "None of it is. The message of the Torah is simple. *Do not do something to another person that you would not have done to you.* Basically. All the rest is commentary." It was his turn to bowl. "Hillel," he said, with a big, final nod. And he went up to retrieve his ball.

"Is my dad giving you speeches?" asked Eli.

"It's interesting," I said.

"He likes to give speeches."

"So does my mom," I said.

There was something really warm about Eli. I couldn't say exactly what it was. He seemed at ease with himself. He was lousy at bowling; his form seemed to be modeled after a fish flopping on the bottom of a boat, and half the time he got gutter balls.

"I'm actually good at a few other things," he said after one gutter ball.

I was curious to know what those things were.

After his next gutter ball, he said to me with a broad smile, "Wow. And I thought *you* sucked."

He reminded me of Adam in a way, I thought later. Both awkward and comfortable with his flaws. Graceful in his gawkiness.

Our team is second-to-last in the league, and tonight we are losing to Ed's Auto Shop.

Eli comes back from the bar with two watery beers in plastic cups, hands me one, and sits down next to me. As if by reflex, he puts a hand on my knee and turns to the lanes to see who's up, what the scores are.

My whole body flushes, being that close to Eli, the warmth of him, his soft arm hairs brushing against mine.

He is watching his dad try to pick up a spare when he seems to notice for the first time that his hand is on my leg. He looks at his hand, then pats me on the knee, says, "I think you're doing pretty well here tonight," and blushes. "I'm sorry. I didn't mean to be so forward. Bad hand. Bad!" he says. "Carpal tunnel. Does its own thing."

I could feel that familiar flutter in my chest. A buzzing in my head. My eyes were tingling. Was this The Anxiety?

It felt, somehow, different.

I remember the way I felt when I first met Paul. This was

that same feeling. "You're not engaged or anything, are you?" I say to Eli, who looks puzzled.

"Well, bowling is a demanding mistress," he finally says. "I'm not engaged. Are you engaged? Or anything?"

"No."

It is your friends, I realize, and your family who smell like dinner. Nourishment. Stability. Comfort food.

Eli smells like dessert.

"Would you want to go out sometime?" I say. "Besides bowling?" I put my hand on his knee. "Carpal tunnel," I say.

"I think," he says, "that would be nice."

For the heroic, heartbreaking, hilarious story
of a woman making her life happen when
it didn't quite happen for her, look for
Shannon Olson's books from Penguin.

Welcome to My Planet

Life just isn't *The Love Boat* for nearly-thirty Shannon, the tongue-
in-cheek heroine of *Welcome to My Planet*. Credit cards don't pay
themselves, no obvious mate has appeared with her name pinned
to his collar, and a job doing new-product research for a fledgling
software company doesn't quite make ends meet in the meaning-
of-life department. Then there's the loser boyfriend, another
boyfriend, her therapist, and unforgettably, Shannon's mom, Flo,
with her unrecognizable leftover casseroles and quirky advice for
her daughter. In a fit of debt and with a bruised heart, Shannon
moves back home to witness the day-to-day tremors of her parents' own marriage. This is a dark-and-light tale—freshly witty
and poignant—told by a young woman with a universal touch.

ISBN 0-14-100177-1

The Children of God Go Bowling

In this much anticipated sequel to *Welcome to My Planet,* we now
find Shannon Olson, our semi-fictional heroine, in her mid-thirties
and still besieged by reminders that her life is anything but normal.
Her friends are blossoming in marital bliss, everyone seems to own
a home, and even her baby sister is having a baby. Why, in the
march to adulthood, has she been left behind? In an effort to be
proactive, Shannon embarks upon a feng shui-inspired campaign
to make room in her life for a future—or at least the hope of one.
She joins group therapy (to meet new people), accepts blind dates
(hey, you never know), and even gives organized religion a go
(with mixed results). Of course, surprises await her in the struggle
against anxiety—coming from some unlikely sources.

ISBN 0-14-303456-1